SLEEPY HORSE RANGE

Jinglebob Jenkins rides into the dusty little settlement of Padre Wells — and straight into the middle of a range war between the Ladder-A and the Bridle-Bit. Lorry Alastair, owner of the Ladder-A, is glad to take on Jenkins and his ever-present concertina. For, in spite of his music and his cowboy ballads, the lanky leather-forker is a tough hombre to cross, and a hand who can jerk a sixgun faster than any man in Dave Scarab's Bridle-Bit gang is a welcome addition to the ranch. The sound of gunplay often echoes against the hills behind the Ladder-A range, and the hot lead spills fast and plentiful before peace finally returns to Padre Wells and Scarab and his gang are wiped out. And only then does Jinglebob Jenkins, the cowboy troubador, find the word to rhyme with "Saskatoon."

SPECIAL MESSAGE TO READERS

THE ULVERSCROFT FOUNDATION
(registered UK charity number 264873)
was established in 1972 to provide funds for
research, diagnosis and treatment of eye diseases.
Examples of major projects funded by
the Ulverscroft Foundation are:-

- The Children's Eye Unit at Moorfields Eye Hospital, London
- The Ulverscroft Children's Eye Unit at Great Ormond Street Hospital for Sick Children
- Funding research into eye diseases and treatment at the Department of Ophthalmology, University of Leicester
- The Ulverscroft Vision Research Group, Institute of Child Health
- Twin operating theatres at the Western Ophthalmic Hospital, London
- The Chair of Ophthalmology at the Royal Australian College of Ophthalmologists

You can help further the work of the Foundation
by making a donation or leaving a legacy.
Every contribution is gratefully received. If you
would like to help support the Foundation or
require further information, please contact:

THE ULVERSCROFT FOUNDATION
The Green, Bradgate Road, Anstey
Leicester LE7 7FU, England
Tel: (0116) 236 4325

website: www.foundation.ulverscroft.com

SLEEPY HORSE RANGE

WILLIAM COLT MACDONALD

SAGEBRUSH
Large Print Westerns

First published in Great Britain by Collins
First published in the United States by Covici Friede

First Isis Edition
published 2019
by arrangement with
Golden West Literary Agency

A catalogue record for this book is available
from the British Library.

ISBN 978–1–78541–565–4 (pb)

Published by
F. A. Thorpe (Publishing)
Anstey, Leicestershire

Set by Words & Graphics Ltd.
Anstey, Leicestershire
Printed and bound in Great Britain by
T. J. International Ltd., Padstow, Cornwall

This book is printed on acid-free paper

Contents

1. Strangers Not Welcome.........................1
2. A Poet With a Punch.........................14
3. Like a Fuse in a Powder Keg..................23
4. A Marked Man.........................36
5. Long Range Shooting.........................46
6. Lorry Gets Her Way.........................62
7. A Man to Be Stopped.........................79
8. Fresh Evidence?.........................93
9. The Marshal Kills a Buzzard..................107
10. Showdown.........................117
11. Trapped Into Admission.....................130
12. "Bring Me His Scalp!".........................142
13. Hannan Gets Smart.........................155
14. Outguessed.........................171
15. Bucky Starts a Trip.........................183
16. Jinglebob Reaches a Decision.................198
17. "You're Covered!".........................214
18. Cornered!.........................226
19. Crooked Plans.........................236
20. Scarab's Proposition.........................246
21. Powder Smoke!.........................257
22. Conclusion.........................265

CHAPTER
ONE

Strangers Not Welcome

He had been staying there three days before old Tarp Jones discovered his camp. Lorry Alastair first heard of the stranger's arrival on Ladder-A range when she went down to the cook shanty to learn the reason underlying old Tarp's tardy appearance for the evening meal. The two elderly cowmen seated at the long table, which was flanked on either side by a bench equally long, hadn't heard Lorry approach the doorway, and the girl had paused just inside the threshold to listen, while Tarp divided his time between the consumption of a warmed-over meal and an enthusiastic relation of the day's discovery.

Lorry mused, listening and looking at the men: "It must be mighty important, when Chris will forget to grumble over making a second supper, and stand there with his ears flapping that way. For once, he is, apparently, speechless."

It was true. Chris Kringle, the Ladder-A cook, was standing, open-mouthed, in the entrance to his kitchen, his bald head shining in the light from the kerosene lamp swung above the board table. His features, normally long and dour, were now animated with

1

curiosity. His lean shanks were covered with an old flour sack, worn in lieu of an apron. In his left hand he held a coffee pot; in his right a long handled spoon.

Matt Alvord, seated across the table from old Tarp, smoking a brown paper cigarette, exhaled a gray cloud of smoke toward the hanging lamp. "Damn' if I ever hear the beat of it," he puzzled, shaking his head, the movement catching silvery reflections in the light. "Man and boy, I've traveled this range for nigh onto fifty year, and I never crossed trails with nothing like what you tell about, Tarp — 'cepting, maybe, in a theayter or opery house. Once, up in Denver —"

"Opry house! Theayter!" old Tarp snorted scornfully. "That stuff ye hear in them places is all made up ahead of time and practised. This Jenkins hombre jest makes 'em up as he goes along, right outten his head." Tarp's sweeping gray mustaches bristled indignantly; his leathery, weather beaten countenance expressed supreme contempt. "Opry house! There ain't a opry house in the country that wouldn't pay big money to get that feller."

"And you say," Chris Kringle prompted, "that he made up one of his poems about *you* — right while you was there?"

"Ain't I been tellin' ye?" Tarp insisted. "It went, '*Old Tarp Jones had rheumatics in his bones,*

'*But he topped a tough bronc mighty handsome,* '*Till his saddle cinch went bust*

'*And he landed in the — tum-ti-tum-tum-ti —*'"

"Don't try to sing it," Matt Alvord said hastily.

"I disremember how the rest of it went," Tarp explained apologetically. "I'll have to get Jenkins to

2

write it down for me. But you got to hear the music to really appreciate it." He paused to shove a forkful of beans through the orifice below his mustache, then started to sing again, beating time with his fork:

"*Old Tarp Jones had rheumatics in —*"

"It ain't your singing, Chris and me's interested in," Matt Alvord interrupted. "We've heard you try to sing before. Your voice may be all right for nighthawkin' a herd, but there's a limit to what the human constitution will stand for. Coming through those beans, it reminds me of a shovelful of gravel slidin' down a congregated roof."

"You mean corrugated roof," the cook said.

"It all sounds the same," Matt said.

Old Tarp looked insulted. He didn't say anything, just chewed moodily on his supper. The girl at the doorway smiled a little, remaining silent, unseen by the men, knowing Tarp would continue in a few moments and was only waiting to be urged.

"You say this hombre made music too," Matt prompted, after a moment.

"Uh-huh," Tarp grunted.

"What kind of music?"

Tarp said sulkily, "What difference does it make?"

Matt Alvord twisted his weather-warped frame around on the bench and commenced to roll another cigarette, as though the subject was closed. He said, "Hmmpf!" contemptuously, to the cook, and added, "I'll bet old Tarp Jones has been smoking loco weed, and dreamed all this yarn about music —"

"You think so? You think so?" Tarp was electrified to indignant contradiction. "You wouldn't say so if you could — could of seen him a-squeezin' and a-pullin' sweet chords outten that little contraption." His knife clattered down against his plate. "And all the time him singin' songs like there wa'n't no end to 'em. I'll betcha I was there three hours or more, and never once did he repeat himself. We —"

"What sort of a contraption did he make this music with?" Matt wanted to know.

Tarp frowned. "He called it by name once, but I disremember. It was a little box, sort of, with six sides to it."

Alvord looked blank. Chris Kringle commenced making jabbing motions at the air, with the spoon in his right hand, mentally counting the sides of an imaginary box. He looked a trifle disconcerted when he had finished.

"I dunno," the cook said, scratching his bald head with the end of the spoon, "that I ever saw a box that didn't have six sides."

Tarp shook his head impatiently. "I ain't counting the sides, just the ends. Each end of the box was a flat piece with six sides to it. The sides of the box was sort of limber and sinewy and kind of stretched when he'd pull the ends. And then he'd squeeze the ends like . . . like . . ." Then with sudden triumph, ". . . like a bellows, that's what it was! It was like a bellows."

"An accordion!" Chris Kringle exclaimed.

"Accordin' to what?" Matt asked blankly.

4

"Yes, yes," Tarp's head bobbed excitedly. "It was something like an accordion, Chris. You've hit it. But that ain't what he called it."

The girl standing in the doorway of the cook shanty stirred a little. Her form was beyond the circle of light cast by the lamp above the table, slightly in shadow. She said quietly, "Tarp, it sounds to me as though you were trying to describe a concertina."

It was a long pull for old Tarp from the stranger's camp on the south fork of Sleepy Horse Creek back to the present. For a moment his consciousness failed to adjust itself to immediate requirements. His mind had been so full, so enthusiastic, regarding his discovery of the stranger on Ladder-A range that words failed him momentarily. He sat, open-mouthed, staring at the slim form framed in the shadowed doorway.

Matt Alvord knocked the ash from his cigarette and twisted about on the wooden bench, saying, "Oh, hello, Miss Lorry."

Chris Kringle moved toward the table, lifted the coffee pot in his left hand and filled old Tarp's cup. He said, "Evenin', Lorry," and retreated in the direction of his kitchen from which presently came a banging and clattering of pots and pans in the process of cleansing.

Tarp Jones' eyes held a half-vacant expression as they focused on the slim, boyish form standing in the entrance to the cook shanty. He saw a tall girl clad in a blue and white calico dress with sleeves rolled to the elbows, exposing forearms that were firm and brown. There were tiny freckles across the bridge of her nose, and where her neck showed at the back, beneath the

5

heavy coil of wavy, blue-black hair, her skin was milk-white. Mostly, though, her features were well tanned, except for a narrow, paler strip across her upper forehead where the band of a Stetson had furnished ample protection from the scorching suns and steadily blowing winds of the southwest cow country.

Tarp found his voice at last, "What's that you're saying, Lorry?" he asked somewhat blankly.

The girl left the doorway and moved into the room. "Concertina is the word you're trying to think of, isn't it, Tarp?" There was a low, husky quality to her tones.

"Concertina! By cripes! Ye've hit it, Lorry."

Lorry Alastair nodded when Matt Alvord moved on the bench to make room for her opposite old Tarp.

"Concertina! That's whut he called it. That's the word," Tarp exclaimed. He seized his coffee cup and swallowed noisily, then slammed the cup down on his saucer. "Matt, pass over that lick, will ye?"

Alvord reached to the pitcher of molasses on the table and handed it across to Tarp. Tarp poured a generous helping into his coffee and made stirring sounds with his spoon. Then he swallowed some more and wiped his mustache with the back of his gnarled hand.

Lorry said quietly, "You finished your supper, Tarp?"

"Jest 'bout, Lorry. Why?"

"All right," the girl said. "Let's have it."

"Huh? Let's have whut?"

"That's no medicine, Tarp Jones. I won't be put off. I gather from what I heard there's a stranger camping on Ladder-A holdings. Now, what's the story? Who is he? What does he want? What's he here for?"

6

"We-ell . . ." Old Tarp looked uncertain. "I don't exactly know . . ." He pulled out a battered old briar pipe and commenced to load it with tobacco.

Lorry's red lips set a trifle grimly. "So! You don't know. Pilgrim?"

"Cripes, no. Cow stuff, from the heels up." Old Tarp wasn't meeting the girl's eyes as he tamped down the tobacco in his pipe and scratched a match. He puffed meditatively for a few moments, the acrid fumes filling the air.

Lorry said testily, "Something should be done about that pipe, Tarp, but we'll forget it right now. So, you don't know anything about this stranger, except that he looked like cow country to you. Tarp Jones, you ought to be playing with a string of spools. You know my orders about strangers. Strangers are not welcome on Ladder-A holdings. Did you tell him to get out?"

"Now, Lorry, there wa'n't nothin' wrong with this feller."

"Did you tell him to get out?" Lorry insisted.

"We-ell," the answer came in uneasy tones, "not exactly. Ye see, I was only there 'bout five minutes or so —"

"Tarpaulin Jones! You're a twist-tongued old liar. I distinctly heard you telling Chris and Matt that you were there about three hours, wherever 'there' is. Where'd you find this man? What was he doing?"

Matt cleared his throat loudly in the silence. From the kitchen the dishes ceased their clatter as Chris Kringle paused to listen.

Tarp blew out a cloud of gray smoke and commenced placatingly, "Now, Lorry, don't you get ringy with me. I know what I'm doing. I haven't rodded this outfit sence you was knee-high to a horny toad without knowin' my business. Yore paw wouldn't have run this feller out —"

"Breck's not running things here, now," Lorry cut in. "I am. With beef stock disappearing right and left, something has to be done. I'm giving orders until Breck recovers. I want those orders obeyed."

"Yes'm, Lorry," Tarp said meekly.

The girl sighed and softened a trifle. "All right, Tarp, give me the story. What about this fellow who sings and makes music? Where'd you find him?"

Tarp commenced, "He's camping up on Sleepy Horse Creek, right at the fork. Says he's been there three days. He's got a bresh shelter throwed up and ain't hurtin' anybody. I was just makin' my mornin' circle around when I run onto him. First time I been over that way in a week —"

"Who is he?" Lorry cut in.

"Name of Jenkins, Jinglebob Jenkins."

"What's he look like?"

"Oh, sort of tall and lean. Red-headed jasper. Kind of an easy-goin' nature. Right pleasant cuss. Sho', Lorry, he wouldn't harm a fly."

"I suppose," Lorry said sarcastically, "he wasn't even wearing a gun."

"No, he wa'n't," Tarp said seriously. "His six-shooter and belt was hangin' on a mesquite limb. He had a

8

thuty-thuty Winchester too. It was leanin' against a tree. Got a saddler and a pack pony —"

"Thirty-thirty Winchester," the girl cut in, thoughtfully. "It was a thirty-thirty that struck Breck —"

"Sho', now, Lorry," Tarp said quickly, "you ain't thinkin' it was Jenkins shot yore paw?"

"I didn't say that," Lorry returned sharply. "At the same time I'm suspecting any stranger who touches our range. No telling who Scarab might hire for his work."

"If it *was* Dave Scarab that was back of Breck's shooting," Matt Alvord said.

"Oh, I know, I know," Lorry said wearily. "We haven't any proof. Scarab came here today . . ."

"Here?" Tarp looked startled. "Here at the Ladder-A?"

Lorry nodded. "Said he wanted to see Breck to try and make a deal for the outfit. I wouldn't let him see Breck. I gave him his walking papers in short order, told him we weren't interested in selling — not at his figure."

Matt Alvord growled. "Wish I'd been here, I'd told him . . ."

"No, you wouldn't have, Matt," Lorry said. "There wasn't a thing said you could have taken exception to. He was as polite as could be. Said he'd try again some time; I told him it wouldn't do any good. Let's forget him . . . Tarp, what else do you know about this Jinglebob Jenkins fellow?"

"I've told you about all there is, Lorry. He's just camping there, enjoying himself. He's harmless."

"But what is he here for? What's he doing?"

9

"I don't know's he's doin' anything in particular. He just travels around makin' up songs and singin' 'em with that concertina-contraption. I sat there and listened. It was plumb enjoyable. Say, Lorry, you don't happen to know a rhyme for Saskatoon, do you? Jenkins wants one —"

The cook spoke from his kitchen, "All's I could think of was balloon."

Lorry spoke sharply. "No, I don't, Tarp. I suppose you were so busy enjoying yourself with this Jenkins that you forgot to go to Padre Wells for the mail."

"That's where you're mistaken," Tarp stated triumphantly. "I went to town. That's what made me late for my grub. If I'd come straight here from Jenkins' camp, I'd been in time."

"The result would have been the same if you hadn't wasted so much time around Jenkins' camp," Lorry snapped. "Was there a letter from the Association yet?"

Old Tarp nodded. "I opened it to see what they had to say. They thanked us for our letter and said everything would be taken care of in due time, when they had another man available."

"They did?" Lorry looked a trifle startled, then she laughed, a little bitterly. "Good grief! One of their operatives killed three weeks ago, and now they'll send another here — in due time. Well, when that time comes, there may not be any Ladder-A to help. However, they can get busy and learn who killed Mitchell, perhaps . . . just perhaps. Nobody else has been able to learn anything."

10

She took the letter Tarp handed across the table and glanced through its contents, then shoved the sheet of paper back in the envelope. "I like the way they end up," she commented ironically. "'Very truly yours.' It sounds so business-like, as if they really intended to help us out . . . some day, when they get around to it. 'Very truly yours, The Artexico Cattlemen's Association.' The much vaunted A. C. A. Those initials should stand for: After Calamity — Arrangements. They're so *damn* slow!"

"Lorry!" Old Tarp spoke reprovingly. "I've taught ye a heap in my time, but I never told you to use language like that."

"No, you didn't," Lorry snapped. "If I ever adopted the vocabulary I've heard you use, it would sound a heap worse."

Tarp's grizzled features took on a deep flush. Something akin to a chuckle was wafted ghost-like from the vicinity of the dishpan in the kitchen. Matt Alvord looked uncomfortable and loudly cleared his throat. Nobody spoke for a few seconds.

Lorry rose abruptly from the bench and started toward the entrance to the cook shanty, her dark eyes hard and unrelenting. She paused at the threshold and looked back. "Tarp," she said, steady voiced, "first thing in the morning you ride up to Jenkins' camp. Make it clear we don't want strangers on our range. Tell him to ride."

"But, Lorry," Tarp protested, "he ain't hurtin' anythin'."

"That's only your opinion," Lorry replied. Her tones carried a metallic ring. "He may be only a traveling troubador, or he may be a sneaking Scarab spy . . . or worse. I'm not taking any chances —"

"A truba-what?" Tarp queried, frowning.

"It doesn't make any difference," Lorry said wearily. "Tell him to ride. The sooner the better."

"All right. If you say so," Tarp conceded in hurt tones.

"I do say so. That's an order. You heard me."

"Want I should ride with Tarp, Miss Lorry?" Matt suggested. "You know, in case this Jenkins turned ornery."

Lorry shook her head. "I don't figure that's necessary, Matt. You know that as well as I do. You continue with building up that south tank, until it's completed. There's no need of both of you becoming concertina-charmed. We've work to do."

"Yes'm, Miss Lorry," Matt agreed meekly.

After the girl had left the cook shanty, the two cowmen eyed each other in a disappointed silence for a moment. Finally, Matt said, "Miss Lorry sounds some proddy."

"She does that," Tarp said sourly.

Chris Kringle stuck his bald head through the doorway of his kitchen. "And why wouldn't she be proddy?" he demanded. "With a hostile outfit pressin' her on the north, her paw bad wounded, and beef critters disappearin'. On top o' that, two ol' coots like you to put up with."

12

"Go on back to yore scourin's, Sourdough," Tarp growled.

"Who you callin' an old coot?" Matt Alvord asked indignantly. "If I ain't ten years younger than you, I'll —"

"It ain't years that counts," the cook cackled derisively. "It's how much a man's brain has been stunted."

"That's plenty in yore case," Tarp grunted.

"Mebbe so, mebbe so," Chris agreed, "but I know enough not to argue when that gal gives an order. She don't want strange riders on Ladder-A range, and by the same token, Tarp, you'll be tellin' that Jenkins hombre to pull his freight tomorrow mornin', like she said."

Old Tarp sighed. "I reckon," he agreed reluctantly, "but I was kind of hopin' she'd let me bring him down here. He could furnish some mighty satisfactual entertainment. But I'll have to tell him to move on."

However, Tarp wasn't called upon to enforce Lorry Alastair's order. When he reached the camp, the following morning, Jinglebob Jenkins was nowhere to be seen. Camp hadn't been broken and the pack horse was still there, so old Tarp knew Jenkins hadn't departed permanently. Tarp turned his pony back toward the ranch.

"I'll jest tell Lorry," he mused, "that I couldn't find hide nor hair of him. She'll probably figure he's left of his own accord."

CHAPTER
TWO

A Poet With a Punch

Padre Wells moved sluggishly beneath the mid-morning heat of the spring sun-glare. Not that Padre Wells showed any particular animation at any time; it wasn't that kind of a town, if town it may be termed. Settlement is a better word to describe it, consisting, as it did, of only one dusty, winding main street and two or three cross thoroughfares. Plank sidewalks flanked each side of the unpaved road, running parallel with an almost unbroken line of hitch-racks. At numerous points wooden awnings reached out, above the sidewalk, from high false-fronted buildings, to contact the supporting uprights to which the hitch-racks were also spiked. Many of the town's structures were of squat adobe construction.

One building of frame, larger than the others, was known as the Padre Wells Hotel. There was a general store, a poolroom, a barber-shop. Two restaurants competed from opposite sides of the main street. One saloon, the Acme, was situated near the center of town; the other, the Red Toro, owned and operated by a Mexican, did business on one of the side streets. There was a Blue Star Livery. A harness and gun shop caught such business as there was of the kind, which wasn't much, and the proprietor would have been glad to sell out, could he have found a buyer. The other business houses were such as might have been found in any other typical settlement in the southwest cow country of that day.

Near the center of Padre Wells was situated a two-story building of plank-and-'dobe, known as the City Hall. It housed as well the offices of the town marshal and sheriff of Truculento County. At the rear was a jail of half a dozen cells which served both officers when there were prisoners to be incarcerated. The cells were empty at present.

Flies droned in the hot dry morning air and about the various cow ponies switching tails here and there at hitch-racks. In the cooler shadows between buildings a few Mexicans dozed or squatted down, drawing on cornhusk cigarettes. Men lounged in tilted chairs in the shadow before some of the stores. A few pedestrians clumped along the plank walks. On the broad porch fronting the City Hall, Sheriff Clem Wagner and his deputy, Bucky Malotte, leaned their straight-backed chairs against the wall of the building and surveyed the dusty street with drowsy eyes.

The sheriff was middle-aged with a bulky middle and iron-gray hair on which a black Stetson was at present shoved back from his forehead. Bucky Malotte was blockily built with short, solid, bowed legs. His face bore a perpetual expression that reminded one of a belligerent bulldog. His nose was snubbed, his mouth wide, his chin pugnacious. His eyes were round and blue, though at present they were nearly closed. Both men wore metal badges, designating their office, on their open vests, and both carried six-shooters.

It was the sheriff who spotted Jinglebob Jenkins first, riding along the center of the street on a roan gelding.

The sheriff spoke to Bucky Malotte. "Ever see that hombre before?"

Bucky straightened in his chair and after a single glance, shook his head. "Stranger to me, Clem."

The two peace officers now surveyed Jenkins more closely, and saw a lean, rangy man somewhere in the vicinity of twenty-five or six, clad in a denim shirt and faded overalls. Brick-hued hair showed beneath the man's roll-brim sombrero of indiscriminate gray. A Bull Durham tag dangled from his vest pocket, the vest, at present, unbuttoned. A cartridge belt was buckled about Jenkins' hips and the sheriff judged, though he couldn't see from where he sat, that its accompanying holster held a six-shooter.

Malotte and Wagner watched while Jenkins rode past their line of vision and turned his pony toward the hitch-rack before the general store. Then, momentarily, they lost interest.

"If he stays in town," Sheriff Wagner commented, "we'll learn who he is. If he don't, I reckon it's none of our business."

"I reckon," Bucky Malotte nodded, and again closed his eyes.

"Just passin' through, probably," the sheriff said. "Likely's not he came through Sabre Canyon, in the Truculentos, since sun-up."

"I reckon," Malotte said again. He didn't open his eyes.

After a minute, the sheriff settled back in his chair.

Jenkins guided his pony to the hitch-rack before the general store and swung down from his saddle. His high heels clumped hollowly on the plank walk as he crossed and stepped to the porch fronting the building. Then he drew open the door and stepped inside.

A long counter ran along one wall of the store. Shelves loaded with merchandise lined the walls. Grouped at various spots about the floor of the big room were boxes and barrels, stacked brooms, shovels. A small showcase at one side contained patent medicines. Across the room another showcase held spools of thread, cheap jewelry, briar and corncob pipes and a card of collar buttons, from which, to date, no purchase had been made. The shelves to the rear of the showcase held bolts of calico and gingham.

There wasn't anyone in the store when Jenkins entered, except the clerk standing behind the counter.

"Something I can sell you?" the clerk asked, looking curiously at the stranger. The clerk was elderly and wore spectacles.

"I reckon I won't ask you to give it away," Jenkins smiled. "Couple of cans of tomatoes, to begin with, and the same of peaches. Oh, yes, two pounds of beans and a chunk of sow bosom. And a pad of writing paper, if you carry it."

He made other purchases: a can of corned beef, dried apricots, salt and sugar. "I reckon that's all," he

17

said at last. "No, wait — a pound of Arbuckle's and a half a dozen sacks of Bull."

When the purchases had been completed and paid for, Jenkins put them into a burlap sack he'd carried into the store with him.

"Strange here, ain't you?" the clerk asked.

"Nope, I'm all right. It's the rest of the town that's strange to me," Jenkins smiled.

"Same thing," the clerk said, nettled.

"Far be it from me to start an argument, mister. Say, where's your post-office in this town?"

"Right here. We take care of the mail. You got a letter to mail? It'll go off on tonight's stage. Let me have it."

From a hip pocket of his overalls, Jenkins produced a sealed envelope and tossed it on the counter. The clerk picked it up, frankly scrutinizing the writing. He looked at the return address, then said brightly, "You must be Jinglebob Jenkins. Must be you're aiming to stay here a spell."

"Right on both counts, mister."

"My name's Wellman, Ichabod Wellman."

They shook hands solemnly. Jenkins said, "Glad to know you, Mr. Wellman."

"Just call me Ichy . . . everybody does."

"How am I supposed to know that?" Jenkins grinned.

"Huh?"

"Never mind. Let it pass."

Wellman returned to an examination of Jenkins' letter. After a moment he looked up. "Well, writing to somebody at the capital, eh?"

18

"Uh-huh. You be right careful of that envelope. I've got some verses in there that I aim to see in print."

"Verses?" Ichy Wellman frowned.

"Verses. Poetry."

"Well, I'll be — Say, you a poet?"

"You called it. Those verses go to a friend of mine who's making arrangements with a publisher."

"Dam'd if you look like a poet," Wellman said bluntly.

Jenkins laughed. "A heap of folks thought that about Shakespeare at one time, too."

A customer entered the store at that moment and Jenkins, picking up the loaded burlap sack, made his escape, leaving Wellman with some fresh gossip to relate to the new customer. Before sundown, everybody in Padre Wells was aware that a poet had arrived in the Truculento Country.

At the hitch-rack, Jenkins tied the sack at his saddle, then leaving his pony, started along the plank sidewalk toward the Acme Saloon to wash out the dust of travel.

Seated on the porch of the City Hall, Sheriff Wagner saw Jenkins leave the general store and start toward the saloon entrance. As Jenkins was about to push through the swinging doors, they flew violently open and a burly-shouldered, red-faced man in range togs came rocking out.

Jenkins stepped swiftly to one side, but he wasn't quite fast enough. His left shoulder struck the big man and sent the fellow staggering clumsily to one side. The man barely saved himself from falling, as Jenkins caught his arm.

From his position across the street from the saloon, the sheriff frowned. "Looks like Raymer's got a skinfull again," he mused.

Jenkins' words came clearly to the sheriff's ears.

"Sorry, pardner," Jenkins was saying. "I didn't see you coming." He could see the big man had been drinking.

Gus Raymer straightened up with an effort, trying to focus his bleary gaze on Jenkins. Then he cursed, violently and loudly.

"That's all right, pardner," Jenkins said. "Just take it easy. Sure, have it that way if you like. It was all my fault. I apologize."

Half laughing, he started to pass on to the interior of the saloon. Raymer caught his arm and swung him around. Then Raymer called Jenkins a name. The word came clearly to the sheriff's ears, as did Jenkins' sharp reply:

"Take it easy, fellow. You're not acting sensible."

Instead of calming Raymer, Jenkins' words seemed to infuriate him. Drawn by the sounds of the loud voice, several men pushed back the swinging doors and stood gazing at Jenkins and Raymer. They didn't say anything.

Raymer repeated the word he had used a moment before and added to it several choice adjectives. Sheriff Wagner saw Jenkins go white, then red. Jenkins' next movement came so fast, the sheriff almost missed it. There came a sudden blur of arms and fists, a quick *thud-thud* sound, and Gus Raymer went sprawling on

20

his back to the sidewalk. A sudden yell sounded near the saloon door.

Bucky Malotte, at the sheriff's side, opened his eyes.

The sheriff said, "You won't want to miss this, Bucky." He sat straighter in his chair.

A tall, spare man stepped out of the saloon at Jenkins' back and caught Jenkins' sleeve. Without looking around Jenkins shook him off. He was waiting for Raymer's next move.

Roaring angrily, Raymer scrambled up from the sidewalk, right hand clawing at his gun holster. Jenkins took three swift steps. His left fist crashed into Raymer's face. His right landed again. Then he hit Raymer a third time. In an instant, Gus Raymer was once more sprawled on the sidewalk. He wasn't out but he made no attempt to get up.

Loud yells of excitement carried along the street. A small crowd commenced to gather.

"The dang fool should have used his gun," the sheriff muttered, "after Gus reaching for his hawglaig."

"He don't need to with a wallop like that," Bucky Malotte said. "Besides, it looks like from here as if his holster was empty."

Sheriff Wagner rose heavily, leisurely, from his chair. "Come on, Bucky. I reckon I'll take a *pasear* across and see who that red-headed hellion is."

Jenkins was still watching the prone Raymer when he felt something round and hard pressed against the small of his back.

"Put 'em high," a voice was ordering. "There can't be no strangers enter Padre Wells and start beating up decent citizens. You're under arrest, feller. I'm warnin' you not to resist."

Jenkins stiffened, then raised his hands in the air. He turned slowly to face the tall, thin man who had tried to grasp his sleeve a minute before. The man had a long horseface, buck teeth and pale blue eyes set too closely together. On his open vest was pinned a metal badge bearing the single word *Marshal* across its narrow, plated surface.

"Look here," Jenkins said quietly, "you've got the wrong slant on this business."

"Oh, no, I haven't," the marshal said coldly. "I saw the whole ruckus. You hit Raymer first."

"You wouldn't expect me to take what he said, would you?"

"That's neither here nor there, feller. You hit him first. I grabbed your arm once, trying to stop you, but you jerked away. You resisted an officer of the law. You're under arrest. Now, are you coming quiet, or do you crave to be carried — feet first — where I'm taking you?"

Jenkins glanced at the faces of the men standing behind the marshal. They were cowmen by their togs, but there was no friendliness, no sympathy, in their eyes.

Jenkins turned back to the marshal. "I'm reckoning to go peaceful with you," he said quietly. "You've got the upper hand for the moment."

"You're acting mighty wise, feller," the marshal sneered. "Stick out your hands till I slip these cuffs on your wrists."

CHAPTER
THREE

Like a Fuse in a Powder Keg

Jenkins shook his head and drew back a little. "You're not putting those bracelets on me," he said steadily.

The tall man with the buck teeth held the handcuffs in his left hand. The six-shooter in his right tilted a trifle. His features hardened. "You're asking for trouble," he warned.

"You're not putting those bracelets on me," Jenkins said again. "There's no need of that."

The ring of curious faces around the two crowded closer. Back of Jenkins, the man called Raymer had gained his feet. He swayed a moment, uncertainly. One side of his face was puffed and darkly bruised. His eyes were bloodshot, wild with hatred. No one in the crowd saw Raymer draw his gun and move in behind Jenkins. So intent was Raymer, his thoughts concentrated only on Jenkins' unsuspecting back, that he failed to notice Deputy Bucky Malotte and Sheriff Wagner closing in at his rear, the deputy walking slightly in advance of the sheriff.

Deliberately, Bucky Malotte drew the six-shooter from his holster, shifted it to his left hand. His stubby, muscular fingers closed about Raymer's gun barrel, turning it out and toward the earth, while at the same instant Bucky's left hand brought the barrel of his own weapon down smartly across Raymer's wrist.

Raymer's right fist flew suddenly open, releasing the gun into Bucky's grasp. At the same time the big man's mouth opened in a heartfelt cry of mingled rage and pain as he seized his wrist and commenced dancing about, calling down curses on the deputy.

Sheriff Wagner took in his deputy's work with a nod of approval. He didn't say anything, just strode on to come between Jenkins and the buck-toothed man with the handcuffs. For the moment, the crowd's attention centered on the deputy and Gus Raymer.

"Damn you, Malotte," Raymer cursed, pain bringing tears to his eyes. "You've broken my wrist."

"I hope so," Bucky said cold-bloodedly. "But I'm afraid not. I didn't hit hard enough. You dirty scut, sneaking in behind a man — why, say, you ought to be telling me 'much obliged.' You were heading straight toward a murder trial."

"By goddlemighty!" Raymer swore hotly. "I'll even matters with you, Malotte, if it's the last thing I —"

"Want to make anything of it right now?" Bucky demanded belligerently. The deputy stood on his sturdy bulldog legs, chin thrust out, his round blue eyes bulging like twin agates.

"You're damn right," Raymer roared. "Let me have my gun." Malotte had thrust Raymer's six-shooter in the waistband of his trousers.

"You, Gus," a sharp voice spoke from the doorway of the saloon, "shut your trap and take yourself out of here."

24

Raymer calmed down abruptly. "You're the boss, Dave," he nodded. He turned without a word and started toward his waiting horse at the hitch-rack.

The voice at the doorway spoke again, "The rest of you boys go along to the ranch with him. Move pronto now."

Three hard-faced cowhands detached themselves from the crowd, near the entrance to the saloon, and followed Raymer out to the hitch-rack. The four men mounted, swung their ponies around and loped swiftly out of town, leaving a cloud of dust to settle slowly in their wake.

A man in the crowd commented to a companion, "Those Bridle-Bit hands sure jump when Dave Scarab cracks the whip."

Bucky Malotte heard the words. He muttered darkly, "And if somebody don't stop Scarab, this whole damn town will be jumping the same way." His solid, bowed legs carried him on to join Sheriff Wagner who was arguing with the man wearing the marshal's badge.

". . . No, Franklin," Sheriff Wagner was shaking his head, "there ain't going to be any need for handcuffs —"

"But, sheriff," the marshal protested, "he already resisted me —"

". . . and," Wagner continued imperturbably, "there ain't going to be any arrest, either."

"That," Jinglebob Jenkins smiled, "is right welcome news."

"Now, look here, Sheriff Wagner," Marshal Franklin commenced, "if you're trying to interfere with my authority —"

"Ain't tryin'," Wagner said heavily. "I'm doing it. I'm not disputing your right to run Padre Wells lawful, when you're needed, but Padre Wells is situated, I'll point out for your benefit, in Truculento County. Being I'm the duly elected sheriff of said county, I top you in rating, Franklin. Making it clear, I have the final say as to who'll be arrested and who won't. There ain't going to be any arrest. Is that plain?"

"Dammit," Franklin said bitterly, "have we got to stand for strangers coming in here and beating up residents of —"

"Gus Raymer had a beating coming," Wagner said a bit wearily. "I was sitting on the porch, 'cross the way, when this cowboy — Say, what's your name?"

"Jenkins. My friends call me Jinglebob, sheriff."

Wagner nodded and continued, "Anyway, I saw the whole business. Jenkins was within his rights. Gus Raymer was spoiling for trouble and he found it. Jenkins tried to avoid a fight. If anybody should be arrested it's Raymer. Only for Bucky taking a hand, Raymer would have shot him in the back, a few minutes since."

"I still insist," Marshal Franklin's voice was high-pitched, querulous, "that you haven't the right to . . . to . . . well to interfere with my authority —"

"Usurp is the word you're looking for," Wagner broke in. "Well, I've already done that, Franklin. What you aiming to do about it?"

"You'll see," Franklin said heatedly. "I'll take the matter up with the proper authorities and see if you —"

26

"Steve," Dave Scarab spoke again from the doorway, "let be." The man had the ability to inject a certain sharp quality into his tones without raising them.

Marshal Franklin quieted immediately. "Just as you say, Dave," he nodded. His pale blue eyes rested hard on Jenkins' features a moment, then, without another word, he backed through the crowd and strode down the street.

Jenkins smiled contemptuously after the man, then turned back to the sheriff and his deputy. "There wouldn't be a little feud on between the city and county authorities, would there?" he asked.

"Such things happen now and then," Wagner conceded shortly. Jenkins could see the sheriff didn't care to continue the subject.

A soft, musical laugh sounded near the swinging-doored entrance to the saloon. Dave Scarab said, "Why not admit, Wagner, it's happening . . . here and now?"

The sheriff looked at Scarab, then back to Jenkins. The cluster of men standing about was breaking up now. The sheriff looked again toward Scarab, then said to Jenkins: "Dave Scarab. Owns the Bridle-Bit. It was Raymer, his foreman, you knocked sprawling. Scarab would like to run this Truculento Country." The words were spoken half seriously, half in jest.

Scarab's soft laugh sounded again. "Don't you believe it, Jenkins. That's all a figment of the sheriff's imagination. Just because I've been successful with my outfit, he has an idea I'm ambitious."

Jenkins smiled, sizing up Dave Scarab. The man was dressed in ordinary cowhand togs, like his men, but something in his manner, his graceful bearing, set him off from the common run. Here, the thought flashed through Jenkins' mind, was a born leader of men. Whether he would lead in the right direction was another matter. Scarab's hair was as straight and black as an Apache's. A thin black mustache adorned his wide upper lip below an aquiline nose. His body was a slim, sinewy wedge, tapering from the muscular shoulders to lean, narrow hips. There was something feline in Scarab's attitude as he leaned indolently against the jamb of the saloon entrance. His stiff-brimmed, flat-topped sombrero was set at an angle above his swarthy features and there were amused lights in his eyes as he met Jenkins' steady gaze.

"At any rate," Jenkins found himself saying, "you aren't holding it against me because of that run-in with your foreman." Even while he spoke, he wondered if he could put any faith in his own words. Scarab was a difficult man to judge.

"Shucks, no," Scarab replied. "Raymer needed a little come-uppance. He's been getting oiled ever since we struck town. It was only a matter of time until somebody stopped him . . ."

"Or he killed somebody," Bucky Malotte spoke harshly.

"Now, Malotte," Scarab protested. "You and the sheriff are too hard on my boys. You won't find a better man any place than Gus is when he's sober. Gentle as a kitten."

"Tiger kitten?" Jenkins drawled the question.

Bucky Malotte said, "Rattler's kitten." The deputy's hard blue eyes challenged Scarab to contradict the statement.

Sheriff Wagner changed the subject: "Jenkins, were you heading for a drink when you encountered Raymer?"

"Nothing else," Jenkins nodded. "I was just about to ask you to join me. I owe you and your deputy —"

"I'm Clem Wagner. Bucky Malotte's my deputy."

The three men shook hands. Scarab didn't offer to take part in the formality of introductions. He said mockingly, "It's nice to see the conventions observed, even in this raw western country." Straightening from his position against the door jamb, he pushed aside the swinging doors and led the way into the saloon, followed by Jenkins and the two peace officers.

The interior of the Acme, empty except for a man behind the bar, was cool and dim after the sun-glare of the street. A long wooden counter ran parallel to the left wall. Scattered about the room were a number of round, wooden-topped tables and straight-backed chairs. Presiding over the bar was a fleshy, round-faced individual with slicked-down hair who, Jenkins learned later, was named Pat Hogan. The walls of the room were decorated with pictures of race horses, prizefighters and wide-hipped burlesque favorites of the day. Kerosene lamps were swung from the low, flat ceiling.

"What'll it be, gents?" Pat Hogan asked.

"Touch of bourbon, Pat," Scarab replied.

The others took the same. Glasses and a bottle were set out. Drinks were consumed. Jenkins placed some coins on the bar.

"What I want to know," the sheriff asked Jenkins, after a few minutes, "is why you aren't totin' your gun? I like to croak when I see your holster empty."

"Didn't expect to find any need for it," Jenkins replied. "I don't know anybody here. I wasn't expecting trouble of any sort. Besides, I didn't know but what Padre Wells might have an ordinance against packing guns in town."

"Sometimes I think it ought," Wagner said gloomily.

"Leave it to the sheriff to take the pessimistic viewpoint," Scarab smiled. "Must be, Jenkins, where you come from, gun toting's growing unpopular."

"Some," Jenkins admitted. "Up Trinidad way we didn't —"

"Cripes! That explains it," Malotte cut in. "Things are pretty peaceful up on that range, now days. Down here we ain't civilized yet."

"You looking for a job, Jenkins?" Scarab asked.

Jinglebob shook his head. "Just sort of loafing around, right at present, seeing the country . . . That reminds me, any of you gentlemen got a word to rhyme with Saskatoon?"

The others looked blank. Jenkins started to explain, "You see, I'm writing some verses —"

"Don't tell me you're a poet," Scarab interrupted.

"You hit it," Jenkins grinned, "first crack. If I could only find a rhyme for Saskatoon I could finish a —"

"Harpoon," Scarab suggested, frowning a little.

Jenkins shook his head. "It has to be a girl's name."

The other men considered the matter. Finally they gave it up. Scarab's eyes held veiled contempt as he listened to the red-headed cowboy explain how he traveled about the country composing verse.

"Where you staying at present?" the sheriff asked, after a time.

"I made my camp up on the south fork of the Sleepy Horse," Jenkins replied. "Nice country up that way. Lots of inspiration. I'll be riding on one of these days though."

Scarab stiffened slightly. "That's Ladder-A range," he said.

Jenkins nodded. "So I understand. I was talking to the Ladder-A foreman yesterday."

"And he didn't run you off?" Scarab persisted.

"Didn't mention anything of the sort to me."

"That's damn funny."

"What is?" Jenkins asked.

"Last I heard," Scarab said slowly, "the owners were warning all strangers off their holdings."

"Including," Bucky Malotte said in his harsh voice, "all Bridle-Bit cowhands as part of said warning."

Jenkins looked at Scarab. "Your outfit and the Ladder-A had some trouble?"

"The Ladder-A has," Dave Scarab nodded carelessly. "They've got suspicions that my outfit is behind it — but they're wrong. They'll see that in time."

Bucky and the sheriff exchanged glances. They didn't say anything. Scarab continued, "Look here, Jenkins, you figuring to take a job with the Ladder-A?"

"I didn't say so," Jinglebob replied quietly. "I told you what I was doing."

Scarab nodded. "If you do," he laughed, and Jenkins sensed a veiled threat in the words, "you'd better wear your iron next time you come to town. My boys might not take gentle to the idea."

"Shucks," Jinglebob laughed, "I'm no gun-fighter. My fists have always been good enough for me."

"You stick around this country, Jenkins, and you may learn something else," Scarab said lightly. He changed the subject, "Ready for another drink?"

Jinglebob shook his head. "I've had enough."

Wagner and Malotte also refused the offer. Scarab said, "Well, I've got to be pushing back to the Bridle-Bit." He started toward the door, then paused and turned. He was laughing now. "I'll ask Gus Raymer if he knows a rhyme for Saskatoon, Jenkins. I'll tell him it's for you."

"Do that," Jinglebob grinned.

The grin was replaced by a look of perplexity as Scarab departed toward the hitch-rack. "What got into him?" Jinglebob frowned. "The minute I said I was camping on Ladder-A range, he seemed to get sort of tense."

"There's a war brewing between the Ladder-A and the Bridle-Bit — if it hasn't already started," Sheriff Wagner said slowly.

"That's no sign Scarab should get suspicious of me."

Bucky Malotte said, "Some time back Breck Alastair, owner of the Ladder-A, was dry-gulched with a thirty-thirty, shook outten a Winchester. It was never learned who did it. The Ladder-A suspects the Bridle-Bit."

"Any reason for that?"

"Dave Scarab wants the Ladder-A," Wagner said. "Oh, he don't make any bones about it. He's offered to buy. But he don't offer enough. Alastair's daughter, Lorry, is running the outfit, until her dad can get back in the saddle. To help her she's got an old fossil who is supposed to rod the outfit, another cowhand that ain't young any longer and a cook that's passed his spryest days. Her cows have been disappearing."

"Looks to me," Jinglebob said slowly, "as though it might be a job for some cowmen's association. Is there such an organization hereabouts?"

"Mostly stock raisers in the Truculento Country belong to the A. C. A. — Artexico Cattlemen's Association," Wagner said. "The A. C. A. was appealed to, and sent an operative here. He was found dead, out on the range, a mite over three weeks ago. No one knows who did that either."

"Bridle-Bit, maybe?" Jinglebob suggested.

"There's no proof of it," Wagner said wearily. "This is the first day I've been in town in a coon's age. I've nigh wore out a horse looking for 'sign' that might lead to clues, but it's got me stopped."

"I've got a hunch it's the Bridle-Bit all right," Malotte said harshly, "but that's as far as it goes. I don't trust Scarab. He's open enough on the surface, perhaps, but underneath there's something else you can't get at. He's tricky. I feel like he was laughing at me all the time. And he hires the hardest ridin', hardest fightin' hands I ever see. But they sure buckle down when he says the word."

"Anyway, Jenkins," Wagner said, "there's the picture. Should it come to open warfare between the Ladder-A and the Bridle-Bit, you can see who'll win. I'm doing what I can to keep the peace, but there's limits I can't control. Here a while back Bucky and I worked out a scheme whereby we flung into a cell every Bridle-Bit rider that created any sort of a disturbance. But, cripes, Scarab just bailed 'em out as fast as we put 'em in, and paid their fines when I could make a charge stick."

"He must have got tired of paying fines," Malotte took up the story, "because he convinces the people in Padre Wells they should have a town marshal. And what does he do? He gets one of his own hands, Steve Franklin, appointed to the job. And Franklin does what Scarab orders done."

Jinglebob whistled softly. "So that's the how of it. I was wondering what a town this size was doing with so much law enforcement."

Wagner nodded. "Ordinarily, Bucky could handle this town in addition to his county duties, and I could be back at the county seat where I belong, but with things carrying on like a lit fuse in a powder keg, I been sticking close for the blow-up."

"Damn' if I blame you," Jinglebob said seriously. "I still don't see though why Scarab should have suspicions regarding me, just because I'm camping on Ladder-A range."

"You don't?" Bucky Malotte said harshly. "Hell's bells! An A. C. A. operative was killed —"

"What's that got to do with me?" Jenkins frowned.

Wagner's gaze narrowed on Jenkins. "You don't see it?" he demanded.

"Not any."

Impatiently, Wagner explained, "Why Scarab thinks you're another operative sent here by the A. C. A."

"And," said Bucky Malotte, confronting Jenkins on his solid bulldog legs, "I wouldn't be none surprised if you were."

A look of amazement slowly dawned on Jinglebob's tanned features. His eyes widened, his jaw dropped as he stared at the two peace officers. Suddenly, he went off into peals of laughter. "I — I think," he choked, "that's just about the funniest thing I ever heard. Me, a poet. And now you're calling me, Jinglebob Jenkins, a cow detective!"

CHAPTER
FOUR

A Marked Man

Jinglebob's laughter subsided after a time. Sheriff Wagner was looking a trifle sheepish. Traces of disbelief still showed in Bucky Malotte's round, china-blue eyes. He wrinkled his snub nose and gestured toward Pat Hogan, behind the bar.

"If you're touchy about speaking out in front of Pat," Bucky said, "you needn't to be. Pat ain't got no reason to love the Bridle-Bit. That crew comes here and busts glasses and raises hell in general, every so often."

"You spoke truth," Hogan growled. "And by the same token, Breck Alastair was always a good friend. If you're skeery to speak in front of me, Mister Jenkins —"

"But I'm not," Jinglebob insisted, still grinning widely. "It just strikes me as being plumb humorous, that's all."

"Maybe it won't turn out so humorous," Malotte spoke in his harsh tones, "when Scarab puts a spy on your tail, to check your actions. Maybe you'll laugh out of the other side of your mouth when a lead slug comes out of nowhere to smash in right where you live."

Jinglebob sobered. "Do you suppose Scarab would do anything like that?"

"What in the name of the seven bald steers do you think he left here for, so abrupt?" Clem Wagner snorted. "Scarab was heading for his outfit to order a man to keep him posted on your movements."

"How do you know that?" Jinglebob asked quietly.

"I don't," Wagner replied promptly. "That is, I've no more than a hunch and my suspicions to go on. But you mind what I say, until Scarab is settled easy in his mind what your business is, hereabouts, you're a marked man, Jinglebob Jenkins."

"Hmmm," Jinglebob considered. "That's a nice pleasant prospect. I'm glad I'm not a cattle detective on the A. C. A.'s payroll."

"You really aren't, then?" Bucky Malotte persisted.

Grinning, Jinglebob slowly shook his head. Sheriff Wagner's gaze bore into Jinglebob's gray eyes. Jinglebob met the scrutiny steadily. Wagner sighed and nodded. There was now no doubt in the sheriff's mind that Jenkins spoke truthfully.

"I reckon you're slinging a straight loop," Wagner said ruefully. "I was sort of hoping the association had sent another man here to help out the Ladder-A. Lord knows, they need help." He paused, then added, "Not that Bucky and I wouldn't do all possible for 'em, but we're not detectives. We're just ordinary peace officers, and when it comes to solving riddles — well, like I said, we're up against a blank wall."

It was pleasantly cool in the barroom. Outside, on the street, there wasn't a great deal of movement. Now and then, footsteps passed, on the plank walk, then died away again.

Pat Hogan said, "How about another drink? This one will be on the house."

"That bourbon you serve is prime tonsil-wash, Pat," Jinglebob said. "It's hard to refuse."

Hogan placed a bottle and glasses before his guests. After a time, Jinglebob said, "I've been thinking about you, Pat."

"About me?" Pat asked, puzzled. "What about me?"

"About you and your whisky. Your bourbon's a real inspiration. I thought up a poem about it."

"You did!" Pat's round face crinkled to an appreciative smile. "You got one of these here . . . what do you call 'em? . . . uh . . . er . . . a name for it?"

"A title? Sure I titled this poem 'Advice to Folks Traveling to Padre Wells, or A Good Reason for Going There.'"

"Gosh," Malotte said, "you don't go for short names, do you?"

"Not if I can help it. I like 'em long. It lets folks know what they're about. Then in case they aren't interested in poetry, they don't have to listen. Here it is . . ." Smiling widely, Jenkins recited:

> "Strangers in Padre Wells should know
> Pat Hogan's bourbon whisky.
> Once you have sipped its velvet glow,
> All other brands are risky."

Hogan's eyes shone with admiration. Bucky Malotte listened with something akin to awe in his features and said, in an aside, to the sheriff, "And we suspicioned that hombre of being a cattle dick. He *is* a poet. He don't even act like he gave a second thought to what we told him about Dave Scarab."

Jinglebob held up one hand for silence. "Listen, here's the other verse:

> "So let Pat pour to the glasses' brim;
>   He'll treat you like a brother:
> For every drink you buy from him,
>   He'll buy for you another."

"Well, I'll be eternally dam'd for a sheep-dipper!" Bucky Malotte burst out.

"It's pretty nice, all right," Wagner said admiringly.

Hogan could only shake his head. When he finally found his voice, his tones were hoarse with emotion, "That . . . that's the finest pome I ever heard. I'll bet that feller — what's his name, Tennyson? — I'll bet Tennyson couldn't do no better."

"Well, I don't know," Jinglebob said modestly. "Tennyson's pretty good too."

"Look, Jinglebob," Pat asked eagerly. "Would you write it down for me? I'll get a copy made to hang over my back bar."

"Sure thing. Got a paper and pencil handy?"

"I have that. I've got another drink handy, too, anytime you say."

"Not for me," Jinglebob laughed. "I've had enough."

While he was engaged in writing down the words of the jingle, Marshal Steve Franklin pushed through the swinging doors. Bucky and the sheriff nodded shortly to the marshal. Hogan reluctantly left off watching Jenkins and moved down the bar.

"What are you having, Steve?"

"I'm not drinking, Pat. I came in to see Jenkins."

"He's busy writing out a pome for me," Hogan said pridefully.

"A poem?"

Hogan nodded. "He made one up about me, right while he was standing here."

Franklin looked dubious. Jinglebob raised his head, saying, "You waiting to see me, Franklin? I'll be through in a second."

He pushed the paper and pencil across the bar to Hogan and sauntered down the bar where Franklin waited. Bucky and Wagner watched in silence. Hogan's lips moved in blissful concentration as he read the words Jinglebob had written.

"What's on your mind, Franklin?" Jinglebob asked.

Franklin's buck teeth showed in an assumed smile. "I got to thinking things over, Jenkins, and I decided maybe I acted a mite hasty. I didn't want you to have a wrong opinion of me."

"I don't reckon my opinion of you is wrong," Jinglebob said dryly. "I figure Scarab sent you here to say that, didn't he?"

Franklin flushed. "We-ell, I wouldn't go so far . . ."

"But it was Scarab's idea, not yours, wasn't it?"

"Now, look here, Jenkins, you can't question me that —"

"I'll question you any way I care to," Jinglebob said directly. "I don't figure you as the kind that would

40

make apologies . . . even when you're in the wrong. And you were wrong — damnably wrong — when you tried to arrest me. And so, it looks to me as though Scarab sent you here to smooth things over."

Franklin stiffened beneath Jinglebob's steady gaze. Abruptly, he allowed his temper to gain the upper hand. His pale eyes flashed angrily. "All right, have it your way," he snapped. "It was Dave's idea. I think he's mistaken. You came here making trouble, Jenkins. I did my best to enforce the law. You got off — but don't try anything else in this town."

"I haven't tried anything yet, Franklin," Jinglebob said softly, "anything that wasn't lawful. Can you say as much?"

"You hinting that I'm crooked?" Franklin rasped.

"I'm not *hinting*," Jinglebob said steadily.

"By God, Jenkins, you're asking for trouble!"

"Maybe you'd like to try arresting me again."

Franklin's buck teeth showed in an angry snarl. He shot a swift glance toward Sheriff Wagner and Malotte, started to speak, then thought better of it. With an effort he held his rage in check, saying, "Jenkins, you're getting off on the wrong foot with me. It's not wise."

Jinglebob repeated in a slow drawl: "Maybe you'd like to try arresting me again."

"It won't be arrest the next time, Jenkins."

"Meaning just what?"

"Work it out your own way."

"Perhaps," Jinglebob said coldly, "you're suggesting I wear my gun the next time I come to town."

Franklin's pale eyes were baleful. "Perhaps," and his tones were venomous, "you get the idea."

Sheriff Wagner cut in: "You'd better bridle that tongue, Franklin, and remember I'm still head man in this county."

Franklin shot a sharp look toward the sheriff. "That condition may be changed too, Wagner."

"You pointing to anything in particular?" Wagner demanded.

Franklin opened his mouth, closed it again. He realized he'd already said too much. "Nothing in particular," he said finally, "except that votes may be lacking the next time you come up for election."

"I'm glad you explained," Wagner responded in a dry, unbelieving voice.

Franklin commenced to back toward the swinging doors.

Bucky Malotte took a six-shooter from the waistband of his trousers. "Wait a minute, Franklin. Here's Gus Raymer's hawglaig that I took off'n him an hour or so back. With so many war rumors floating around, I'd hate to see Gus left without his gun."

"Leave it with Pat," Franklin half snarled. "Gus can get it from him. Why ask me to tote Gus's iron?"

"I figured you'd see him before Pat does." Bucky's snubnosed face was innocent. "Ain't you figurin' to ride to the Bridle-Bit and report to Scarab now?"

Franklin swore and took two quick steps back into the room. Then he stopped, swore some more, and turning, headed for the street.

There was a moment's silence, after the marshal had left. Then Malotte chuckled harshly and handed Raymer's gun across the bar. "You heard Franklin refuse it, Pat. You can give it to Raymer, next time he comes in."

"Never knew it to fail," Wagner rumbled heavily. "Put a town marshal in where there's already a sheriff's office, in a town like this, and there's trouble."

"Hell, he's no real marshal," Bucky said. "You know's well as I do, Clem, that he'd never got the job, except that Scarab wanted some of the law on his side —"

"You mean," Jinglebob interrupted, "Scarab wanted somebody to interpret town law — in Scarab's way."

"Nothing else," Wagner nodded. "Jinglebob, that was war talk Franklin was pushing in your direction."

Jinglebob smiled. "I had a sort of a hunch it was."

Wagner snorted. "Hunch, hell! Don't you recognize a threat when it's thrown in your face?"

"I reckon," Jinglebob said nonchalantly.

"Great Godfrey, man! Don't you realize Franklin's out to get you? I'll do what I can to prevent it — and Bucky too — but we can't be everywhere at once."

"I suppose not." Jinglebob was silent for a moment, then, "Gosh, I wish I could find a rhyme for Saskatoon. If you hombres think of one, let me know, will you?"

Malotte looked disgusted. Wagner groaned.

"Under some circumstances," the sheriff grunted peevishly, "*loon* might fit your case."

Jinglebob chuckled. "Nope, it's got to be a girl's name. What's fretting you, sheriff?"

"I wish you'd forget your danged poems for a few minutes," Wagner said irritably. "Here's Franklin all set to puncture your hide and —"

"What do you want me to do?" Jinglebob asked innocently.

"That's what we want to know," the sheriff half yelled. "What are you going to do?"

"Well," Jinglebob faced the sheriff and his deputy squarely, "I'm going to get my horse and ride —"

"You running away?" Bucky demanded disappointedly.

". . . back to my camp," Jinglebob continued placidly, as though he hadn't heard the interruption, "and work on a few poems I've started. My gun is there. Next time I come to town I'll be wearing it, and if Marshal Steve Franklin is still looking for trouble, he's going to find it —"

"That's the talk," Bucky Malotte said enthusiastically.

". . . and maybe," Jinglebob drawled on, "he'll find said trouble a heap hotter than he reckons on. And the same goes for any other Bridle-Bit hand that takes a notion to disrupt my poetic studies. If I'm suspected of being a cattle dick, I might as well act like one, until such time as I can have some peace and quiet for my life's work. The more I see of Scarab and his methods, the more the Bridle-Bit annoys me. And if you see any of that outfit, I'll appreciate your telling 'em what I said . . . *Adiós*, gents."

He'd passed through the swinging doors, on the way to his waiting horse at the hitch-rack, before the men in

44

the Acme Saloon had time to make a reply. There was nothing to be seen of Marshal Steve Franklin on the street. Climbing into his saddle, Jinglebob turned his pony and loped out of town.

Back in the Acme, the sheriff and his deputy were staring, tongue-tied, at each other. Hogan, speechless, was trying to draw their attention to the bottle he kept shoving toward them. In the sheriff's features was a dawning look of elation.

"By God! He will fight, if he's pushed," the sheriff said finally.

Bucky's bulldog head bobbed up and down in enthusiastic agreement. "Pushed hell!" Bucky half yelled. "I know his breed. All he needs is a little nudge — and he won't wait long for that. By cripes! I'm commencing to wonder now if he *is* a poet!"

CHAPTER
FIVE

Long Range Shooting

The sun had passed meridian by the time Jinglebob departed from Padre Wells. By two in the afternoon, riding west, he was ten miles from town, following a wagon-rutted trail that led to the Ladder-A Ranch. Far to the west, the rugged Truculento Range raised serrated peaks toward a sky of sapphire. To the north floated a fleecy bank of white, against which were silhouetted the dipping, wheeling forms of a pair of buzzards, which dropped nearer and ever nearer to the earth.

"Must be a dead cow or something over that way," Jinglebob mused, and thinking of buzzards, he thought, at the same time of Dave Scarab and the Bridle-Bit outfit. "Yes, this is a country for wearing guns," his thoughts ran, and changed abruptly to "Cripes! I wish I could think up a rhyme for Saskatoon."

It was all rolling grass-country through which he was riding. The trail, well defined, coursed ribbon-like up low slopes, crested the top and dipped gently to meet wide hollows, in some of which Jinglebob saw white-faced cattle, bearing on the left flank the Ladder-A brand, a four-runged ladder design with one of the rungs forming the cross piece of the connecting A.

Occasionally, the trail, along which the roan gelding was kicking up puffs of white dust, swerved to one side to avoid tall outcroppings of rocky granite. Here and there, jumbled heaps of bowlders barred the way. Mostly, though, it was good grazing country through which Jinglebob passed, dotted now and then with clumps of sage brush, low mesquite bushes or thorny prickly pear.

Two miles farther on, Jinglebob reined his pony off the trail running to the Ladder-A and took a more direct course toward his camp, located on the south fork of Sleepy Horse Creek. There wasn't any trail to follow now, as the pony pushed steadily through the long grass, at places almost reaching to its rider's stirrups, when Jinglebob dropped down to cross shallow hollows.

Gradually, horse and rider commenced climbing higher slopes as they neared the foothills of the Truculento Range, closer now, under the bright afternoon sun. They were approaching a long, bare ridge with a rather steep ascent, and Jinglebob slowed the pony's gait to meet the barrier.

By the time the roan had reached the crest it was breathing heavily, and Jinglebob drew rein to breathe it a moment before commencing the descent. He had stopped near an upthrust of jagged red granite that reached several feet higher than his head. In the bright sunlight his form stood out clearly against the rough, mottled rock.

Jinglebob drew out his sack of Durham and fingered one vest pocket for a cigarette paper. Shaking the tobacco into the paper he deftly rolled a smoke, then scratched a match and lighted the slim cylinder. He inhaled deeply, broke the match in two pieces and tossed it away. The pony shifted weight from one foot to another, the movement bringing Jinglebob around to face off toward the south.

He sat, smoking quietly, idly surveying the wide stretch of terrain that lay before his eyes. Thirty-five miles off, he knew, lay the Mexican border. To the west and south, high ridges of the Truculento Mountains grew hazy in the distance. Nearer, some seven or eight hundred yards away, rose a rock-cluttered slope, rising somewhat higher than the ridge upon which Jinglebob rested his pony. Between these two higher points lay a long, wide grassy depression across which Jinglebob's gray eyes idly roved. Still drawing on his cigarette, Jinglebob lifted his gaze up the rock-cluttered slope to range along the uneven, rock-strewn crest.

Abruptly, he stiffened, lifted one hand to his lips and tossed away the cigarette. From the top of the opposite ridge had come a brief, momentary gleam, as of sunlight reflecting from bright, moving metal. Then, the metallic glint vanished as quickly as it had appeared.

Jinglebob wasn't taking any chances. He paused but a moment longer, then, loosening his feet from stirrups, he flung his arms in the air and pitched abruptly from the saddle. Even as he plunged toward the earth, his ears caught the vicious whine of a leaden slug as it passed dangerously close. He heard it spatflatten against the rock at his back, and an instant later, the distant crack of a rifle came to him.

He lay silent, still, as he had fallen, his long form huddled awkwardly, close to the gravelly earth. His sombrero had rolled three feet away. His head rested, sidewise, on a small clump of sparse grass, red hair forming a patch of bright color against the gray-green foliage. The roan pony had jumped nervously at the shot, the movement carrying the saddle from beneath Jinglebob's body as he fell. Now it had quieted and stood a few yards off, idly cropping at some small growth and, from time to time, pausing to turn a questioning head toward its prone master.

Scarcely a muscle moved while Jinglebob's narrowed eyes scrutinized the rocky slope from whence had come the rifle shot. There wasn't a movement to be seen, strain his gaze as he might. No sign of life appeared on the opposite ridge.

Thoughts coursed swiftly through Jinglebob's head: Yes, this *is* a country for wearing guns. My hunch was right. It's lucky for me I dropped when I did. That's long range shooting — damn fine lead-throwing. I wonder who did it? Scarab? One of his men? Was I mistaken for someone else, someone connected with the Ladder-A? Or did that hombre know who he was drawing a bead on?

There hadn't been a second shot. Evidently, the hidden rifleman had figured the single bullet was enough, when he saw Jinglebob drop from the saddle. That showed confidence in his shooting, the confidence of an executioner who knew his work. The apparent results of that single shot had been no more than the ambushing assailant had expected. When a second shot had failed to follow the first, Jinglebob commenced to breathe easier. But not yet did he dare make a move. He lay as before, wishing he had brought a gun with him, motionless, like a dead man.

The seconds dragged into minutes and the minutes moved sluggishly on leaden feet. A small insect crawled into Jinglebob's left ear, and out again, tracing a tiny, tickling path across one cheek. That in itself was torture of a sort, but Jinglebob made no move to brush it off, put an end to its wanderings.

A quarter-hour passed and merged into twenty minutes. The sun moved steadily overhead. Flies droned about the prone man's head, while the shadow of the tall rock near which he lay commenced to lengthen. He waited, a moment longer, then slapped smartly at the exploring insect on his cheek. Swearing softly under his breath, Jinglebob rose cautiously to his feet.

For a moment he held himself tense, expecting no further activity, but ready to move swiftly if any appeared on the opposing rocky ridge. Then he exhaled a low whistling breath and relaxed. The cigarette he had been smoking when he dove from his saddle had long since gone out and lay where he'd dropped it. He reached for his "makin's" and rolled and lighted another cigarette with cool, steady fingers.

"I reckon that dry-gulching son has high-tailed it," he said, half aloud.

He moved toward his pony, caught the reins, and climbed into the saddle. Then he directed the roan down across the wide hollow and toward the slope from which the hidden rifleman had fired.

Ten minutes later the pony was picking its way up the rock-strewn slope. At the top, Jinglebob again drew rein and dismounted. He glanced back across the depression he'd just crossed and quickly calculated the approximate point from which the shot had come.

On the other side of the crest of the ridge lay a long gradual slope. Along the top of the ridge were heaps of jumbled rock. Halfway to the bottom, a stunted mesquite tree grew at an angle. Jinglebob paused, then cast his eyes around the surrounding country.

His glance was just in time to catch, far to the east and south, a rider dipping down over a rise of land, heading in the direction of Padre Wells. The man was riding hard, moving fast, and in an instant was out of sight. The rider was too far away to be distinguishable from any other mounted man who might have been crossing the range.

"An honest hombre," Jinglebob mused, "wouldn't be riding that hard to leave this vicinity. I wish I could have seen him sooner. I might have recognized him. Shucks, at this distance I couldn't even determine the color of his horse. Well, there's no use taking up his trail now. He's heading for Padre Wells, but he'd lose himself in town before I could get there."

Jinglebob hesitated but a moment more before moving down the slope to where he had seen the stunted mesquite tree. Once more he had guessed correctly. It was here the would-be assassin had tethered his horse. There was "sign" on the ground to denote that. Jinglebob moved out from the tree and circled it. There were hoofprints to be seen, here and there, wide-spaced hoofprints.

"Rode like hell getting here, before I come along," Jinglebob told himself. "Then moved plumb speedy after figuring he'd rubbed me out."

Jinglebob moved in a crouching position, now, again scrutinizing the earth beneath the stunted mesquite. Here, there were more marks to be seen, imprinted on the earth, fainter marks than those made by the horse. Footprints. There was too much gravel scattered about for the prints to be numerous, but Jinglebob managed to follow them to the top of the hill.

The footprints led him, almost in a straight line, to a wide, sandy nest among the rocks. The prints became plainer when they reached the sandy footing, though even now they were none too easy to follow.

Here the rocks were piled breast-high, forming a sort of breastworks from behind which the would-be murderer had fired. Jinglebob cast a quick glance across the hollow, to the point where he had dropped from his horse.

"A good seven hundred fifty yards," he cogitated. "This sure made an ideal spot for dry-gulching. That hombre could look right down on me from here. Damn lucky for me I saw that movement. If it had been a cloudy day there wouldn't have been any gleam for me to glimpse. Wonder what it was? Rifle barrel, maybe. No, it was small, brighter, than a reflection from a gun barrel."

He moved carefully around, inspecting the earth and the footprints. A tiny metallic glint caught his eye, off to one side. Jinglebob stooped and retrieved an exploded rifle cartridge. He examined it carefully. It was of thirty-thirty caliber. After a few seconds he placed it in his pocket and continued his search for evidence.

Then, close to the spot at which the rifleman had stood, Jinglebob picked up a cigar stub. The cigar had gone out when half smoked. One end was still slightly damp, but it was drying rapidly in the hot air.

"Probably tossed this away when he spotted me coming," Jinglebob mused. He placed the cigar stub carefully on a rock and returned to an examination of the footprints. Where the man had ascended from the mesquite tree below, the prints, for a distance of three or four yards at one point, were clearly discernible.

Walking parallel to the prints, Jinglebob paced off several steps. Then he returned and knelt down close to the spot from which he had started. Here, moving slowly forward, he compared his own prints with those of the man who had fired upon him. Finally, he straightened to his feet, something of satisfaction showing in his gray eyes.

"Prints about the same so far as depth is concerned," he reckoned mentally, "so he's probably about my weight. He takes longer steps, though. His legs are longer than mine. He's a mite taller than I am. Probably a sort of a tall and skinny cuss. High-heeled boots. Left foot about like my own. The heel of his right boot is run over on the outside. Walks on the outside of his right foot, when he puts it down. Well," grinning cheerfully, "I've learned a right smart more than I hoped for. I'll give this some thought, and maybe arrive at the identity of the dry-gulching son who tried to put his quietus on me."

By the time he had concluded his examination, the sun had moved far to the west and was already hovering above the distant Truculento peaks. Jinglebob retrieved the cigar butt from the rock where he had left it. By this time the tip was dry and stiff. He drew out his bandana and wrapped the cigar butt, together with the exploded rifle shell he had found, carefully in the handkerchief before putting it back in his pocket. Then he moved down the slope and again mounted his pony.

Twenty minutes later, once more riding in the direction of his camp, Jinglebob spied a rider approaching from the north. As the horse drew near, Jinglebob recognized old Tarp Jones. The weather-beaten old cowman sat easily in his saddle, unconsciously accommodating his movements to those of the horse he straddled.

"Hi! Jinglebob!"

Jinglebob drew rein as old Tarp came up and checked his own pony.

"Hi-yuh, Tarp? How's tricks?"

Tarp put forth a gnarled hand. Jinglebob took it gravely. Tarp said, "Tricks don't look so good."

"What's wrong?"

Tarp cursed and spat a long stream of tobacco juice. "Back yonderly," jerking his head toward the northeast, "'bout fifteen mile, I found three of our Ladder-A cows."

"Anything unusual about that?"

Tarp cursed some more. "They'd been hamstrung. It was done sometime yesterday, I figure. The coyotes done *their* work last night."

Jinglebob remembered now the buzzards he'd noticed earlier in the afternoon. He said quietly, "That's right tough, Tarp. Any idea who did it?"

"Them Bridle-Bit skunks, a-course."

"Got proof of that?"

"No, I ain't got no proof. Don't need no proof. Dave Scarab is doing his damndest to scare us out. Cripes dammity hell! Wanton slaughter, thet's whut it is! I can almost forgive a cowthief, when I think on it. Anythin' a cowthief takes is used to feed somebody. But when it comes to slaughterin' cow critters for coyotes and stink birds to fatten on, it shore riles my innards. If I only had proof agin the Bridle-Bit —"

"It might not be the Bridle-Bit, Tarp. I came from town a spell back. Some of the outfit was in Padre Wells . . ."

"You see Scarab?" Tarp demanded.

Jinglebob nodded. "Scarab. Raymer. Three others whose names I don't know."

"Cripes a'mighty! That's only about half the crew. There's three or four more hands on Scarab's payroll. Anyway, them cows was cut sometime yesterday, I figure. The coyotes got in their work last night, judging from signs —" Old Tarp broke off, "Did ye talk to Scarab any?"

"Some."

"What ye think of him?"

Jinglebob just shrugged his shoulders.

Tarp looked disappointed. "Some folks like him," he said. "Did ye talk to Gus Raymer too?"

Jinglebob smiled. "Didn't have much time to talk to him. He needed knocking down."

"He whut?"

"Raymer had been drinking. He got sort of tough. I had to wallop him a couple of times."

"Ye did?" eagerly. Tarp's eyes bulged in his excitement. "Well, by all the long-sufferin' old maids! Tell it."

"And then," Jinglebob grinned, "Marshal Franklin aimed to put me under arrest."

"Great palpitatin' prophets! Whut happened? I want all of it."

"There isn't much to tell. Sheriff Wagner interfered. I passed a few hard words with Franklin —"

"That measly coyote!"

"That's about all there was to it." Jinglebob related details of the story as briefly as possible.

Tarp Jones looked serious when he had concluded. "Ye'll have the hull Bridle-Bit outfit on yore tail now, boy. Ye'll have to look sharp. You won't have much time for makin' up pote-ry. Say, have ye made up anythin' new since I saw ye, yesterday?"

Jinglebob nodded. "Next time you're in town, ask Pat Hogan to show you the one I did for him."

"I'll do that. I was up to yore camp this mornin'. Ye was gone to town, then, of course."

"I'm heading back now. What you doing over this way, Tarp?"

Tarp frowned. "A short spell after I found them hamstrung critters, I kind of thought I heard a shot over this way — mebbe a mite farther to the east. Did ye hear anybody burnin' powder?"

Jinglebob nodded. "I heard it. And damn near felt it."

"Ye don't say. Come close?"

"Missed me by inches. I dropped out of the saddle and played possum . . ."

"Well, by all the long-sufferin' old maids! Who done it? Did you see him?"

Jinglebob again gave brief details. Not wanting Tarp to repeat his words, he failed purposely to mention the finding of the cigar stub and the reading of the footprints. "Yes," Jinglebob concluded, "I looked over the ground. I did find a thirty-thirty shell."

Tarp swore a blue stream, ending, "It was a thuty-thuty that downed my boss, Breck Alastair. And a thuty-thuty that ended Mitchell, an A. C. A. man that was sent for. I didn't tell ye that yesterday, but it's God's truth. Damn them Bridle-Bits for cold-blooded, murderin' —"

"There's no proof against the Bridle-Bit."

"Me, I ain't needin' proof," the old man said doggedly. "I know what I feel in my bones."

"Mebbe so," Jinglebob nodded. "Well, I've got to be pushing on. My stomach tells me supper isn't far off. I didn't eat any dinner. I'll see you some more, Tarp. Come up to camp, any time."

"I'll do thet, thankee. I got to be driftin' on, myself, and tell Lorry about them hamstrung critters."

"Lorry?"

"Breck Alastair's datter. She's runnin' the outfit, sence Breck's laid up."

"Oh. Well, *adiós*."

"*Adiós*, Jinglebob."

Jinglebob put spurs to his pony and continued on his way. Muttering to himself, old Tarp took a northwesterly course that brought him into the Ladder-A ranch yard just before sundown.

Lorry spied the old-timer when he was unsaddling near the corral. She left the house and came out to speak to him.

"Howdy, Lorry." Tarp busied himself with his cinch.

The girl, sensing something unusual in his manner, asked, "What's wrong now, Tarp?"

Tarp told her about finding the three hamstrung cows. Lorry's dark eyes flashed angrily. Neither the old cowman nor the girl mentioned the Bridle-Bit, but the name was uppermost in their minds. The girl bit her lip. Tarp employed polite cuss words.

Lorry went on, "Did you ride up to that Jenkins' camp and order him to move on, as I ordered?"

"Sho' enough."

"Did he give you an argument?"

"He wa'n't there."

The girl frowned. "Wasn't there? Do you mean he's pulled out for good? Had he broken camp?"

"We-ell," Tarp fumbled for words, "I don't rightly know, Lorry. Fact is, I got an idee that feller is all right —"

"Tarp Jones! When I give an order I want it carried out. You know very well he hasn't broken camp. For all you do know, he may have been the one that hamstrung those cows —"

58

"Now, wait a minute, wait a minute, Lorry. Ye don't know whut ye're sayin'. I'd stake my poke thet boy's all right. After him cleanin' Gus Raymer's clock —"

"Tarp Jones, what are you talking about?"

"We-ell, you see, Lorry, I crossed Jinglebob's trail a spell back and he said —"

"Did you tell him to pick up his camp and get?"

"I sort of forgot thet." The oldster scratched his jaw reminiscently. "You see, we got to talking —"

"You forgot!" Lorry's face colored angrily.

"Yes, demmity blazes, I forgot," Tarp snapped defiantly, in righteous indignation. "Ye would've, too, in my boots. Now, now, wait a minute. Put a hobble on that tongue o' yourn, Lorry, and listen to me . . ."

Skepticism struggled with belief in the girl's face as she listened to Tarp's story of his meeting with Jenkins.

"So there," Tarp concluded, "ye'll see how it was. I say it's a mistake to run off a man who licked Raymer, tangled with Steve Franklin and was shot at for his pains. He might prove a good friend to us. Gawd knows we could use a couple."

Lorry considered a moment, then shook her head. "Maybe it's as you say, Tarp, but we can't take chances. How do we know that fight with Raymer wasn't faked?"

"Whut would be the reason?"

"To pretend an enmity for the Bridle-Bit while he spies out the situation on the Ladder-A. We can't chance it, Tarp."

"By the seven palpitatin' prophets! Yo're jest a stubboring female, like all wimmen," Tarp exclaimed angrily. "Don't ye figure I got any sense?"

"Sometimes I doubt it," Lorry snapped.

"But size up the situation, gal," Tarp shouted angrily. "They already tried to dry-gulch him."

"You heard a shot. How do you know Jenkins didn't fire it himself?"

"Common sense tells me that ain't true —"

"Maybe common sense told you to ask to see the thirty-thirty shell he claimed he found, too."

Tarp looked exasperated. "I didn't think to do thet. Why should I? One thuty-thuty looks like another. Lorry, I'm old enough to be yore paw —"

"Grandpa."

"All right, all right, hev it yore own way. Common sense tells me I'm right. Ye better go back in the house, afore I loses my temper and quits this job right this minute."

Even while he talked, Tarp was unsaddling his horse. He muttered angry oaths under his breath. Lorry, too, was angry.

After a minute she said, "I'm still giving orders, here, Tarp. Quit if you want to, but I want one thing settled now — Jenkins must get off Ladder-A holdings."

"All right, all right," Tarp said sulkily. "Ye can have yore way. I'll ride up, fust off, in the morning and see him."

"You needn't. He'd give you another song-and-dance and you'd forget some more. Chris can take care of Breck. I'll ride up and talk to this Jenkins man, myself. And if he doesn't break camp when I tell him to get out, I'll take back everything I've said, Tarp Jones."

60

"Yo're makin' a mistake," Tarp growled. "I've talked to that boy. I know he's right."

"My mind's made up," Lorry snapped. "Jenkins moves on!"

CHAPTER
SIX

Lorry Gets Her Way

It was noontime before Lorry had an opportunity to leave the following day. The doctor had arrived at the Ladder-A in the morning, on his weekly visit from Padre Wells, to see Breck Alastair. When the doctor's horse had clattered out of the ranch yard, Lorry returned to her father's bedroom, located on the eastern side of the ranch house to catch the rays of the early sun.

For a few moments, Breck Alastair didn't hear his daughter at the doorway. He half-reclined in an easy chair, bundled in blankets. A few months before, Breck Alastair had been a fine, upstanding man in the prime of middle age, with broad shoulders and an unruly shock of wavy hair the color of iron. Now, he had wasted away to a mere shadow of his former self. The iron-gray mop of hair had turned to silver. His face was pale and drawn with suffering. Remained only the finely chiseled nose and the square jaw from which Lorry had inherited her determination. There were deep hollows beneath the once keen eyes, and the hand that picked fretfully at the blanket covering was almost fleshless.

A wave of pity swept through the girl as she stepped into the room, then as her father's eyes slowly came around at her step, she forced a warm smile. She went to him and knelt on the floor by his chair.

"You see, Breck, I told you you weren't strong enough yet to dress and move out."

"Doc Roberts doesn't know what he's talking about," the invalid muttered peevishly. Even the slightest exertion of speaking seemed to cause difficulty in Breck Alastair's breathing. "I'm certain sure, could I once get out, I'd be in the saddle in no time. There's no sense in Roberts holding me down forever."

"Look here, Breck Alastair," Lorry smiled, "you should know well enough that you can't take a thirty-thirty slug through your lungs and dance at a *baile* the same day. It takes time to recover from these things."

"Don't want to dance at a *baile*, or any place else," Alastair spoke querulously. "I just want to get back in a saddle and get on the trail of the skunk that did this to me."

"And you will, Breck. But you must be patient. Doctor Roberts told me you were coming along fine, far faster than he'd hoped for. You've had a pretty narrow escape, but the danger's past now. All you've got to do is rebuild yourself, get back your strength and your weight . . ."

"That's all right for you to say, Lorry, but how about the outfit?"

"You stop worrying about the outfit. Everything's going fine." The girl forced a short laugh. "You're just jealous because I'm running things as well as you ever did."

"Apparently," the invalid said with a touch of dry humor. "I heard you scrapping with old Tarp this morning —"

"Just as you used to do," Lorry cut in. "He riles me something awful at times. He's so set in his ways."

"Tarp's a good man, Lorry," Breck Alastair said seriously. "You can count on him. After your mother died, when I sort of went all to pieces, it was Tarp Jones who held the outfit together."

"Shhh, Breck. Let's not think of that." Lorry changed the subject, "I'm going to leave you in Chris's care, this afternoon."

"Where are you going?"

"I want to get away for a short spell. I figure to take a short ride over near the south fork of Sleepy Horse —"

"You're not going to Padre Wells?" Alastair asked anxiously. "There's always some of that Bridle-Bit outfit —"

"Now, quit your worrying, Breck. I'm not going anywhere near Padre Wells. I just want to ride and get some air."

Alastair nodded slowly. "You should get away. You've stayed too close to home. You're losing weight, girl. Go ahead, and have your ride."

"You promise to eat your milk and toast when Chris brings it?"

"I promise. Aren't you going to wait for dinner?"

Lorry shook her head. "I'll have Chris make me a beef sandwich to take with me."

A short time after, Lorry left the bedroom and stepped out of the house. Seeing Matt Alvord just emerging from the bunkhouse, she called to him to saddle her horse, then went to her own room to change to riding things.

A little over an hour later, Lorry was pushing her pony across the hills toward Jenkins' camp. There wasn't a cloud to be seen against the deep-blue expanse of sky. Ahead of her, almost seeming to tower over the girl, rose the precipitous heights of the Truculento Mountains, one or two of the higher peaks still clad in a mantle of white, from which long twisting fingers of snow filled the lower ravines, though on the grassy slopes across which the girl traveled the sun was bright and hot.

Now Lorry saw the long, marching line of tall cottonwood trees bordering the stream, where the south fork of Sleepy Horse Creek wended its lazy twisting way through the foothills of the Truculentos. She guided the pony down the gently sloping bank and into the water, drawing up her high-heeled, booted feet as the pony moved out, belly-deep, into the stream and paused to bury its nose in the limpid depths. While the horse sucked the cool water in noisy draughts, Lorry twisted in her saddle and gazed along the other side toward a thick clump of tall cottonwoods where she thought she saw movement.

Splashing out on the opposite bank a few minutes later, the girl directed the pony toward the clump of

65

cottonwoods that had caught her eye. There was plenty of low brush on this side of the stream and the trees grew closely together. Abruptly, girl and mount emerged on the edge of a wide clearing, not far from the stream, and here Lorry saw the man she had visited for the purpose of telling him to move on. The girl drew her pony to a halt and waited for Jinglebob to glance up.

He was seated on the earth, his shoulders resting against a rock, seemingly engrossed in scribbling on a pad of paper he held in his lap. To his left was a brush shelter with beneath it a neatly spooled bed-roll. A cartridge belt and holstered six-shooter hung from a low branch near the brush shelter, and against the trunk of the tree stood a Winchester rifle. Farther on, a roan saddler and gray pack pony were pegged out where the grazing was satisfactory. Not far from the seated man, a small iron kettle, braced on two chunks of rock, between which were glowing coals, bubbled and steamed and gave off savory odors.

A right comfortable camp, was the thought that passed through Lorry's head. She was still waiting for Jinglebob to glance up, but he continued writing, writing and crossing out, and writing again. He muttered to himself as his pencil moved across the paper. Once he smiled, but the smile was quickly replaced by a disgusted frown, and he made a number of vigorous obliterating marks over what he had written.

Lorry had been watching him for a full minute, commencing to believe he hadn't heard her arrival, when he spoke without raising his head, as though he had known she was there all the time. He said, "You haven't a rhyme for Saskatoon, have you?" His tones were quiet, evenly questioning.

The girl felt a flush mounting to her cheek. She commenced to feel angry, without knowing why. Or perhaps she did know. Here was this trespasser on Ladder-A property, displaying no interest in an owner's arrival, acting as though he had as much right as she to be there, when he should have been apologizing, at least asking leave, for his presence. Instead, he wanted help in the composition of some silly jingle.

Lorry gasped, then caught her breath. She said tartly, "No, I haven't."

At the first sound of the girl's voice, Jinglebob raised his eyes to see a tall slim girl in a mannish flannel shirt and patched and faded overalls. A fawn-colored sombrero was pulled low on her black hair. Looking at her eyes with their long dark lashes, Jinglebob thought, And now I'll have to find a rhyme for violet. And one for lovely, too.

He rose quickly from his seat on the earth and spoke as though addressing the cottonwood trees, "Ye gods! I sit here wasting all my time in trying to write a poem, and now one comes riding to me on a buckskin pony." He turned to the girl with a grin, "Light and rest your saddle, lady. I'm Jinglebob Jenkins." He gestured toward a rise of land, seen through the trees beyond the stream, a mile and a half away. "I saw you coming when you topped that slope. Too far away to recognize a girl though."

67

Lorry swung easily down from the saddle. Jenkins took her reins and draped them over a convenient mesquite limb. "Sorry, I haven't a chair to offer you."

His smile was warm, infectious. Lorry steeled herself to the duty at hand. This wasn't going to be easy. It didn't seem hospitable, somehow, to tell this smiling stranger to move on. Still, an order was an order. If Tarp Jones couldn't obey, it was up to her to see it was carried out.

The girl said stiffly, "I'm Lorry Alastair."

"I figured that. Tarp Jones mentioned you."

"This is Ladder-A property —" the girl commenced.

"I know. Tarp told me. He said it was all right, my camping here."

Lorry clenched her fists. The old scoundrel. Well, that permission would have to be rescinded. She moved toward the fire and seated herself on the earth. Jinglebob resumed his position. If he noticed the girl's chilly manner, he gave no sign. Lorry was silent for a few moments, endeavoring to marshal words, phrases, to explain her visit.

Jinglebob broke the quiet: "So you haven't a rhyme for Saskatoon?"

Lorry spoke an abrupt "No," and no more.

Jinglebob scratched his red hair and grinned. "If I don't get a rhyme for that word soon, it's going to be tough. I've done a lot of work on —"

"Tarp mentioned that you wrote nursery rhymes or something of the kind," Lorry said in chilly accents. She tried to make her voice sound contemptuous, but didn't quite succeed.

"Nursery rhymes?" Jinglebob looked dubious. "Tarp must have got mixed up. I never did figure 'em for nursery —" He broke off, then, "This poem I want the Saskatoon rhyme for is called 'Traveling is a Good Education, or A Pleasant Way to Learn Geography.'"

"Short and sweet, isn't it?" Lorry murmured politely.

"Well," Jinglebob grinned, "it's not very short. The poem isn't either, for that matter. You see, it commences like this:

"I've got a girl in Santa Fe
    And a girl in Saskatoon;
The first girl's name is Dora May,
    The other's . . ."

Jinglebob stopped, then, "You see, that's as far as I can get on my first verse, until I get a rhyme for Saskatoon."

Lorry said icily, "How about using buffoon?"

Jinglebob shook his head. "No, that wouldn't do," he explained earnestly, "it has to be a girl's name. I'm just waiting for that to end up with. Let me give you some of the other verses. You'll see what I mean. After that first verse the next one goes:

"There's Rosy Belle in San Antone'
    And Flossie in Cheyenne
And Samantha Jane in West Tyrone,
    In Douglas, Lucy Ann."

"You certainly cover a lot of territory," Lorry commented sweetly, her dark eyes hard.

"You understand," Jinglebob said seriously, "this is just a poem. I don't really mean all this." He went on with the next verse:

"In Lincoln town lives Sally Joe
    And Maude calls Austin home,
While Molly dwells in El Paso,
    Helena lives in Nome."

"It's just too bad," Lorry spoke coldly, "you couldn't have kept Helena in Montana."

Jinglebob grinned cheerfully. "We think along the same lines, don't we? I thought of that, too, so I made up a verse for that state. Listen,

"In Butte, there's Berta, sweet as pie,
    In Rawlins, Effie Lou;
Amanda waits in New Delhi
    And Betsey in Saint Lou'."

"Well," Lorry said ironically, "it's nice that you have enough sense to keep 'em apart, anyway."

Jinglebob said slowly, "Well, I didn't exactly aim to do that. It was just the way the rhymes fell. But you can see how it goes. With all the cities there are and girls' names, I could keep on and on —"

"I've been afraid of that."

"But I just intend to write a few more, then when I get the right rhyme I'll bring Saskatoon in again."

Lorry took a long breath. "Is this all you do, write this — this kind of stuff?"

70

Jinglebob grinned. "It's fun. I just ride around the country, seeing things, and then settle down and write. Lots of times I write while I'm riding."

"I was wondering what made your lines so jerky."

"Uh-huh. Some of 'em do need a smoothing down."

"I'd suggest sandpaper. Or at least try walking instead of riding when you write."

"No cowhand likes walking, Miss Alastair. That reminds me, I've got a song about why cowboys don't like walking. I'll sing it for you."

"Without any urging, eh?"

But Jinglebob missed the last words. He had gained his feet, crossed to the brush shelter and was rummaging in his bed-roll. He returned and seated himself, holding in his hands a somewhat battered old concertina. He drew a few wheezing notes from the instrument, then said, "I call this one 'The Repentant Cowboy, or A Tragedy of the Range in Sixteen Lines.'"

"You sound quite technical, Mister Jenkins." Lorry had to bite her lip to keep from laughing by now. It all seemed so ridiculous, with tragedy brewing on her own range, and this stranger who only yesterday had been fired on, sitting here playing an old musical instrument. This visit was turning out entirely different from what the girl had intended.

The next notes drawn from the concertina were mournful, plaintive, as Jinglebob commenced his song:

"A gay caballero rode over the hills-s
    A-forking a fast-stepping gray-y-y,

71

Looking for whisky and feminine thrills-s
  On which to spend all of his pay-y-y."

"Very elegant voice," Lorry murmured with something akin to sarcasm. "Did I suggest sandpaper a few minutes back?"

The concertina wheezed and groaned to the second stanza:

"The feminine thrills he unluckily found
  Led straight to a gamb-o-ling hell-l-l:
Horse and money were lost; in whisky he drowned,
  And woke up in an iron-barred cell-l-l."

"Hmmm." Lorry looked surprised. "Drowned? Woke up? Oh, I see. Resurrection from the dead. Sort of a miracle, eh?"

Jinglebob's hands and arms worked vigorously with the concertina. The buckskin pony's ears flattened against its head and it snorted nervously as the song continued:

"The judge the next morning was very severe,
  And threatened three months in the clink-k-k,
Unless the poor cowboy, by all he held dear,
  Would forswear future use of strong drink-k-k."

Jinglebob paused and eyed the girl uncertainly. "Maybe," he suggested, "it would be better without the music."

Lorry shook her head. "I don't see how it could be," she said politely. She was finding it difficult to suppress a smile.

Jinglebob nodded and concluded:

"The promise was given; once more on the street
    The buckaroo started for home.
By the time he arrived there, the state of his feet
    Made him swear he would nevermore roam-m-m-m."

Jinglebob put down the concertina. "The music isn't very good," he admitted apologetically. "I don't know much about writing music."

"But you are a poet?" Lorry's dark eyes were dancing now.

"Oh, yes," Jinglebob nodded, grinning widely. "I'm probably the best poet in this country."

"You have proof of that, I suppose?"

"Don't have to prove it," Jinglebob said brazenly. "I admit it."

The girl laughed. Despite herself she was liking this red-headed cowboy with the infectious, white-toothed smile. She nodded suggestively toward the kettle bubbling over the fire. "What's in there?"

"Stew. Slum. You know, a little of everything I can find to put in. Tomatoes, spuds, beef, onions." He rose, went to the brush shelter and returned to ladle out two platefuls of the concoction. He handed her a tin plate and a spoon.

"Don't burn yourself, lady. I've tortured you enough for one day."

Lorry said, "I was commencing to remember that all I had for dinner was a chunk of beef and bread, eaten on my way here." And a minute later, "Mmmm, it's good."

"You admit that," Jinglebob grinned, "now that you've had verse?"

The girl wrinkled her nose at him. "That one was pretty bad, Jinglebob Jenkins." She sat cross-legged, spooning the contents from her plate, and ate a second helping when that was finished. Finally, when the plates had been put aside, Jinglebob said seriously,

"Well, what's on your mind, lady?"

"What makes you think there is anything in particular?"

"This wasn't just a friendly visit. When you first arrived I figured you aimed to scratch my eyes out."

"I reckon you're right," Lorry said at last. She sat hunched up, knees cradled in her arms, gazing on the sunlight streaming spottily through the cottonwood leaves. A short distance away, Sleepy Horse Creek made soft, purling music between its sandy banks. Lorry turned to the man abruptly, "I gave Tarp Jones orders to tell you to move on."

Jinglebob said gravely, "Any particular reason?"

"Not where you're concerned . . . personally. It's just that we're having trouble."

"I heard something of that. The Bridle-Bit?"

Lorry nodded. "I gave orders that strangers weren't to stop on our holdings. You see, my father was shot, left for dead, out on the range . . . by someone. I suspect the Bridle-Bit. Our cows have been disappearing. Again, I suspect the Bridle-Bit."

"I've heard about that too. But why the Bridle-Bit? There are other outfits in this neck of the range."

"Scarab," the girl replied, "wants the Ladder-A."

"A matter of needing water, maybe," Jinglebob nodded. "This stream would be right valuable to any stock raiser."

The girl shook her head. "That can't be it. Scarab's holdings border on the north fork of Sleepy Horse. The north fork is bigger than this — at spots, almost a river. No, it's not water he's after. He has plenty of his own."

"Grazing lands, then?"

"Scarab's grass is as good as ours and he has more of it under his brand. He insists on trying to buy the Ladder-A. He won't offer a decent price, or I'd accept. So now, he's trying to scare us out, or steal enough stock to break us."

Jinglebob frowned. "I can't see any other reason for Scarab to want your property, then, except plain greed. He must be ambitious for large holdings."

"That's not the reason, either," Lorry said moodily. "If it was just land he wanted, there's plenty of open range to the east and north of him. He could have his hands pretend to homestead that and then buy their patents. He could get land in that direction a heap cheaper than the price he offers me."

Jinglebob frowned thoughtfully. "There might be valuable ore of some sort in that section of the Truculentos that borders your property."

"I doubt it. The Truculentos have been pretty thoroughly prospected. Besides, the Bridle-Bit property borders the Truculentos above Sleepy Horse. Mountains are mountains, mister, and if there was ore of any sort on Ladder-A property, there'd probably be ore on Bridle-Bit. No, there's some other reason for Scarab's persistence. I wish I knew what it was."

"It'll take a mite of thinking over," Jinglebob said gravely.

"Anyway," the girl said, "maybe you'll realize why I hate to see strangers on our land. You haven't seen them bring in your own father, after he'd been left for dead out on the range, shot by a murdering rat. Mebbe you'll see why I've grown to distrust every strange face I see, or hear of." The girl's voice was rising.

Jinglebob put out one hand. "Take it easy, Lady Lorry. I know what it is to be shot at. Yesterday —"

The girl nodded, quieting under his words. "Tarp Jones told me about that, and about your fight with Raymer. At first, I thought the whole thing might be faked, that you might be a spy for the Bridle-Bit, planning to do us further harm —"

"And now you've changed your mind?"

"I've changed my mind," the girl nodded simply. "You're — you're not quite like I expected you to be. This afternoon has made things seem different."

"*Muchas gracias, señorita.*"

"Thanks aren't necessary, Jinglebob. I'm only telling you how I feel."

They talked on and on while the shadows lengthened. It wasn't long before the girl found herself

76

laughing at Jenkins' dry humor during their conversation. The wall of fear that had hedged her in for the past few months no longer appeared so ominous, so unsurmountable. Something in the man's very manner bred a new confidence, courage, in the girl's being. Before the two realized the fact, the sun was dipping toward the higher peaks of the Truculentos and forming purple shadows in the deepest ravines.

"Good grief!" Lorry exclaimed, leaping to her feet. "The day's almost gone. I've got to be drifting back before Breck decides to send out a searching party for me. He'll worry, if I'm not back before dark . . . No. No, thanks. No need of you coming along. I'll be all right."

Jinglebob tightened the cinch on the buckskin pony. He didn't miss the lithe ease with which the girl gained the saddle. She turned the pony and sat looking down on him, noticing how the dying sunlight picked out bright highlights in his red hair, seeing and appreciating the open admiration in his frank gray eyes.

"Well," the girl hesitated, "thanks for a nice afternoon."

Jinglebob smiled, one hand resting on the horse's bridle. "I'm not a stranger any more, then?"

"Not any more."

"Friends?"

The girl reached out her hand. It was cool and firm in his grasp. "Friends," she nodded, smiling. After a moment she removed her hand and tightened the reins.

He detained her a moment longer. "I won't have to break camp and get off your range, then?"

A tiny wrinkle appeared between Lorry's eyes. "I've been thinking about that, too. You see, I can't go back on what I told Tarp. I told him you'd have to break camp. I said I'd see to it, or know the reason why. Tarp helped Breck raise me. He has a sort of an idea he can boss me around, now and then. If I retracted what I said, now, that old tyrant never would quit riding me."

Jinglebob said, "What's the answer?"

"You break camp," Lorry said firmly. Then she smiled, "Then move your duffle down to the Ladder-A bunkhouse. You're welcome to stay as long as you like. I know it will please the boys — if you'll forget their age and call 'em boys. I think you might cheer Breck up, occasionally." She took a long breath. "That solves the problem, if you'll do it . . . and I won't lose prestige with old Tarp."

Jinglebob grinned. "I'll do it, Lady Lorry. I'll break camp in the morning. And look — Tarp didn't say so, right out, but I judged from his manner that the Ladder-A could use an extra hand —"

"We can't afford to pay wages, Jinglebob," Lorry said. "We're playing 'em too close to our vest."

"Did I say anything about wages?" Jinglebob chuckled. "I'll take my wages in making you listen to my poetry."

"Cowboy, you're hired."

He watched her ride off through the trees, musing, No, there couldn't be any rhyme for lovely. That one word says it all . . .

CHAPTER
SEVEN

A Man to Be Stopped

Clem Wagner was still an hour's ride away from the fork on the Sleepy Horse when, glancing off to the southwest, he spied a rider with a pack horse. Before the rider were being herded along two other animals that looked like Hereford calves. Apparently, the rider had, a short time before, emerged from among the trees bordering the southern widening of the south fork of the Sleepy Horse, where it commenced to spread out on its way toward the Mexican Border.

The sheriff frowned. "Now, I wonder who that could be? Reckon I'd better drift over thataway and find out what that jasper's doing."

Turning his horse, the sheriff struck out toward the distant stranger. A moment later the animal dropped down a long slope and the rider was blotted from view. By the time Wagner's horse had again carried him to higher ground, the sheriff saw that the stranger had stopped and dismounted. Nearby, stood the pack horse. The two calves had been roped and thrown to the earth.

Again, the grassy slopes dipped down before the sheriff was close enough to recognize the man who had dismounted.

"Looks to me," Wagner muttered, "like that hombre was fixing to do a mite of branding. Some investigation seems to be called for."

Twenty minutes later when the sheriff's horse emerged on a long stretch of open range, the sheriff recognized Jinglebob Jenkins. Jenkins was bending over a small fire he had built. The two calves were still on the earth, resting on their sides, making plaintive bawling sounds.

Crouched above the fire, Jenkins suddenly lifted his head and recognized Wagner. He raised one arm in greeting and called, "Come on in, sheriff," and went on with the work he was doing.

By the time Wagner had arrived and dismounted, Jinglebob had taken a branding iron, improvised from baling wire, from the fire, and walked to the nearest calf. He put one knee on the calf's side, braced his other foot against the calf's legs, and applied the cherry-red iron to the small animal's flank.

A stench of burning hair and flesh rose on the air. The calf struggled and bawled frantically. Jenkins swore once or twice, good-humoredly, and continued his work.

Frowning, the sheriff came close and saw that Jinglebob was branding the calf with a Ladder-A brand.

The sheriff breathed a little easier. "What in hell you think you're doing?" he demanded.

"It's known as calf-branding, sheriff," Jinglebob grinned cheerfully.

"Dammit, I know that, but what —?"

"Take a look at this critter's eyes," Jinglebob said, rising from the calf's side, "while I reheat this iron and slap a brand on that other doggie."

He returned to the fire and thrust the iron among the glowing embers. In a few minutes he went to the other calf. Frowning, Wagner stooped near the head of the calf that had been branded, lifted its head. The calf had ceased struggling now, and had returned to its plaintive bawling.

From the other calf now came frantic, struggling noises. Again rose the odor of scorched hair and flesh. Jinglebob returned to the fire and tossed his iron on the ground. He wiped the perspiration from his forehead and smiled at the sheriff, just coming up to the fire. Wagner was still looking puzzled.

Jenkins commenced rolling a cigarette. He held out the sack and papers to the sheriff who took them and also started to fashion a smoke. Jenkins stooped down and plucked a coal from the fire, holding it by the still unburned end and proffered a light for the sheriff's cigarette. The sheriff inhaled gravely, still waiting for Jenkins to explain. Jenkins blew a long cloud of gray smoke into the air and tossed the burning wood into the fire.

"Mavericks," he said quietly. "I figured the Ladder-A needed 'em worse than anybody — inasmuch as they're probably Ladder-A stock, anyway. Did you take a look at that critter's eyes."

The sheriff nodded, without speaking.

Jenkins went on, "The other one's the same way. Wait a minute, I'll let 'em up."

He crossed to the two calves and quickly jerked off the piggin' strings that had bound their feet. The animals rose with clumsy swiftness and awkwardly lumbered away, pausing now and then to lick their burns.

Jenkins went to his pony and carefully recoiled his lariat and disposed of the piggin' strings. Then he returned to the sheriff. "First day I came into this country," he said, jerking one thumb toward the row of cottonwoods that fringed Sleepy Horse Creek, a few hundred yards to his rear, "I crossed the stream right about there. It's a heap wider, but shallower, than farther up where I had my camp. There's a regular jungle of growth down in those bottoms. I heard sounds in the brush and figured them to be made by cows. Didn't pay much attention. Yesterday I was talking to Lorry Alastair. I got thinking over one or two things, and decided to come down here and investigate after I broke camp."

"You figuring to pull out?" Wagner asked.

"Miss Alastair invited me to stay at the Ladder-A. Anyway, I come down here first and found those two doggies with not a brand on their hides. They were plumb wild and inclined to hide out. I was going to drive 'em to the Ladder-A, but it was too much of a job to keep 'em headed — with a pack horse to think of."

Wagner glanced at the pack horse, standing quietly beyond the roan pony, with its pack saddle and roll of duffle. He came back to the calves, still wanting certain things explained. "I reckon they missed those calves at calf-branding, this spring," the sheriff commented.

"That must have been it," Jenkins replied with dry irony.

The sheriff looked narrowly at Jenkins. "What was wrong with those critters' eyelids?" he asked. "They didn't look natural . . . they were sort of droopy."

Jenkins laughed softly. "I can see you're learning a new one. Look, sheriff, at spring round-up, how do you know what brand to burn on a calf?"

The sheriff looked surprised. "Anybody knows that. The calf follows its mother and you give it the same brand the mother wears. Everybody knows that a calf will follow its mother until it's weaned, even when it's big enough to eat grass."

"Sure enough. Now, listen to me. I don't say this actually happened, but it could have. Suppose some rustlers, we'll say from the Bridle-Bit, run across a bunch of Ladder-A cows, over on the Ladder-A east range, before calf round-up had taken place and before Lorry Alastair issued her order about strangers keeping off her range. We'll say some of the cows had calves following 'em, calves old enough to be weaned."

"I got you," the sheriff nodded, puzzled. The two men were squatting down by the fire now, from force of habit more than from any need of warmth. The sun was climbing high by now. Besides the fire was fast reducing itself to dead ashes.

Jenkins went on. "We'll say the rustlers cut out a dozen or so of those calves — maybe more — and drove off the mother cows, then herded the calves over this way and left 'em down in those river bottoms. What would happen?"

Wagner frowned. "We-ell, it's always been my experience, that a calf separated from its mother will try to find its way back to the spot at which the separation took place."

"Right — usually. But suppose the calves were prevented from returning there."

"I don't figure," Wagner said scratching his head, "that the rustlers would dare stay on Ladder-A range, just to keep those calves from straying back."

"No, they wouldn't," Jenkins conceded, "but they could do something else. They could take a knife and sever the muscles that held up the calves' eyelids —"

"And their eyes would drop closed!" The sheriff's mouth dropped open. "And then the dang critters wouldn't budge from the place where they'd been left."

"You guessed it, sheriff. They'd just hang around and bawl for a spell. Eventually they get hungry, and, blind or not, they'd start sniffing around for food. That'd start 'em eating. Once weaned, they'd forget they ever had mothers. In time the severed muscles would heal, but the eyes would always have a droopy appearance."

Wagner swore suddenly. "Eventually, the rustlers could come back and pick up those animals and slap a Bridle-Bit on 'em, feeling quite sure the calves wouldn't stray far from the river and the fodder they'd learned to graze on. Any Ladder-A hand rounding up strays would likely pass up those river bottoms. By God, Jinglebob, is there any way we can hang this on the Bridle-Bit. I'll —"

Jenkins shook his head. "I'm just giving you an explanation for the lack of a natural increase Miss

84

Alastair mentioned, when I talked to her yesterday. There's nothing we can do without proof — but Lord knows how many calves have been run off that way. Those two I found may have been missed by the rustlers. Probably calves have been driven to Bridle-Bit range and the same trick worked. So long as they go unbranded they are any man's property — mavericks. Once they carry a brand they belong to the owner of that brand."

"Well, I'll be damned. That's a new stunt on me — cutting their eyelids."

"I ran across — that is, I heard of the stunt being worked down in southern Texas one time." Jenkins changed the subject, "Where you heading this morning?"

Wagner tossed his cigarette stub on the ashes of the fire. "I was riding to talk to you a mite. Then, before I got to your camp I spotted you over here and rode over to see who it was."

"You saved yourself a longer trip. I broke camp this morning, like I said, but what's on your mind?"

"Tarp Jones was in town yesterday afternoon," Wagner said. "He tells me somebody tried to dry-gulch you, after you left Padre Wells, day before yesterday."

Jinglebob nodded. "Yeah, he tried."

"With a thirty-thirty, Tarp said."

"Dang Tarp Jones for a garrulous old wag-tongue," Jinglebob said ruefully. "I was hoping to show up in town and give my dry-gulching friend the surprise of his life. He left me for dead."

"The news is all over town now."

"I suppose," Jinglebob said.

"Tarp said you picked up the shell."

Jinglebob nodded.

Wagner continued, "I examined the country pretty well after Mitchell, that A. C. A. operative, was killed and Breck Alastair was shot. Found the places where the ambusher had holed up, waiting for them to appear." The sheriff paused a moment, then, "I found the shells that did that work too. They were both thirty-thirties. Out of the same gun, I think. I've saved 'em. I'd like to compare 'em to yours."

Jinglebob drew out the handkerchief containing the cigar butt and exploded rifle shell he had found. He handed the shell to Wagner. Wagner drew from a pocket two similar shells. The three shells were compared carefully for several minutes by the two men. The tiny indentations made by the rifle when it was fired came in for special attention.

Wagner looked up at last and handed one shell back to Jinglebob. "All three centerfire," he observed casually.

Jinglebob nodded.

"It's my guess," the sheriff went farther, "all three came from the same gun."

"I don't think there's any doubt of that, either."

Wagner swore suddenly and forcefully, ending, "Dammit, Jinglebob, if I could only find the owner of that Winchester, I'd have him on three counts, one for murdering Mitchell and the other two for attempts on your life and Alastair's."

"He's a dang good shot," Jinglebob said. "Better than ordinary. It was long range lead-throwing." He expanded on the story, telling Wagner what had taken place. "I located the spot he'd fired from," Jinglebob concluded. "Picked up sign here and there that told me one or two things."

"What sort of sign?" Wagner demanded.

Jinglebob opened the handkerchief to disclose the cigar butt. "He smoked a cigar while he waited for me to come along."

Wagner glanced at the cigar. "There's a hell of a lot of men smoke cigars," he said irritably. "I don't want to know his habits. I want to know who he is."

"A man about my weight," Jinglebob said quietly, "but tall and thin."

Wagner's eyes opened wider. "T'hell you say!"

"He puts his weight down on the outside of his right foot."

"You expecting me to go around looking at everybody's boots?" Wagner said.

"Maybe that won't be necessary," Jinglebob drawled. "Look at this cigar butt. The end is stiff and dry where it was held between the fellow's teeth. There are two upper teeth marks showing plainly. Examine them closely. They'll tell you considerable . . . See this tooth mark? Now, look at this one, sheriff."

Frowning, Wagner bent closer to the cigar butt.

Jinglebob went on, "The hombre who smoked this cigar has a pair of protruding, front teeth in his upper jaw. He didn't hold this cigar in the middle of his mouth, but slightly to one side. He may have bit down extra hard when he saw me coming. The mark of the right center tooth is set about an eighth of an inch in advance of that of its neighboring tooth. Anyway, there's a bit of prime evidence —"

"By God!" Wagner exclaimed. "It's —"

Jinglebob cut in quietly, "It was the reflection of sunlight on metal that caught my eye and warned me in time, sheriff, the sort of reflection that might be thrown from a badge, say, for instance, a marshal's badge."

"Marshal Steve Franklin!" the sheriff half shouted.

Jinglebob nodded slowly, "Steve Franklin."

Silence fell between the two men. Jinglebob commenced rolling another cigarette. He offered tobacco and papers to Wagner. Impatiently, the sheriff shook his head, his eyes fixed absent-mindedly on some far-off vista. A soft breeze ruffled the grass tips. Cigarette smoke slanted diagonally across Jinglebob's tanned features and was whisked away to vanish in thin air.

Jinglebob spoke at last. "Do you know if Franklin is any good with a rifle?"

"I've been thinking about that, cowboy." The sheriff paused a moment, frowning at the dead fire-ashes. He cleared his throat. "Three years back," he said, "we held a sort of Fourth of July celebration in Padre Wells. Things were peaceful those days. The feature of the day's entertainment was a shooting contest at marks. Six-shooters and rifles. All distances. I just happened to remember that Steve Franklin was top man, that day, with a Winchester."

"It ties in," Jinglebob said calmly.

"Here's something else that ties in," Wagner growled. "I should be cussed for not thinking of it before. The day you were dang nigh dry-gulched, I saw Steve Franklin riding into town, 'bout an hour before sundown. His horse was lathered a right smart. He'd been riding hard. I didn't think anything of it at the time, except that probably he'd been to the Bridle-Bit to report on his meeting with you, in the Acme."

"Did he have a rifle with him?" Jinglebob asked.

"I don't remember seeing any. 'Course, he could have hid it some place outside of town."

"Probably that's the answer."

Another silence ensued. The sheriff rose, grim-faced, at last, from his crouching position. "Well, I reckon I'll ride in and place Steve Franklin under arrest."

"And then what?" Jinglebob queried, straightening up and placing one booted toe on his discarded cigarette.

"Then what?" the sheriff asked. "Why, let the law take its course. Franklin's got to be stopped right pronto."

Jinglebob smiled. "You might have hard work making the evidence stick, sheriff. Dave Scarab would bail him out . . ."

"What? With three shootings against him?"

"You've said yourself that Scarab is pretty powerful in Padre Wells. Once out on bail, Franklin would fan his tail out of this section so fast you'd never see him again. Look here, sheriff, I'd like to tie the evidence a little tighter, before any action is taken. Suppose you leave matters to me?"

Wagner snorted. "You don't know Franklin like I do. You start making any accusations to his face and he'll jerk his iron so fast that you'll —"

"I'll be wearing my own gun, next time I meet Franklin," Jinglebob smiled.

"Hell's bells, boy! You don't know Franklin. He's lightning with a hawglaig. *I* wouldn't risk him alone. I'll have Bucky Malotte to back me up —"

"Look here, sheriff, I've uncovered your man for you, haven't I?"

Wagner nodded promptly. "And a right smart job you did, too, Jinglebob. You've got a head on you."

"We'll pass that. But don't you think I'm entitled to ask for a delay before anything is said to Franklin — or anyone else?"

"We-ell, yes, I reckon you are."

"Will you wait and let me handle it, then?"

"What are you aiming to do?"

Jinglebob smiled. "I'm not ready to say yet. Maybe I'm not sure what I'll do. But I'm asking you to leave this to me. If I fail in producing more evidence, you've still got your chance."

"Franklin may run out on us."

"Not if you keep secret what we've discovered. He wouldn't have any reason for making a run for it . . . Will you do it?"

"Leave the handling of Franklin to you?"

"That's the idea, sheriff. And don't say a word to a soul — not even Bucky. He might drop something by accident."

90

"We-ell, yes, I reckon I can favor you to that extent," Wagner conceded reluctantly. "Sure, I'll do it, Jinglebob, and you be plumb careful how you talk too. Remember, Franklin is heap bad medicine to fool with."

"Thanks, I'll remember . . . It's getting on toward dinner time. I reckon I'll be heading for the Ladder-A."

"I've got to get back to town, too."

Jinglebob scuffed the ashes of his fire to make certain it was extinguished, then, stooping, retrieved his now cold, improvised branding iron. Folding the lengths of flexible hay-wire into a small compact bundle he thrust it into his pocket.

Wagner eyed him queerly. "Some hombres," he observed, "would make me mighty suspicious if I saw 'em totin' a section of baling wire around that-away."

"I reckon," Jinglebob nodded. "It's an old habit." He didn't make further explanation, but sauntered off in the direction of his pony. Frowning, the sheriff followed and swung heavily up to the back of his own horse.

"*Adiós*, Jinglebob."

"*Amigo, adiós.*"

"When'll I see you?"

Jinglebob replied, gathering his reins, "I'll maybe ride to Padre Wells tomorrow."

"I'll be looking for you." The sheriff kicked his horse in the ribs and started off, heading due east. Jinglebob, with his pack pony trailing behind, rode toward the north. He was some distance away when he heard the sheriff yell:

"Hey! Jinglebob! Are you just a poet, nothing more?"

Jinglebob raised his voice, "What do you think?"

"I'm damned if I know what to think, now."

Jinglebob grinned. "Suppose we let it ride at that," he called back. "I'm never very certain in my own mind."

An oath floated to him on the rising breeze, a puzzled, disturbed oath that held, nevertheless, a great deal of friendly feeling.

The two riders continued on in their separate directions. The wind was blowing hot across the range now, flattening the grass in graceful undulations.

CHAPTER
EIGHT

Fresh Evidence?

Jinglebob was met by old Tarp Jones, down near the corral, when he trailed his pack pony into the Ladder-A ranch yard that afternoon.

"Howdy," Tarp greeted. "Thought I recognized ye, when I fust sighted ye ridin' this way. Ye'll be stayin' for chow, of course."

"It sort of looks thataway," Jinglebob replied. "The owners usually feed their hands, don't they?"

"Certain, but say . . ." Tarp paused, puzzled. "Say, you ain't figurin' to ask for a job, are ye? 'Cause if ye are, it'll be wasted time. The Ladder-A ain't hirin, can't afford to hire." A frown crossed Tarp's grizzled features. "I don't rightly know how Lorry'll take this. Was she right proddy yistiddy?"

"Well," Jenkins grinned, "we didn't pull any guns on each other. And it was Miss Alastair suggested I tie on with the Ladder-A."

"Wha-a-a-at?" Tarp exploded. His eyes bulged.

"Sure enough. What's queer about that?"

"Well, by all the long-sufferin' old maids! Dang that gal for a deceivin' female! She never tole me thet. How can I be expected to run things when I don't know what's a-goin' on? An' she was so perky like when she come in last night and told me she'd give you yore walkin' papers and tole you to break camp."

"So she did. But it was on her suggestion I'm here."

"Great palpitatin' prophets! I never heard the beat of that gal." Grudgingly, "Well, she made you break camp like she said she would. But I certain feel like I'd been deceived. Howsomever, I can find it in my heart to forgive her, seein' as her connivin' around brung you here. And you'll be stayin'?"

"For a spell, I reckon."

"Did ye bring yore concertina?"

"I couldn't leave that behind."

"By the seven bald steers, this is the best news I've had sence David slewed Goliath. Well, throw yore pony in thet corral. I'll unravel yore pack critter while ye're unsaddlin'."

While they were working with the two horses, Jenkins glanced around, searching for Lorry Alastair. The girl was nowhere in sight, and his wandering gaze took in the big, rambling ranch house built of rock and adobe and timber. Cottonwood trees surrounded the house and a short distance away a windmill clanked and whirled in the breeze blowing across the range. There were other buildings: the combination bunkhouse and mess shanty; stables, blacksmith-shop and big barn. It was a good looking spread, though at present somewhat in need of painting and minor repairs.

With ponies turned into the corral, the two men picked up the saddle and Jenkins' other belongings and headed for the bunkhouse.

"Ye get yore choice of most any bunk," Tarp Jones said, gesturing toward the double-tiered line of bunks. "Spread yore blankets where ye're a mind to. There ain't only me and Matt Alvord and Chris Kringle sleepin' here now. I don't know where Matt is. Out hopin' to find strays, I reckon. Chris should be in his kitchen —"

"Somebody mention my name?" The cook's dour countenance popped through the entrance to the kitchen. He grunted sourly, "*Hmmph!* 'Nother mouth to feed for supper, I suppose. Now I got to put 'nother spud in the pot."

"You, Chris," old Tarp bridled. "None of yer grumps, now! Jenkins ain't no ordinary grub-line rider. He's the feller I —"

"Jenkins?" Chris pricked up his ears. "You, Jinglebob Jenkins?"

"That's the name," Jenkins smiled.

Chris looked him up and down, then snorted contemptuously, "I always knowed Tarp Jones was a liar. You just look like any other cowhand."

Jenkins chuckled. "Any reason why I shouldn't?"

Chris seemed uncertain. "We-ell, mebbe not," he conceded at last, "only Tarp allowed as how you could make up pomes right outten your head and sing 'em too. Ain't no ordinary human can do that —"

"Now, you just put a dally on that tongue of yourn, Chris," old Tarp broke in hotly. "Jest as soon's Jinglebob gets settled 'round proper he'll show you."

"Wait a minute, Tarp," Jenkins smiled. "You can't hardly blame Chris for doubting me. Fact is, I sort of doubted him, too."

"How you mean, you doubted me?" Chris demanded suspiciously.

"We-ell," Jenkins explained, "it's sort of hard to put into words, only after what I'd heard about your cooking, I sort of half expected to see a French chef with a long white apron and a big cooking hat on your head. Why, accordin' to Tarp, those biscuits you bake always have to be clipped —"

"Clipped!" Chris Kringle looked puzzled.

Jenkins nodded gravely. "So they won't fly right out of the oven when you open the door — they're that light."

Slowly a grin crinkled Chris Kringle's dour features and he put out one flour-dusted paw. "Put 'er there, Jinglebob. I reckon we're both regular hombres, after all. But I'm sure cravin' to hear you make music on that bellows Tarp has been talkin' about."

"I hope Tarp hasn't made it too tough for me."

Tarp said, "I didn't exaggerate none. Chris, where's Matt?"

Chris shrugged his bony shoulders. "I ain't seen him sence he et dinner. Heard him say somethin' about forkin' his bronc and ridin' out to see if he'd find any more of our critters hamstrung."

"I'm shore hopin' he don't," Tarp growled.

"That reminds me," Jenkins put in, "on my way here, I ran across a couple of mavericks."

"Ye did?" Tarp said quickly. "Where 'bouts?"

"Over in the bottoms on the south fork of Sleepy Horse. I slapped a brand on 'em."

"Never thought of lookin' in them bottoms," Tarp said. " 'Course, a critter or so is bound to get past us, now and then —" He paused abruptly.

"Did you say you branded 'em?"

Jenkins nodded carelessly.

"Where'd you get your iron?" Tarp wanted to know.

Jenkins reached into his pocket and produced the compact bundle of flexible hay-wire, showed it to Tarp and then put it away again.

Tarp stiffened and exchanged quick glances with Chris. Then Tarp said slowly, "I've seen the time, Jinglebob, when a bunch of wire, the like o' thet, would brand a man havin' it in his possession as a cowthief. Now I ain't callin' you no names, but I crave to know —"

"I branded those calves with a Ladder-A, Tarp," Jenkins smiled. "You don't need to take my word for it. Ride over and hunt those calves out. Or ask Sheriff Wagner. He was there when I burned those hides."

Tarp nodded hastily. "No offense meant, Jinglebob. I just got to wonderin' about thet wire . . . Say, how did you know they were Ladder-A critters?"

"I didn't. But they were any man's property. I figured the Ladder-A was entitled to 'em."

"Right you are — but, there, throw your things in a bunk. We been standin', talkin', and —"

A step was heard at the doorway to the bunkhouse and Lorry Alastair entered, looking cool and sweet in fresh gingham. The girl smiled and extended one hand.

"Hi-yuh, Jinglebob."

"Hello, Lorry. I didn't get in quite as soon as I'd expected, but —"

"I saw you through the window when you came. I knew Tarp would take care of you. I was busy with Breck."

Old Tarp was surveying the girl suspiciously. "You, Lorry," he demanded, "what you doin' all dressed up in the middle of the day? What's the occasion?"

"Occasion?" the girl asked innocently. "I don't know what you mean, Tarp." Her cheeks were flushed. "Can't a gal get out of overalls once in a spell without it being an occasion? Anyway," laughing, "you've got to admit, Tarp Jones, that I made Jinglebob break camp and move on."

"Fummydiddles!" Tarp snorted disgustedly. "You used underhand methods, so you did. 'T'warn't fair, nohow. Anyway, I proved what I said in the first place. Jinglebob's already proved friendly. He branded us two mavericks today."

"That so?" the girl queried.

Jenkins nodded. "Ran across 'em over near the bottoms of the Sleepy Horse. Slapped your brand on 'em." To forestall the girl's thanks, he changed the subject, "Say, you didn't think of a rhyme for Saskatoon, did you?"

"How about rigadoon?" the girl offered.

Jenkins shook his head. "That rhymes, but it isn't a girl's name."

"That's right. I'd forgotten. Anyway, Jinglebob, we're much obliged for saving those mavericks for us. Come on up to the house and meet Breck. He's so sick of

98

looking at the same faces all the time, he'll welcome a new one. You can tell me more about those calves on the way to the house."

Jinglebob and the girl left the bunkhouse, leaving Tarp and Chris looking rather disappointed. On the way to the house, Jenkins told Lorry of finding the two mavericks. When he had finished:

"That's a new stunt, isn't it?" Lorry frowned. "I never heard of cutting eyelids to prevent calves from following their mothers."

"It may be new in these parts," Jenkins nodded.

"It's the Bridle-Bit's work, of course," the girl continued. "I may be jumping to conclusions, but —"

"I've a hunch you're jumping in the right direction," Jenkins said slowly. "We haven't proof, but I'd lay aces to tens that that same method accounts for the loss of a good many of your calves."

They were almost to the house, now. Lorry hesitated near the back door. "Don't say anything to Breck about that eyelid cutting stunt. He doesn't know how things are, at present. It would only worry him. We want him to get well as soon as possible. We'll just let him think they were two strays the boys missed."

"That'll be best," Jenkins replied. He followed the girl into the house.

Meanwhile, Chris and old Tarp faced each other with something akin to disgust on their features.

"Ain't that jest our luck?" Tarp growled. "Jest as I was about to ask Jinglebob to unlimber his music contraption, Lorry has to come in and take him away. By the seven bald steers, sometimes that gal riles me

99

worse'n pizen! Anybody'd think she was roddin' this outfit, the way she acts."

"I reckon she is," Chris said.

"Yaah! You would," Tarp grunted morosely. "Well, it's just as well Jenkins didn't get started on his entertainin'. I'd had to stop him."

"*You'd* had to stop him?" Chris jeered. "How come?"

"You wouldn't have been able to get your work done. Don't you forgit, cookie, they's a supper to be got ready. It's nigh to four o'clock now. Ye better get busy. And try not to burn no more food than is possible. It'd be plumb nice if we could fool Jenkins and serve a good meal for once. You know, don't let on but what we have good food every day, and that you really know how to cook. If ye can only deceive him the fust night, might be he'll take a likin' to the place and stay a long time, that is, until he realizes his stomach has sudden gone bad —"

That was as far as Tarp got. Chris had edged back toward his kitchen and reached around the edge of the doorway. The next instant, an iron skillet appeared in Chris' hand and then, abruptly, crashed against the wall, not far from old Tarp's head. A lurid flow of profanity accompanied the missile through the air.

Tarp rose with considerable haste and beat a retreat for the outside, chuckling dryly. At the doorway, he paused and eyed Chris with severity. "Tryin' to add murder to yore crimes of cookin', be ye? Ye'll come to no good end, Chris Kringle, ye mark what I tell —"

100

The words came to a sudden end as Tarp dodged a wet dishrag that came hurtling through the air. Still chuckling, ignoring the wave of invective beating against his retreating back, Tarp headed for the corral where he had spied Matt Alvord just unsaddling.

"I shore reckon Matt's eyes will bug out when he hears Jenkins is here," Tarp mused. He hurried on to break the news.

That night, Tarp, Matt Alvord and Chris sat in the big main room of the ranch house, their eyes bulging and their mouths agape, while Jinglebob entertained with song and concertina music. Lorry, eyes sparkling, sat near Breck Alastair who had been carried from his bedroom and made comfortable in the warmth reflected from the wide stone fireplace where mesquite roots blazed and crackled. The room was simply furnished with large easy chairs; Indian rugs and animal skins were spread about the floor; on the walls were mounted animal heads and a few old-fashioned pictures in frames. An oil lamp stood on a heavy oaken table and nearby were a box of cigars and a bottle of bourbon Lorry had resurrected to please her father: Breck had insisted that the new hand be given a proper welcome to the Ladder-A.

As for Jinglebob Jenkins he was just about proving himself to be "just what the doctor ordered" through providing a new interest for Breck Alastair. Under the spell of the entertainment, the invalid was smiling more than he had for weeks; already there was a sparkle to his eyes and his skin was taking on fresh color. Though Breck didn't say so in so many words, Lorry gathered that the presence of a younger man on the Ladder-A did much to ease her father's troubled spirits.

The Bridle-Bit outfit hadn't been mentioned all evening, and when bedtime arrived and Alastair was helped off to his room, he went to bed and instantly fell asleep. Lorry finally emerged from her father's room, her eyes a trifle moist. Jinglebob was standing near the door with the three elderly Ladder-A hands, preparing to leave for the bunkhouse.

The girl came up to Jinglebob and held out her hand. "You've done Breck a world of good already," she said simply. "It seems ages since he laughed the way he did tonight."

"That's fine," Jinglebob said.

"Damn' if I ever see the like of it," Matt Alvord said enthusiastically. "Jinglebob, yore better nor a reg'lar sawbones at curin' folks. It was mighty enjoyable tonight —"

"Gosh," Jenkins broke in, somewhat embarrassed at the praise, "I should have told Breck about my Saskatoon poem and asked him if he knew of a rhyme for it."

"I thought of that," Lorry smiled, "but something happened and it slipped my mind. You can ask him some other time, though I doubt it will do much good. Breck's long suit doesn't run to rhymes and such."

"I was goin' to mention it a coupla times," Tarp Jones stated, "only with Jinglebob runnin' from one song to another, I didn't want to interrupt."

Lorry accompanied the men to the back door and prepared to lock up for the night. Just as Jinglebob

102

stepped into the open air he heard the creaking of saddle leather, then a rider took form in the darkness, not far from the house. A voice carried through the night.

Tarp Jones answered: "Who is it?"

"Me. Bucky Malotte," came the response. "Is Jenkins here?"

"It's Deputy Malotte," Lorry said. "Come on in, Bucky."

"Yes, I'm here," Jinglebob put in. "What's on your mind?"

Malotte reined his pony nearer. In the light from the open back door they could see his pugnacious bulldog features wrinkled in something that was very like a grin. He swung his sturdy bowed legs down from the saddle.

Jinglebob said, "Anything wrong, Bucky?"

Malotte replied, "Depends how you look on it. I say no. Everybody else says no. Pat Hogan says yes. Looking at it from his viewpoint, I agree with him. Jinglebob, you sure made the Acme Saloon one mighty popular hangout. Too popular the way Pat looks at it. He says it's all your doin's, Jinglebob, and he's hopin' you'll see your way clear to get him out of the jam he's in."

Jenkins was mystified. "What did I do?"

Malotte chuckled harshly. "It's that pome you wrote for Pat — you know, regardin' his bourbon."

"What about it?"

"It's the last two lines that done the damage," Malotte said. "As near as I can remember, the pome ends like this —"

“For every drink you buy from him,
  He’ll buy for you another.”

“Well, what about it?” Jenkins sounded puzzled.

The deputy explained. “Pat had a copy of the pome made to hang over his bar. He was right proud of it at first, until hombres commenced takin’ the words at their face value. The word soon passed around town. Now everybody that goes in the Acme buys a drink, then waits for Pat to serve one free —”

A sudden laugh broke from Jenkins’ lips. Lorry and the three Ladder-A hands joined in. Bucky Malotte was grinning widely. He went on, “Pat says it’s up to you to help him out, Jinglebob, seeing as how it’s you started this. He’s been beggin’ folks’ to come get you, but nobody was willing of course — not while they could cadge so many free drinks from Pat. The whole of Padre Wells is roarin’ at Pat and advisin’ him to get in large stocks of whisky. Pat’s takin’ it good-natured, but he’d sure like to see you, Jinglebob. He says his profits is all goin’ into free drinks.”

Jinglebob chuckled. “I’ll have to see what I can do to change the meaning of that poem. How’d you know where to find me, Bucky?”

“Sheriff Wagner said I might find you here. He took pity on Pat and told me to ride out and tell you what had happened.”

“Right kind of Clem Wagner, I’d say,” Lorry commented, “to send you riding this far, Bucky.”

“I tried to talk Clem out of the idea,” Bucky grinned, “tried to point out to him he was just cheatin’ himself

104

out of a lot of free drinks, but he ordered me to ride, so here I am. At that, if the news gets out that the sheriff tried to help Pat, it'll mebbe cost him votes, next election."

Lorry put in, "Well, you don't need to make that twelve mile ride back to town tonight, Bucky . . . Tarp, you dig out some blankets and spread a bed in the bunkhouse."

"Thanks, Miss Lorry," Bucky said.

They talked a few minutes longer, then Lorry said "good night" and closed the door. The men started off toward the bunkhouse. Malotte walked at Jenkins' side, leading his pony. Jenkins accompanied him over to the corral and stood near while Bucky unsaddled.

"Funniest thing I ever saw," Bucky said, "the amount of trade the Acme is getting all of a sudden."

"I'll bet," Jinglebob said, absent-mindedly. He glanced across the ranch yard, and saw, in the light from the stars, that Tarp, Matt and Chris were just entering the bunkhouse.

Jinglebob turned to Malotte, tugging at a cinch, and said, "All right, Bucky, what did you really come here for? I know Clem didn't send you riding this far, just to tell me about Pat."

Bucky straightened up and faced Jinglebob. "Clem wants to know if you can come in tomorrow. He's got something to show you."

"What is it?"

"I haven't the least idea." Bucky seemed a trifle aggrieved. "Usually, Clem tells me things, but he's plumb secretive. He said to tell you it concerns what happened day before yesterday. That was the day old Tarp hit town with the news you'd been shot at. I'm putting two and two together, but I ain't got the answer yet. Are you saying anything?"

Jinglebob's eyes narrowed. "Bucky, I think I know who shot at me, and I think he's the same coyote that killed that A. C. A. operative and wounded Breck Alastair. Until we could get more proof I asked Clem not to say a word to anybody. It's my fault he didn't tell you. Perhaps by this time, the sheriff has discovered further evidence . . ."

"Sufferin' cats! If you can catch that dry-gulchin' son — say, who is he?"

"Is Marshal Steve Franklin still around town?"

"Certain . . . spending most of his time in the Acme . . . sa-a-ay, you ain't claimin' Franklin is the one —"

"Think it over, Bucky. Keep it quiet. We can't talk now before old Tarp and the other two. I'll give you the story on our ride to town, tomorrow morning."

"You aimin' to put the deadwood on Franklin?"

Jenkins frowned. "Bucky," he said slowly, "I'm not sure yet just what I intend to do. We'll have to play the cards as they're dealt out . . ."

"Hope for winners if you go against Franklin, cowpoke."

"Play 'em as they're dealt out," Jenkins repeated quietly, "and hope for winners, Bucky. That's our game. Tomorrow should tell the tale."

CHAPTER
NINE

The Marshal Kills a Buzzard

Bucky Malotte's round blue eyes narrowed angrily as he absorbed the facts Jenkins had marshaled against Steve Franklin. The deputy's stubby fingers contracted on his pony's reins and harsh lines tightened his belligerent, bulldog features.

Malotte and Jinglebob were trotting their horses along the trail leading to Padre Wells. The hot morning sun brought out streaks of perspiration on the animals' hides, as they kicked up small clouds of dust along the way. To their rear, the serrated peaks of the Truculento Range formed a jagged frieze against the billowy cloud banks which, apparently, were resting on the mountain tops. Overhead the sky was a dazzling blue. The trail to town coursed ribbon-like across rolling grasslands, or dipped down to shallow hollows that were often thickly grown with mesquite and prickly pear.

". . . and that," Jinglebob concluded, "is the way the evidence stacks up at present. Everything points to Franklin as the dry-gulcher . . ."

"The dirty, back-shootin' son," Bucky spoke with bitter intensity. "He should have a taste of his own medicine. Prison is too good for him. He should be gunned out. 'Course, no matter what Sheriff Wagner does, it's going to earn us the bad feelin's of Dave Scarab and his Bridle-Bit thugs. S'help me, if I'd known this yesterday, I'd been inclined to take a shot at Franklin —"

"That's exactly what I was afraid of," Jenkins cut in. "It's my fault you didn't know. I asked Clem Wagner not to say a word about this — to anybody. I was afraid something might happen that would tip Franklin off to what evidence we had. I'd have told you all this last night, only with old Tarp Jones and the others around, I didn't want to say anything that might be repeated."

Bucky nodded and said ruefully, "You're right, of course. It's just as well I didn't know about Franklin yesterday. I'd been plumb tempted to throw a gun on him. If that had happened . . . well, it would have been just too bad for me. I'm admittin' I'm no match for Franklin."

"He's bad with a six-shooter, eh?"

"Poison! You already know what he can do with a Winchester. He's just as accurate with a hawglaig."

"How would Sheriff Wagner stack up against Franklin's shooting?"

Bucky said definitely: "Clem wouldn't have a chance."

Jenkins looked thoughtful. He didn't say anything. The two men covered the next three miles in silence, each occupied with his own abstractions.

Malotte said finally, "What you thinkin' about?"

"Nothing much." Jinglebob smiled. "I was just sort of wondering what I could write for Pat to get him out of that free drink fix."

108

"T'hell you say!" Bucky was astounded. "I figured you had your mind on Steve Franklin. Me, I can't think of anything else."

"I'm all thought out on that subject. No use wasting more time."

"But what are you going to do, what are *we* going to do?"

"Just what I said last night, Bucky, play the cards as they're dealt out and hope for a winning hand."

Malotte frowned. "Seems like we should be making some plans of some kind."

"I suppose," Jenkins said softly, then repeated, "I suppose."

He wouldn't say any more. The ponies trotted on.

Before long they were riding into Padre Wells. It wasn't yet ten o'clock. A few ponies stood at hitch-racks along the dusty street. Here and there a wagon and team waited before a store. A few men sat, half dozing, in the shadow beneath porch roofs, their chairs tilted back against front walls.

Bucky and Jinglebob drew rein before the long tie-rail fronting the City Hall building, dismounted and then climbed the steps to the wide, open doorway. Following Bucky, Jenkins found himself in a long hall with doors on either side. A closed door bore words reading: City Marshal. Steve Franklin's office. Jenkins wondered if Franklin was inside. Through an open doorway across the hall, Jenkins saw Sheriff Clem Wagner frowning over his monthly expense accounts.

Light came into the sheriff's office through a window in the side wall of the building. Besides the sheriff's desk, several straight-backed wooden chairs were scattered about the room. A rack on one wall held guns and handcuffs. Several reward bills were posted about. Back of the sheriff's desk hung a topographical map of Truculento County. A firearms company's calendar, with an illustration depicting the Battle of Bull Run, ornamented another wall.

The sheriff looked up as Jinglebob and Bucky entered. When the greetings had been disposed of, Wagner said, "Grab a chair, Jinglebob. Bucky told you I wanted to see you?"

Jinglebob nodded as he sat down, near the desk. Bucky Malotte, at a word from the sheriff, closed the door leading to the hall, then returned to perch his sturdy form on one corner of the desk.

Wagner seemed at a loss as to how to proceed. He looked a trifle uncomfortably at Bucky, then at Jenkins. "We-ell," he commenced uncertainly, "it's like this —"

"Look here, sheriff," Jenkins cut in, "if this has anything to do with Steve Franklin, you can speak out. I've already told Bucky what I've discovered . . . gave him the story on the way in, this morning."

Wagner looked relieved. "That's good. I sort of hated to ask you to step out, Bucky, but Jinglebob wanted this matter kept quiet and —"

"Sure, sure, I know," Malotte interrupted. "You got any new evidence, Clem?"

"I sort of reckon so," the sheriff said slowly. He tossed a sack of Durham and papers on his desk. The three men rolled and lighted cigarettes.

110

"It's like this," Wagner commenced. "Yesterday, Jinglebob, after I'd left you heading for the Ladder-A, I came direct to town. I've been putting off my expense report for the past week, and I figured I'd just have time to get down to business. When I came in here, Steve Franklin's door, across the hall, was open and he saw me. I'd just got seated at my desk when he came strolling in. I pretended to be too busy to talk, but he sat down and commenced to josh me . . ."

"'Bout what?" Malotte demanded belligerently.

"Oh, one thing and another. Mostly about failing to get the feller who tried to dry-gulch Jinglebob, here. He asked me if I'd been out looking for 'sign.' I allowed as how I had, but couldn't find any. With that, Franklin got right sarcastic, and commenced throwing out hints about this county needin' an efficient sheriff. Said he had a notion to run himself, next election and see could he beat me out . . ."

"That's probably what he has in mind," Jenkins nodded.

"Wouldn't surprise me none." The sheriff continued, "Well, he was commencin' to rile me some with that sort of ribbin'. I told him I was busy and didn't have any time for talk, but he stayed on. I was just about ready to tell Franklin to get out, when old Pablo Gonzales come looking for me."

The sheriff broke off long enough to explain to Jenkins: "Pablo Gonzales is an old Mex that lives down in the Mex Quarter — if you can call it that. Anyway, there's a bunch of Mexicans living on the east edge of Padre Wells. Pablo's a pretty square old cuss. I've

111

known him and his wife for years. We've exchanged favors now and then —"

"One of said favors," Bucky broke in, talking to Jenkins, "being the time Pablo and his wife were flat broke and Clem give him enough cash to buy some chickens and supplies. I don't know what favor Pablo ever done for Clem."

"Now, you hush up, Bucky," Wagner said with some irritation. "I'm doing this talking. Pablo brings me and my missus fresh eggs every so often. Last Christmas time he brought us a nice fat hen . . . Anyway, it was about his chickens Pablo came to see me. One of his hens had recent hatched out a litter of young 'uns, and Pablo was plumb worried for fear he'd lose some of 'em to a buzzard that had been hangin' around his house for the past couple of days."

"What did he want you to do," Bucky asked, "get a warrant swore out for the stink bird's arrest and then enforce it?"

"If you'll keep your trap shut I'll tell this," Wagner growled. "Pablo wanted to borrow a shotgun. He'd been plugging away at the damn buzzard, as it sailed overhead, with an old six-shooter, but without results. I reckon he didn't even scare that damn bird as it kept coming back as soon as the smoke had blowed away, Pablo said."

"That buzzard sure must have had his mind set on young chicken," Jenkins commented.

Wagner nodded and went on, "All the time Pablo and I were talking, Franklin sat here, taking it all in. Well, I told Pablo he could borrow a shotgun. Next

112

thing, Pablo wanted me to come down to his place and do the shooting. I told him I was too damn busy. Franklin cuts in with a sarcastic remark to the effect that I probably couldn't hit the bird anyhow. Well, that gave me an idea. I sort of strung him along, letting him think he was getting the best of the argument. It wa'n't long before he got to boasting and when I asked him if he thought he could shoot the buzzard, he allowed as how he could and he wouldn't need a scatter-gun either."

"I see what you're getting at, I think," Jenkins smiled.

"I reckon. Well, I led Franklin on some more and told him I knew he was a right good shot with a rifle, shooting at a target, but that shooting at a flying bird was a damn sight different. One thing led to another and he was getting sort of hot under the collar. First thing I knew he was offering to bet me five bucks he could get that bird. I hated to lose my five bucks, but it was worth it. The upshot of the matter was that Franklin got his rifle and him and Pablo and me went down to Pablo's place. That damn buzzard bird was still floating around and the hen squawking frantic and them little yellow chickens dashing around like leaves in a wind."

"And Franklin shot the buzzard?" Jenkins asked.

Wagner said grudgingly, "It was as pretty a shot as I ever see. When the bird dropped, Franklin levered another ca'tridge into his chamber in case it was needed, but it wa'n't. His slug had carried the buzzard's head just about off. He come running back with the bird in his hand, yelling for me to pay my bet.

I paid it and I tried to look put out, but I don't know if I succeeded. You see, when Franklin ran to get the bird, I picked up the empty shell his rifle had ejected."

"Good work, Clem," Jenkins said. He took from his pocket the bandanna handkerchief containing the cartridge shell and cigar butt he had found and placed them on the desk. "Let's compare," he suggested.

Wagner produced an exploded thirty-thirty shell from his pocket and rolled it across the desk. The three men examined the two shells.

Jenkins said finally, "Both from the same gun."

Wagner and Malotte nodded. Wagner added, "This shell that killed the buzzard compares with the shells I picked up after that A. C. A. operative was killed and Breck Alastair was downed."

Malotte said in his harsh voice. "This sure puts the deadwood on Steve Franklin. It's time to act."

The sheriff nodded grimly and started to arise from his desk.

Jingebob said, "What you aiming to do?"

"Arrest Steve Franklin for murder and attempted murders. I've got the evidence I need and with your word —"

"Sit down a minute," Jenkins said.

Reluctantly, Wagner resumed his seat and looked inquiringly at Jinglebob.

Jinglebob continued, "Suppose Franklin resists arrest?"

The sheriff's face went hard. "I know what you mean. Well, it will be up to Bucky then. He'll take my place . . ."

"And only too glad to —" Bucky commenced, then paused, in some confusion, "Not that I'd want you rubbed out, Clem."

"Look here," Jinglebob said, "if we don't move careful everything may be spoiled. We'll say that both you and Bucky arrest Franklin, Clem — you know, get the drop on him. What then?"

"In that case," Bucky growled, "Dave Scarab would bail him out immediate. This ain't an arrestin' matter. He'd never come to trial."

"And if he did come to trial," Jinglebob said, "which I agree is doubtful, you might have a hard time proving how long he's had that rifle."

"What do you mean?" Wagner demanded.

Jinglebob explained: "Franklin would admit firing the shot that killed the buzzard, but he might swear the gun had only recently come into his possession."

"Why he's had that gun for a couple of years or more that I know of —" Wagner commenced.

"Can you swear to that?" Jenkins asked. "You're probably right, but have you proof of that statement?"

Wagner remained silent. Bucky said triumphantly, "But with the evidence you've got, Jinglebob —"

"That's the point I'm trying to make," Jenkins nodded seriously. "I've got certain evidence. I figure this is my job. You'll try to take Franklin in a lawful manner. He may kill one or both of you. Such evidence as I have has got to be presented in such a way that Franklin's reactions to what I tell him will convict him. Will you leave this matter to me?"

"What you aiming to do?" the sheriff asked.

"I can tell better when I see Franklin. Is he in town?"

Wagner said, "I saw him leave his office about an hour before you came in. I reckon he's over at the Acme. Ten to one the Bridle-Bit crew is there, too, taking advantage of Pat Horgan's free drinks . . ."

Jenkins grinned suddenly. "That's right, I've got to see what I can do for Pat, too. But . . . this Franklin matter . . . will you let me see Franklin before you act?"

Wagner frowned uncertainly. "I don't know what you intend doing, but if you know some way of tying Franklin up — we-ell, yes, go ahead, Jinglebob. If he gets proddy, Bucky and I will come to your rescue."

Jenkins said dryly, "Thanks, Clem. That's a comfort. Come on, let's drift over to the Acme."

Wagner rose, took his belt and holstered gun from a nearby peg and strapped them about his waist. Then he lifted his sombrero from another peg and placed it on his head.

"I'm ready," he announced.

Bucky and Jinglebob filed out, with the sheriff at their heels. The sheriff paused only long enough to close the door to his office, then with a deep sigh he followed the other two to the street.

CHAPTER
TEN

Showdown

Pat Hogan's eyes lighted with sudden relief when he saw Jinglebob enter the Acme Saloon, followed by Sheriff Wagner and Deputy Malotte. There were several men in the saloon, among whom were Marshal Steve Franklin, Dave Scarab, Gus Raymer and a couple of other hard-looking cowhands whom Jenkins judged were Bridle-Bit men, inasmuch as they stood at one end of the bar, drinking and talking with Scarab, Franklin and Raymer. Jenkins and his companions nodded to the Bridle-Bit men and took up a position a short space farther along the bar.

Scarab replied to the greeting cordially enough. Raymer's face flushed. He didn't reply. Franklin nodded curtly. The others remained silent.

Jenkins said, grinning, "Hello, Pat. I hear my poem got you into some trouble."

Pat smiled ruefully, and jerked one thumb toward the offending jingle hanging back of the bar. "Sure I wouldn't say it made trouble, Jinglebob, but it cut into my profits something awful."

"Why didn't you take it down?"

Pat looked aghast. "What! Take down that elegant pome? I'll go broke first. But I was kind of thinking

117

maybe you could change the wording a bit and fix it up some way."

"Maybe I can add an extra verse," Jenkins suggested.

"That would be fine, if you would —"

A man at the bar, farther down, commenced to laugh. He called up to Jenkins, "Hey, stranger, before you order, let me give you some advice ... order bourbon, then Pat will give you another drink. See? It says so on that pome of his'n —"

"Shut your trap, Meecham," Pat spoke to the speaker. "This is Jinglebob Jenkins, the poet who wrote me those lines. But he's going to fix 'em up. There won't be so many free drinks for you hombres."

"Sure enough," Jenkins laughed, nodding at the man. "It's all my fault. I reckon the laugh's on me, the laugh and the cigars, too." He tossed some money on the bar. "Let me have some of your smokes, Pat."

There was a great deal of laughter in the barroom as Hogan placed a box of cigars on the bar. Smiling, Jenkins flipped back the cover and removed a double handful of the weeds. "This will help serve to introduce me in Padre Wells, too," he said.

Commencing with the sheriff, Jenkins made his way around the barroom distributing cigars and nodding in friendly fashion to men he hadn't seen before. Bucky Malotte accompanied him, mentioning names and making introductions. Jenkins came last to Scarab and his companions standing at that end of the bar nearest the entrance.

"Have a cigar, Scarab?" Jenkins said cordially enough.

118

"Thanks, Jenkins." Scarab laughed softly. "I sure hate to see you making any changes in Pat's poem. His free drinks have been right gratifying."

"I reckon, but all good things have to come to an end . . . Here, Franklin, toss away that cigar you're smoking and try a fresh one."

Franklin hesitated. Jenkins went on, "Go ahead, take a cigar. Just because you and I don't quite agree on one or two matters is no sign you should turn down Pat's cigars."

"That's right, Steve." Scarab laughed again. "When a man offers a peace-pipe, you shouldn't refuse."

Jenkins smiled good-naturedly. "I don't say it's a peace-pipe. I reckon we can still keep our own opinions."

Somewhat reluctantly, Franklin accepted a cigar and lighted it, after tossing the cigar he'd been smoking on the floor. Jenkins had turned to Gus Raymer by this time.

"I don't want none of your damn smokes," Raymer growled.

"You, Gus," Scarab cut in, still speaking softly, though his words carried an edge now, "think twice. Jenkins is trying to be friendly. You've no scrap with him. It was your own fault he knocked you down a few days back."

Raymer didn't object further. He accepted his cigar. Jenkins quickly disposed of the remainder of the weeds, then returned to the center of the bar. "All right, Pat," he said, "hand out some paper and a pencil and I'll see what I can do toward writing another verse for you."

119

Pat procured a sheet of paper and pencil and placed them on the bar. As Jenkins thought a few moments and then commenced to write, the men in the saloon gathered closer to watch him. He hadn't finished a complete line before they were hedging him against the bar, stretching to peer over his shoulder and cramping his movements. Even Scarab, Franklin and the other Bridle-Bit men moved along to see better.

Suddenly, Jenkins laughed and moved back. "Gosh, I've got to have room to write," he chuckled. "You hombres aren't even giving me elbow room. Now, don't crowd me. I'll read this to you when it's finished."

The crowd scattered somewhat, grinning and offering advice as to the way he worded the lines. Jenkins returned to the bar, carrying his paper and pencil. This time he took up a position to the right of Steve Franklin and again resumed writing.

The men once more hemmed him in. Jenkins would write a word or two, then pause, lost in thought, then he'd go on again. Once, as he straightened up and took a deep breath, his elbow brushed the paper from the bar and it fell to the floor at Steve Franklin's feet.

Franklin immediately shifted position and placed his right foot on the paper. His pale blue eyes held contemptuous lights as Jenkins stooped to retrieve the sheet.

"I'll be much obliged, Franklin, if you'll move your hoof," Jenkins said good-naturedly.

"Huh! What? Oh, I stepped on your pome, didn't I?" Franklin said with exaggerated courtesy. "Say, I'm sorry about that, Jenkins. It's too bad I'm so clumsy. I

120

wouldn't have done that for anything . . . Here, Pat, get Jenkins another piece of paper."

As he removed his foot, Jenkins picked up the paper. "Never mind, Pat, this piece is all right . . . No, don't mention it, Franklin. Shucks! No, no apology is necessary."

Franklin's eyes held a sneering light as he watched Jenkins turn the paper over and again take up the writing. Finally, Jenkins ceased and looked up. "I reckon maybe this will do, Pat. Your poem as it stands now, ends with:

> . . . For every drink you buy from him,
> He'll buy for you another."

"That's right," Pat was beaming now. "Them's the words that nearly put me out of business."

Jinglebob chuckled, "We'll have to qualify that last statement, Pat. You just buy drinks for your customers when you happen to remember it, like you've always done. The next two verses take care of that. Listen to this . . ." Jinglebob read aloud the words he had just written:

> "He'll buy another drink in kind
>   To the best of his ability;
> But should it chance to slip his mind,
>   Remember your civility.

> "The gratis drink just comes, perforce,
>   By special recollection;

For all the other drinks, of course,
There'll be a small collection."

Applause, laughs, yells filled the Acme barroom. Pat, grinning from ear to ear, was setting out bottles and glasses and shouting himself hoarse to the effect that the drinks "are on the house in honor of a great pome-maker." Glasses clinked. Other customers entered from the street. Jinglebob was forced to read the words a second time.

"From now on," Pat was chuckling, "no more free drinks unless I happen to remember it."

"We'll see that you do," a man exclaimed. "We'll jog yore memory."

"That wouldn't be polite," Pat said triumphantly and quoted from the jingle, " 'Remember your civility.' "

"Who gives a damn about his civility when he can get free drinks," the man persisted with a loud guffaw.

The smile vanished from Pat's face and he looked appealingly at Jenkins. "You see," he groaned, "there's always bound to be some hawgs in the trough."

"Well, if anything like that happens," Jenkins laughed, "you'll just have to boost the price of your drinks enough to take care of the one you give free."

Pat nodded. Then he had another idea: "But suppose a hombre came in, just wanting one drink. I couldn't overcharge him —"

"You don't need to worry about that," Scarab's soft laugh cut in, "I don't think there's a man in Padre Wells that stops after one drink."

122

A howl of laughter went up. That seemed to settle the matter, and from that day on the Acme Saloon resumed its customary business procedure.

Pat said, after a few minutes, "Jinglebob, let me have those extra verses. I'll get a printed copy made."

"I'll have to rewrite this first," Jenkins returned, glancing at the sheet. "I've crossed out and rewritten so many words that nobody could read it but me."

The room again broke into small groups. Scarab and his companions remained near Jenkins, Malotte and the sheriff. Scarab spoke to Jenkins:

"You figuring to stay in the Truculento Country a while?"

Jenkins nodded, facing Scarab squarely, "I've hooked on with the Ladder-A spread. They can use an extra hand."

For just a brief instant, Scarab stiffened, then he nodded, "Yes, I reckon they can. They've been short-handed for some time. Fact is, I sort of had a hunch you might tie on with Alastair. Well, good luck."

"Thanks."

"You'll need good luck —" Raymer commenced.

"You, Gus!" Scarab cut his man short. Raymer fell silent, eyes savage on Jenkins.

Jenkins spoke quietly, "I might take that up, but I'm not going to. Maybe I will need luck. I don't know. I do know this much. I'm not looking for trouble, but I'm not dodging any either."

"Spoken like a man, Jenkins," Scarab nodded.

"I hear tell," Steve Franklin put in, "that you had good luck dodging a lead slug the other day, Jenkins."

Jenkins nodded. "How'd you know that, Franklin?"

Malotte and the sheriff tensed, waiting for Franklin's reply. Franklin, for a moment, seemed at a loss to answer the question. His eyes shifted before Jenkins' steady gaze.

"Why — why," he said at last, "I reckon everybody knows it. Old Tarp Jones spread the story all over town."

Jenkins said dryly, "Oh." He didn't say anything more, just waited for Franklin's next words. He could feel the eyes of the other Bridle-Bit men watching him narrowly.

Franklin said, after a moment, "Of course, you haven't any idea who tried to dry-gulch you."

"That," and Jenkins laughed softly, "is just where you're wrong, Franklin."

Franklin frowned. "You — you mean you know who done it?"

"I know who tried to do it."

"You do?" Franklin's voice cracked sharply.

"I'm telling you."

Franklin commenced to look uneasy. Silence fell on the barroom as other men gathered around to listen. Franklin spoke after a few moments:

"What's the matter . . . did he get away . . . leave town?"

Jenkins slowly shook his head. "The dirty, dry gulching coyote is still in Padre Wells."

"Why hasn't he been arrested?" Franklin's voice trembled a little. "The sheriff and deputy lose their nerve? Tell me who he is. I'll go after him."

124

Jenkins said sarcastically, "Yes, I can see you saddling up right pronto. But —"

"Who is he?" Franklin demanded.

"The same coyote who killed that A. C. A. cattle detective and tried to kill Breck Alastair."

Franklin looked relieved. "Oh, you're just guessing, eh? Just because a couple of other men were shot at, you've jumped to conclusions . . ."

"I'm not jumping to conclusions, Franklin. I'm telling you straight."

"You've got proof, of course." The words were made to sound casual.

"Plenty proof. I've been all over it with Sheriff Wagner. Anybody that wants to, can check with him. I picked up a lot of sign after I was shot on. The man who tried to kill me fits your build, Franklin. I read that from his footprints. He wore a badge that glinted in the sun and warned me, just before the shot came. I picked up his empty shell and it checks against the shells that got Alastair and Mitchell, the cattle detective. They're all from the same gun. There's another shell, one that killed a buzzard yesterday. That checks too . . ."

"Great God, Jenkins! You accusing me —"

Franklin had gone white and started to back away.

Scarab cut in, "You'd better make sure what you're saying, Jenkins. Franklin used to work for me and I know him. He's no dry-gulcher —"

"You don't know your man, then, Scarab," Jenkins snapped.

"You can't build a case like this against me," Franklin said angrily. He was commencing to get his

125

nerve back. "Maybe that rifle I used on that buzzard does mark a shell like the others that were found. I'm not surprised. I just bought that gun, yesterday morning, and I wanted to try it out . . ."

"Got it from that hobo that was passing through town, didn't you, Steve?" Scarab said calmly.

"That's it, that's it," Franklin said swiftly. "This feller was bumming his way across country and he was broke and wanted to sell the rifle and . . ."

"You'll have to think faster than that," Jenkins said sternly.

Scarab cut in again, "There's no use of all this talk. Jenkins, if you think Franklin is guilty, I think the best way to settle the matter is to have Sheriff Wagner arrest him. We'll bring him to trial and if you have other evidence . . ."

"I figure this has gone beyond the arresting stage," Jenkins said grimly. "I'm offering proof now." He turned to Bucky, "A spell ago, when I passed cigars, Franklin threw a butt away. Did you get it, Bucky?"

"Here y'are." Bucky handed a partly-smoked cigar butt to Jenkins. "I saw him toss it away, and got it a minute later."

Jenkins accepted the dead cigar butt and gave it a quick glance. Then he raised his head, his eyes resting momentarily on the faces gathered around him. Scarab's features still held a supercilious sneer. The Bridle-Bit hands had tensed somewhat, wondering what was coming — as was every man in the Acme Saloon.

126

Steve Franklin was as pale as the proverbial ghost. He cast furtive glances from side to side, though he couldn't as yet understand what Jenkins was proposing to show. Fear and curiosity mingled in his manner, causing the muscles of his face to twitch convulsively. His tongue licked at dry lips.

"You — you ain't got nothin' on me," he stammered. "Maybe you've worked out some sort of story, but you haven't got proof. I've already told you where I got that gun. Anybody could have had something shiny pinned to his shirt. You just thought it was my badge you saw. And — and there's lots of fellows built like me. My footprints — those footprints," he corrected himself quickly, "don't prove a thing —"

"Franklin," Jenkins cut in dryly, "there's a certain type of bullets named after you, I reckon."

"Bullets?" Franklin queried. "What do you mean . . . named after me? What are they?"

"Dum-dum," Jenkins snapped. "In your case it's spelled d-u-m-b. Nobody but a dumb, cold-blooded murderer would leave as much sign around as you do."

Franklin backed away a step. "You — you ain't got proof," he repeated.

"I'm asking for proof too," Scarab cut in coldly. "There's a lot of talk been spilled, but I can't see yet, Jenkins, where you've got anything on Steve. What's all this fol-de-rol about cigar butts?"

"I'll show you in a moment," Jenkins said calmly.

He produced the cigar butt and cartridge shell he had found the day he'd been shot at, and opened the handkerchief in which they were wrapped, spreading

127

the objects on the bar. Franklin gazed at them as though hypnotized.

Jenkins continued, "That shell is from your gun, Franklin. It's the one that came close to finishing me. You tossed that cigar butt away, while you were waiting for me to ride into your trap —"

"But look here —" Scarab commenced an angry protest.

"I'm doing the talking, Scarab," Jenkins cut in sternly. "You keep quiet until I've finished, then you'll have your opportunity to talk . . . and you'll have to talk fast. Remember, I've been over all this proof with Sheriff Wagner. We've covered every detail. For instance, there are tooth marks in both these cigar butts. They match perfectly. Franklin has the sort of teeth that leave very definite 'sign'."

Franklin acted as though he were gasping for air now. He backed away another pace, as Jenkins' quiet words beat like hammers against his now tumultuous mind.

"I've already mentioned footprints," Jenkins went on. "The man who shot at me that day walked on the outside of his right boot. Franklin, we won't bother to examine your boot. I've already got an imprint. A short spell ago, when I was writing that verse for Pat, my paper slipped to the floor. You stepped on it. The bottom of your boot was soiled, soiled enough to leave the imprint on this paper."

Jenkins turned over the sheet of paper in his hand. Outlined on the paper was the imprint made by part of a boot.

128

"You see," Jenkins said softly, "this print, if it was in sand, would leave exactly the sort of mark left by the man who shot at me that day, the man who shot Breck Alastair, the man who killed Mitchell, the cattle detective. You've asked for proof, Franklin, Scarab, all the rest of you. There's your proof. It couldn't be any plainer. Franklin, your game is finished!"

CHAPTER
ELEVEN

Trapped Into Admission

A sudden silence had descended on the Acme, a silence that almost seemed to crackle, so charged it was with the bitter intensity of pent-up hate and violence. Jenkins had scored, one by one, and so swiftly, his various points of condemnation, that even Dave Scarab was, for once, stunned to speechlessness by the irrefutable indictment.

There was something of awe and terror in the gaze Steve Franklin bent on Jenkins. Franklin tried to find his voice to shout out convincing denials, but the words wouldn't come. He backed away two more paces, the scraping of his booted feet sounding unusually harsh in the pregnant quiet. He swayed a little bit, still striving for speech and failing to find it.

Jenkins stood as before, right elbow resting on the edge of the bar, left arm hanging loosely at his side. A thin smile curved his lips, but there wasn't any smile in his cold gray eyes.

"You've run your course, Steve Franklin," Jenkins was saying quietly. There wasn't any malice, any hate, in the tones. It was simply the chill, implacable voice of a designated executioner speaking.

130

Steve Franklin gulped, shaking his head. He opened his lips but no sound issued. The fingers of his left hand played restlessly about his throat as though already feeling the harsh, rough burn of the hangman's noose. His features were paper-white.

And then, Jenkins did an apparently careless thing: he swung halfway away from Franklin, his back against the bar, both elbows resting on the edge of the long counter. His left boot heel was hooked nonchalantly, almost too nonchalantly, over the bar rail. Only his cold eyes remained steadily on Franklin's lean form as it retreated still another pace.

Bucky Malotte saw it coming and tried to shout a warning to Jenkins, but Bucky's vocal cords seemed paralyzed. Only a choked gurgling issued from his throat.

If Jenkins heard the sound he gave no sign. His chill gaze still knifed into Franklin's eyes. And his tones were still level, quiet, when he said, "You won't shoot any more men in the back, Franklin." And added one more word, "Murderer!"

That single word was like a spark in a powder keg. A long exhalation of breath sounded through the room before Franklin ripped out a sudden curse. With the swiftness of a striking diamond-back, the man's right hand flashed down toward holstered gun.

Jenkins still had both elbows resting on the bar, when the movement came. Abruptly, his right arm flicked at his side. Two spurts of white fire flashed momentarily against the dark background of the bar-front. Where those two flashes had appeared a leaden slug ripped into the wood. Three thundering detonations sounded almost simultaneously, shaking the rafters of the building.

Through a thick fog of powder smoke, the occupants of the Acme Saloon saw Steve Franklin whirled half around by the impact of the shots, saw the gun drop from his nerveless fingers and heard it clatter to the floor. The man's eyes were wide with horror and surprise. He stiffened rigidly to tip-toe, his glaring eyes staring, as though hypnotized, at Jenkins. Then, quite suddenly, Franklin's body jack-knifed and he pitched forward on his face. His right knee moved a trifle; a tremor ran through his long form. After that, he didn't move again.

There came the soft rasp of metal against leather as Jenkins' gun slid back into holster. He hadn't stirred away from the bar. Some of the hardness had left his eyes, now, as they gazed down on that motionless form, sprawled on the planks.

Jenkins spoke and his voice sounded a trifle weary and toneless, "His own actions convicted him. He knew he was trapped. There was nothing left except to kill off his accuser, shoot his way out."

Jenkins darted a swift glance about the room as though seeking someone to deny the words. No one did. The powder smoke thinned and disappeared.

Sheriff Clem Wagner was the first to reach the body, stoop down and turn it over. The sheriff whistled softly, noting the narrow space between two wounds, then he glanced up at Jenkins and nodded.

"That's all, Jinglebob," the sheriff said, trying to hold his voice steady. He rose to his feet.

There were yells on the street now and a rapid thudding of footsteps near the entrance to the Acme. Men crowded inside to stare down on the silent form of the town marshal. Abruptly, everyone started talking at once.

In the same toneless, weary tones, Jinglebob said, "God, I hate killing." He looked at Scarab, but Scarab refused to meet his eyes.

Bucky Malotte was saying something to Jenkins, but Jenkins didn't hear what it was. He was already nearing the door, pushing his way through a crowd reluctant to let him pass. A few moments more and he was through the entrance and on the street.

An hour later, Sheriff Wagner and Bucky Malotte pushed open the door of the sheriff's office to find Jenkins seated inside.

"I figured we'd find you here," Wagner said.

Jenkins rose to his feet as they entered. "I wanted to get away. There are always damned fools who want to buy a man a drink after a shooting like that, just so they can hear a lot of talking. I didn't want to talk about it."

"I reckon I know how you feel."

"Am I under arrest, sheriff?"

Wagner stuck out one hand. He didn't say anything for a moment. Jenkins took the hand and gripped it hard.

"Arrest, hell!" Wagner snorted. "Everybody in the Acme saw Franklin go for his gun first. You did a good job, Jinglebob. I'm thanking you. I didn't know what you were up to when you asked me to leave things to you, but you had the right idea. I wasn't fast enough to draw against him. Arresting Franklin would only have been a waste of time. Your way was best."

"It was the only way," Jenkins said soberly, "much as I hated to take it."

Bucky Malotte had been making spluttering noises behind the sheriff ever since he had entered the office. Now he shoved in front of the sheriff and confronted Jenkins on his sturdy, bulldog legs.

"Damn you, oh, damn you, Jinglebob," he uttered with a great deal of feeling. "Why didn't you tell me?"

"Tell you what?" Jinglebob frowned.

"If I'd only known," Bucky spat in his harsh voice, "that you had speed like that in your holster, I wouldn't near died of fright. I was watching Franklin, I saw he was ready to draw, and you, you cow-blasted son of an idjit, leaning against the bar like you was discussing the weather. I tried to warn you, but it was like my voice was stuck in my throat. Damn your hide, why didn't you tell me you was fast enough to —"

"I didn't know for sure if I was," Jenkins said quietly. "I didn't know, Bucky . . ."

"Fast enough," Bucky sputtered. "Is that what I said? Cripes A'mighty! You had speed and to spare. But, dang your easy-goin' ways, anyhow! I never will forgive you for the way I felt when —"

"Bucky's right," Wagner interrupted. "I know how he felt. Over there in the Acme, they're still talking about your speed, Jinglebob. How in God's name do you do it? One instant you was standin' there, easy as you please; the next, you was shaking lead outten your barrels. It was like magic, like you had that gun on a spring, or something. How do you do it?"

"I was lucky —" Jenkins commenced.

"Lucky, hell!" Bucky exclaimed. "Here, I forgive you for scaring me to death, but don't do it again." He stuck out his stubby-fingered hand. Jinglebob shook it warmly.

"The lucky ones," Bucky continued, "are those Bridle-Bit hombres who were probably figuring to throw a gun on you, first chance, but didn't get around to doing it."

The three men dropped into chairs and started rolling cigarettes. Jinglebob said, "How about those Bridle-Bit men, Sheriff?"

Sheriff Wagner looked serious. "It means you have a fight on your hands, Jinglebob. That crew —"

"Are they making threats?" Jenkins asked quickly.

"They started to, after they'd recovered from the shock," Wagner replied, "but Scarab shut them up."

"What did Scarab have to say?"

"Scarab is a fast thinker. He disclaims all connection with those shootin's of Franklin's. He told me he was glad you got Franklin and that he had never suspected Franklin was the sort of hombre who would do what he's been doing."

"Scarab," Jenkins said quietly, "is drawing a red herring across his path."

"There's sure something fishy about him," Bucky Malotte snapped.

"I mean," Jenkins went on, "that Scarab is trying to get us off his own trail. Franklin was useful, so long as he lived. Now, Scarab will try something else."

"What?" from the sheriff.

"I haven't the least idea," Jenkins said soberly. "I wish I knew. Did he have anything more to say?"

"Wanted to know where you'd gone," Wagner replied. "I told him I didn't know. I asked him if he was itching to take up Franklin's fight. He denied that, emphatically, of course. I asked him next if he wanted to stand funeral expenses for Franklin, seeing Franklin was a friend of his —"

"And," Bucky Malotte put in, "Scarab acted plumb indignant when Clem asked that. He allowed as how Franklin had brought the Bridle-Bit into disrepute and that he didn't want anything more to do with Franklin and that the county could bury him or throw his carcass to the coyotes for all he cared. He appeared to act like Franklin had double-crossed him, or something."

"Franklin did," Jenkins put in, "by being careless. Nobody but a fool would leave as much sign around as that hombre did after his dry-gulchings."

Jenkins dropped his cigarette butt on the floor, extinguished its fire with the tip of one boot, and rose to his feet, "Well, I reckon I'll drift out and get a breath of air."

"It's getting along toward dinner-time," Bucky said. "How about some chow?"

Jenkins shook his head. "Not this noon," and his lips curved in a slight smile. "I just don't feel hungry."

136

"I reckon not," Clem agreed. "There's something about letting daylight through a hombre, even when he deserves it, that plumb takes away a man's appetite —"

A knock sounded on the door. The sheriff called, "Come on! It ain't locked."

The door opened to admit Dave Scarab. No one said anything for a moment. Bucky Malotte swore under his breath. The sheriff remained at his desk, looking questioningly at Scarab. Jenkins stood as before. He stiffened a trifle, but didn't say anything. They all waited for Scarab to speak.

Scarab said quietly. "I've been looking around for you, Jenkins."

"I reckon I wasn't there," Jinglebob drawled.

Scarab's face flushed a little. "I wanted to see you."

"You looking to take up Franklin's fight?" Jinglebob demanded.

Scarab shook his head. "Far from it. Look here, Jenkins, you got me wrong —"

"I don't know any other way I could get you, Scarab."

Scarab forced a thin smile. "You and I seem to be getting off on the wrong feet, Jenkins."

"We not only seem to be — we are."

"Look here, Jenkins, there's no use of all this wrangling. I came here to see you. I'll make my say and get out."

"Shoot!"

"I came here," Scarab commenced, "to apologize and congratulate you."

137

"Thanks," dryly. "Which comes first and what's it all about?"

Scarab kept his temper. "First, I want to apologize. You were right about Franklin. I was wrong. I never realized what a crook he was before. I congratulate you on putting him out of the running. You're damnably fast with a six-shooter, Jenkins."

"Thanks some more. Now, if that's all —"

"Just a minute. I don't suppose you'll believeme if I tell you I didn't know what Franklin was doing."

"I can't do that, Scarab."

Scarab nodded cheerfully. "No, I don't suppose you can. I didn't expect you to. All I ask is that you consider me not too harshly. I tell you frankly, I didn't know what Franklin was doing. He worked on the Bridle-Bit at one time. I thought he was straight. You proved he wasn't —"

"It don't wash down, Scarab. If Franklin wasn't pulling those dry-gulchings on your orders, what was his reason for them?"

"Great Scott, Jenkins! Why should I order those shootings?"

"I'll let you figure it out, Scarab. The Ladder-A brought a cattle detective in here to determine who was stealing its cows —"

"Now, look here, Jenkins, the Bridle-Bit has lost cows too —"

"The Bridle-Bit wants the Ladder-A —"

"Granted," Scarab said frankly. "I've tried to buy it —"

"And failing to get the spread cheaply, you've tried to intimidate the Alastairs. You had Franklin shoot Breck Alastair."

Scarab laughed softly. "You certainly haven't a very pretty opinion of me, Jenkins, but you're badly mistaken. I'm sorry it works out this way. I came here, wanting to be friends. In fact, I intended to offer you a job where you can earn better wages than —"

"The Ladder-A suits me, Scarab. And I'll continue to hold a poor opinion of you until you can prove to me that Franklin wasn't working under your orders."

"The way I figure it," Scarab said, "Franklin must have needed money. He gambled a lot. I happen to know he lost, a great deal of the time. I think robbery must have been the motive for those shootings —"

"Mitchell's money hadn't been touched," Sheriff Wagner broke in heavily. "Breck Alastair's money was intact —"

"And there wasn't any effort made to rob me," Jenkins said, "that day I was left for dead."

"Franklin was sore at you, that day," Scarab put in quickly. "I sent him to the Acme to smooth things over, but he lost his temper and —"

"You're wasting time, Scarab," Jenkins interrupted. "You should know I can't believe anything you say . . ."

"You refuse to be friendly then?" Scarab's face darkened.

"I don't trust you, Scarab."

"I'll make a lot better friend than I will an enemy," Scarab pursued softly.

"That," and Jinglebob's eyes were stony cold, "sounds a heap like a threat, Scarab."

A silky smile crossed Scarab's face. "Suit yourself. In this country, folks are either with me, or against me. There isn't anything halfway about it."

"You look here, Scarab," Sheriff Wagner said hotly, "you better go easy. You're none too clear on the Franklin shootings yet —"

Scarab whirled, almost savagely, to face the sheriff. "You talk like a fool, Wagner. I don't bluff easily. Any time you can get proof of my connection with Steve Franklin, you're entitled to act. *But get proof.*"

Wagner gulped. He didn't have proof and Scarab knew it.

Scarab smiled suddenly, turning back to Jenkins. "It's war then?" he asked lightly.

"It's war," Jenkins said coldly.

"I'm glad to know where we stand," Scarab nodded. "Anytime, Jenkins, you catch me employing crooked methods to gain control of the Ladder-A, come with your guns smoking. But, remember, you'll have to *catch* me, first. *Adiós.*"

He turned toward the doorway, then hesitated at the threshold, smiling, "By the way, Jenkins, you were looking for a rhyme for Saskatoon. How about 'lampoon'?"

Jinglebob shook his head. "It doesn't fit the subject, Scarab," he smiled thinly.

"Sorry," Scarab nodded carelessly. "I'll keep trying. You do the same."

140

"That," Jinglebob said dryly, "sounds like a challenge."

Scarab nodded. "Suit yourself, Jenkins. Think it over. I'll see you again one of these days."

And with that he was gone.

Bucky Malotte swore and, jumping to his feet, slammed the door shut. "That hombre is dangerous," he growled.

Jenkins nodded soberly. "He's all of that, Bucky . . . Well, anyway, we each know where the other stands."

"Trouble is," Wagner rumbled, "you'll fight in the open. You can't tell when or where Dave Scarab will strike."

"Well, there's no use of fretting about it now," Jinglebob said. "Bucky, do me a favor."

"Certain, what is it?"

"Drift out to the Ladder-A and tell 'em I won't be coming back today."

"What you aiming to do?"

Jinglebob shrugged his shoulders, smiled. "I don't know just yet. Drift around and look the country over a mite. Maybe catch up on my poetry . . ."

"Yaah! You and your poetry," Bucky scoffed.

"You can tell Breck Alastair what's happened. It'll save me talking about it, Bucky. Just tell Breck there's no more need of his wanting to get well so he can hunt the man who shot him. His recovery can be normal, restful, now. I'm aiming to keep it thataway."

CHAPTER
TWELVE

"Bring Me His Scalp!"

Gus Rayner and Utah Hannan waited in front of the barber-shop on Padre Wells' main street. Hannan was a slim, wiry man with ash-yellow hair and hard-lined features, his form almost dwarfed by Raymer's heavier bulk. He wore bibless overalls, and a Colt's forty-five hung at his right thigh.

". . . and if you ask me," Hannan was saying bitterly, "I'd say we ought to gather the boys and go to the Ladder-A and clean 'em out. Dave is taking all this too cool."

Raymer shook his head. "I'm not agreein' with you, Utah. It's best to leave the brainwork to Dave. He knows what he's doing."

Hannan laughed sarcastically. "You don't seem any too anxious to buck Jenkins. That brush you had with him, a few days back, must have shook your nerve some."

Raymer flushed. "My nerve is as good as it ever was."

"Mebbe it's Jenkins shootin' Steve this morning, that's the trouble."

Raymer's flush deepened. "You saw the shooting. You've got to admit Jenkins is fast. I was plumb stunned when he beat Steve to the shot."

142

Utah Hannan nodded. "That's because you haven't taken time to think things out. It hit me the same way at first. But I've been doping out just what happened. I figure Jenkins ain't so fast. He's just smart."

"I suppose," Raymer sneered, "you'd be willing to face his gun."

"Certain," Hannan said promptly. "He wouldn't outsmart me."

"T'hell you say," Raymer snorted. "Just how do you figure Steve was outsmarted?"

"It's plain as the nose on your face, when you think it over. First, Steve's nerve was shook some, when Jenkins commenced piling up the evidence on him. Under those conditions, no man can shoot straight. Jenkins was ready for him. Every man in the Acme knew Steve was getting ready to shoot, when he started backing away and going into that sort of crouch."

"Maybe so, but it didn't look like Jenkins knew it. He was leaning back against the bar, easy-like —"

"Yeah, easy-like," Hannan said dryly. "I know it looked that way, but Jenkins was a heap more ready for action than he looked. Sure, he was lounging back against the bar; one elbow was resting on the edge of the bar. But if you'd took notice of things, you'd seen that Jenkins' right hand was hanging just above his gun butt . . . ready for a fast draw. He wasn't as careless as he seemed."

"Mebbe so, mebbe so." Raymer was unconvinced. "The fact remains it was Steve who died . . . but not Jenkins. Call it speed, call it being smart, call it anything you like, Utah, you can't deny the facts."

"All right, have it your way, but I wish Dave would do something about it."

"He will, don't you worry. But he'll do it in his own way."

"That's just the trouble. We never do know what Dave has in mind. He never tells us anything. He didn't even tell us what Jenkins had to say when he went down to the sheriff's office, beyond saying he was trying to assure Jenkins that none of us knew anything about Steve being a dry-gulcher."

"When you've known Dave Scarab as long as I have," Raymer said heavily, "you'll realize, it's not Dave's way to talk. I been through a lot with him. He uses his head and he always come out, top side up. You let him do the thinking, Utah. Our part is to carry out orders when he gives 'em —"

"There's Jenkins now," Hannan said suddenly. He added a profane curse.

From in front of the barber-shop where they were standing, both men glanced diagonally up the street a short distance, to see Jinglebob emerging from the building where the sheriff's office was located. In his right hand, Jinglebob carried a white oblong bit of paper that, from this distance, looked like a letter. He strode out to the hitch-rack, mounted his pony and turned it. A moment later he was riding past the barber-shop. He didn't glance toward Hannan nor Raymer, but both men felt Jenkins was conscious of their presence. In front of the general store, Jenkins drew to a halt, stepped down from the saddle and entered the store. Within a few minutes, he was back, mounting his horse. Then he continued on, out of town.

"Where do you reckon he's going?" Hannan commented.

"I don't reckon," Raymer said.

"But the Ladder-A lies in the opposite direction."

"How do you know he's heading for the Ladder-A?"

Utah Hannan didn't have any answer for that one.

Raymer said, "You wait here for Dave. I'm going to drift down to the general store."

Except for Ichy Wellman, the elderly, bespectacled clerk, the store was devoid of occupants when Raymer entered. Raymer purchased a sack of cigarette tobacco, and opened it to roll a cigarette before leaving.

Ichy said, "Quite some excitement in town, this morning, Gus."

Raymer pulled the string of the tobacco sack with his teeth, thrust the sack into his pocket and glanced at the clerk. "Meanin' what?" he asked.

"Marshal Franklin."

"Oh, that dry-gulchin' son. Hell, he deserved to die if a man ever did."

"I reckon so, from what I hear. You and him used to be right good friends, didn't you?"

Raymer shook his head and struck a match. "Not for a long time. Dave Scarab and me, we been suspecting Franklin of some sort of crooked business. We never had any proof, though, so we just kept our mouths shut."

"It takes that Jenkins feller to get proof. They say he's fast with a gun, too."

"Tolable. Fast enough for Steve Franklin, leastwise."

"And him a poet too. I always thought poets had long hair and were kind of sissy like . . . He was in here, just a short spell back."

"Who, Jenkins?"

"Yep, come in to mail some more of his poems up to the capital."

"You don't say so."

"Yep. He must write 'em plumb fast," Ichy commented. "T'ain't only three-four days back he come in and mailed some. He told me then he was aiming to get 'em printed."

A couple of customers entered and Raymer left the store to head back toward the barber-shop where Hannan was waiting.

Hannan said, "What was Jenkins doing in the general store — buying ca'tridges?"

Raymer spat and shook his head. "Mailin' a letter . . . with poems in it."

Hannan frowned. "You figure he wrote a poem, already, about shootin' Steve?"

"I don't know and I don't give a damn," Raymer scowled.

The door of the barber-shop opened and closed. Dave Scarab came out, wiping a bit of talcum powder from his blue-black, cleanly shaven chin.

Scarab said, "Where's Hank gone to?"

"I chased him back to the ranch," Raymer said. "There's those three new broncs to be topped off. I figured he'd better get it done. Did you want him for anything?"

146

"You're the foreman," Scarab said. "No, I didn't want him . . . just wondered where he'd gone."

"Look here, Dave," Utah Hannan put in. "What are you going to do about Jenkins?"

Scarab looked level-eyed at his employee. "When I make up my mind to that, Utah, I'll let you know."

Raymer cut in, "Utah has got an idea he'd like to face Jenkins' gun. He don't think Jenkins is so fast." The foreman's voice was scornful.

"There," and Scarab's dark eyes held lights of cold amusement, "there speaks the confidence of ignorance."

"But, Dave," Hannan defended himself, "Jenkins just outsmarted Steve . . ." Hannan continued, giving the reasons he had given Raymer to explain Steve Franklin's sudden demise.

"I know, I know," Scarab nodded, when his henchman had concluded. "I look at the whole business pretty much the same way, myself. But don't underrate Jenkins. He's a man to be reckoned with. He's smart, but he's fast too. When a man's just fast, you more or less know what to expect, but you never can tell what a fox will do to augment his speed. We've got to move very, very carefully where Mr. Jinglebob Jenkins is concerned."

"Just the same," Hannan maintained stubbornly, "I'm not convinced that Jenkins can beat me to the shot."

"Maybe," Scarab said dryly, "you'll have an opportunity to prove the truth of your statement."

"When?" Hannan asked eagerly.

"When I say the word and not before. I'm paying you to take orders, Utah. I don't want you going off half-cocked."

"Sure not, chief. You're the boss."

Scarab said, after a moment's musing, "You haven't seen Jenkins leave the sheriff's office, have you?"

Raymer nodded. "Probably fifteen or twenty minutes ago."

"Where'd he go?"

"Down to the general store to mail some poems. Then he got back in the saddle and headed east out of town."

"East?"

"East," Raymer repeated. "We wondered about that."

"How did you know he was mailing his poems, as you call 'em?"

"After he left the store," Raymer explained, "I went over and bought me a sack of Bull. Then I just let Ichy talk. You know how he runs off at the head."

Scarab nodded thoughtfully. After a minute, "I guess I'll drift over to the general store and see if Ichy can find any of those Red Devil pitchforks."

"I can save you a walk," Raymer said. "You ordered a half a dozen, last fall. We took 'em out to the ranch and —"

"I'm sure I ordered a dozen." There was something mocking in Scarab's thin smile as he walked away, leaving Hannan and Raymer frowning after him.

When he entered the store, Ichy Wellman was busily engaged in stacking some canned goods on a shelf. There weren't any customers in the place.

Wellman turned as Scarab came in.

"Howdy, Dave."

"Hello, Ichy."

Wellman came up to the counter. "Lots of excitement in Padre Wells, eh, Dave?"

"Some," Scarab admitted. "It just goes to show that you never know who you can trust. You couldn't ask for a finer hombre than Steve Franklin when he was working for me. But he changed, after he got to be marshal. He gambled too much, lost money right and left. No wonder he took to pot-shooting men in the back and robbing them."

"So that's what his game was, eh?"

"So I understand," Scarab said carelessly. "Well, the community is better off without him. Jenkins should receive a vote of thanks from Padre Wells."

"I reckon. You and Franklin used to be right good friends, too . . ."

"We weren't as close, after he left the Bridle-Bit, as folks thought. I've never talked about it, but Steve and I had a disagreement one time. Well, that's over and done with now. Ichy, while I'm in town, and Gus and Utah are with me, I reckon we'd better take the rest of those pitchforks back —"

"Pitchforks?" Wellman frowned. "What pitchforks?"

"Those Red Devils."

Wellman shook his head. "Jupiter, Dave! You got them last fall."

"Not all of 'em."

"There was only six."

"We ordered twelve. We took six of 'em last fall."

"Seems like you just ordered half a dozen." Ichy looked troubled.

Scarab smiled. "You go look in your storehouse, Ichy. You'll find 'em. Betcha a dollar on it."

Wellman nodded. "I'll take that bet. You wait here. If any customers come in, tell 'em I'll be right back."

Wellman disappeared through a doorway at the rear of the store.

The clerk had scarcely disappeared, when Scarab, moving with quick, light steps, rounded one end of the counter and made his way toward a small wire cage, set into the counter, which represented the Padre Wells' post-office. There was a desk there, a counter drawer containing stamps and small change. At one side a mail sack hung on a hook. The door to the cage was unlocked, as Scarab had expected. He gave another quick glance toward the front and rear doors of the store, then stepped quickly inside the cage.

It required but an instant for Scarab to plunge one arm into the mail sack and draw out a couple of dozen stamped letters which were waiting to go off on the evening stage. Scarab glanced quickly over the return addresses written on the envelopes selected one letter, and dropped the rest back in the mail sack.

With the letter in his pocket, he swiftly returned to the position before the counter he had held when Wellman went to the storehouse.

In a few minutes, Wellman returned from the storehouse, a triumphant look on his lined features.

"You owe me a dollar, Dave."

"Yeah? Aren't those forks there?"

150

"Nary a Red Devil. We've got some Blue Labels . . ."

"Those Blue Label forks don't stand up."

"Most folks like 'em better than Red Devils."

"It's a matter of taste, I suppose . . . Well, that's funny. I could have sworn we ordered a dozen." Scarab tossed a silver dollar on the counter and smiled genially. "Don't say I don't pay my bets, Ichy."

"Thanks, Dave. I'll speak to Hub about those forks. We can order what you want. He'll be in later."

Hub Hodkins was the owner of the general store.

Scarab shook his head. "Let it go, Ichy. As a matter of fact, we don't need any more forks yet. I just thought if they were here, we'd take 'em. I must have been mistaken."

"Reckon you were," Ichy cackled. "Too bad it had to cost you a dollar, Dave."

"It was worth that . . . anyway," Scarab smiled, "just so I could make sure in my own mind."

He said "So long" and sauntered out of the store.

Utah Hannan and Raymer were waiting where Scarab had left them.

Raymer said, "Was I right about those pitchforks?"

"You certainly were," Scarab smiled.

While the two men watched him he took a letter out of his pocket and glanced at the address. "Hmmm," he muttered, "a publishing house doesn't usually have a general delivery address." He drew a knife from his pocket, opened one blade and slit the envelope. Inside was a second addressed envelope. A frown passed momentarily over his face as he opened this second envelope.

Light suddenly dawned on Raymer. "So that's what you were up to," the foreman chuckled. "Cripes! You and your pitchforks."

"Keep quiet," Scarab said impatiently. He had drawn a sheet of paper from the second envelope and quickly perused its contents. It contained only a short message:

All signs point to Bridle-Bit. Mitchell's murderer taken care of this morning. Will write again, later. Jenkins.

Hannan and Raymer watched their chief's face as he read the contents of the envelope. Finally he restored the paper to its container and slipped the envelopes into his pocket. He didn't say anything for a moment. His features were cold as he gazed musingly at some undetermined point down the street.

Hannan finally broke the silence: "What sort of a poem did he write, boss?"

"One that's not at all to my liking," Scarab said softly. "I'm aiming to see it never sees print."

"What's it like?" Raymer wanted to know.

Scarab smiled, though his eyes were still cold and thoughtful. "Well, it might be like the 'Ode to a Grecian Urn' — only it isn't."

"Owed? Earn?" Raymer asked blankly. "That's got a sort of a money sound, somehow."

"It won't mean any money to us, if we don't act mighty quick," Scarab frowned.

"I don't get you, chief."

"There's no reason you should, Gus — yet . . . Utah, you still feeling as though you'd like to put a stop to Jenkins' poetry writing?"

"I can't think of anything I'd like better."

"You have my permission."

"Good," Hannan spat. "I'll stick around town and when Jenkins shows up, I'll —"

"You'll do nothing of the sort, Utah," Scarab contradicted. "I don't want it to happen in town. That would only call down on us more . . . well, it would only bring in more hombres like Jenkins. We're in a tight, boys. We've got to stop Jenkins before he stops us."

"We're waiting for orders, Dave," Raymer said.

"You'll come back to the ranch with me, Gus," Scarab stated. "Utah, you're a pretty good trailer. You get on Jenkins' tail. Find out if you can, why he headed east when he left town."

"Right. But when do I —"

"That's up to you, Utah. Jenkins will be crossing a lot of range before he gets back to the Ladder-A. Some place along his route you should be able to —"

"I get you, Dave."

"And, Utah —"

"Yes, chief?"

"You saw this morning what happens to damn fools who leave sign around for everybody to read and use as evidence. Don't get careless."

"Not me, Dave."

"You don't dare to get careless, Utah. All right. You've said your say. Now, let's see you outsmart

153

Jenkins. There'll be a nice piece of extra cash . . . when you bring me his scalp."

"I'll get it," Hannan said confidently.

"If some of us don't," and there was just a trace of weariness in Scarab's tones, now, "he'll get ours, sure as hell. Get going, Utah."

CHAPTER
THIRTEEN

Hannan Gets Smart

The trail eastward out of Padre Wells was too hoof-chopped and wheel-rutted for Hannan to distinguish the marks of one horse from another. Jenkins had left town riding east. Why? To the east, a distance of some forty miles, was located the town of Greyville. Jenkins was apparently headed toward Greyville. Again, Utah Hannan frowned and muttered "Why?" and jabbed impatient spurs to his pony's ribs.

Greyville was quite a sizable town and marked the westward termination of rails for the T. N. & A. S. Railroad. Could Jenkins be leaving the country? Hannan's judgment decided against that. No, there must be some other reason for Jenkins' heading east.

A short distance out of Padre Wells, just beyond a plank bridge crossing a dry wash, a well defined trail left the main road and traveled in a north-easterly direction across the rolling grass lands, toward the Thompson T-Bench outfit.

Hannan cast a predatory glance toward the T-Bench trail. "Seems to me," he mused, "Dave could pick up some right nice T-Bench beef from time to time, if he wasn't so wrapped up in this Ladder-A business.

Maybe, after the Ladder-A is settled to his satisfaction, he'll have us give our attention to the T-Bench. Old man Thompson runs some pretty nice stock . . . Get along, hawss."

The pony quickened pace, kicking up as it moved small clouds of dust that were lifted on vagrant puffs of wind to settle on the bordering hillsides of the road. Three miles beyond town, Hannan rounded a curve in the trail to see a small rock and adobe shack standing beside the road. A giant cottonwood spread wide branches above the small house, and not far from the door a couple of small Mexican children, practically naked, played in the dust. Half a dozen chickens scratched futilely at the gravelly earth and standing near the trunk of the cottonwood was a tiny, shaggy-furred burro.

On the small porch, fronting the house, sprawled a round-faced Mexican in tattered overalls and a dirty white shirt, half asleep. The Mexican straightened up, when Hannan hove into sight.

Hannan turned his pony toward the house, checked it and dismounted. "I'm thirsty, greaser," he announced.

The Mexican waved one languid hand toward an *olla* hanging from the porch rafters where it would catch the breeze. "It is yours, señor," he replied courteously, in Spanish.

"Cripes! Speak American, can't you?"

"Eef you wish eet. I'm spik ver' good American. But help yourself of the water."

Hannan's spurs tinkled as he stepped to the rickety porch and tipped the *olla* on its hangings. He drank

156

long and deeply and gave a long sigh of satisfaction when he had finished and returned to the edge of the porch.

"Got any *tequila* around, greaser?"

The Mexican shook his head. "None of the *tequila*, señor."

"*Vino?*"

"Crips!" There was a sly twinkle in the Mexican's eyes. "You can't spik American — no?"

Hannan swore. "All right, wine, then. Got any wine?"

"None of wine, señor."

Hannan swore some more. "I reckon you haven't any ambition, either. And don't try to get funny with me. Layin' around here all day, half asleep. You spies don't have much self-respect, I reckon."

"Self-respec'? Ambition? Señor, I'm work for my living . . ."

"Yeah? What do you do?"

"I'm chop the wood and sell heem in Padre Wells," the Mexican replied with some dignity. "Before the sun rise' I am at work. Now, when my day is finish', I'm take my res'. I'm sit here and watch the worl' go by . . ."

"Mebbe you saw a red-headed jasper go by recent?"

The Mexican shook his head. "He did not take theese road, señor."

"Sure he did. A tall, red-headed hombre on a roan *caballo*."

The Mexican definitely shook his head. "That one deed not pass my house."

"T'hell you say!" Hannan frowned. "You sure?"

"I could be more sure of nozzing else."

Hannan was nonplused. Where had Jenkins gone then? He had started out on this road. Unless he had cut across the range at some point . . .

"How long you been sitting here?" Hannan demanded.

The Mexican shrugged his shoulders. "Maybee one hour, maybee more."

"Asleep most of the time, I reckon."

"Not so sleep I do not see who pass."

"Cripes! That's what you say. Look, this hombre is my pal. I'm trying to catch up to him. He's a lean, slim jasper with red hair and rides a roan horse. You must have seen him. Think hard."

"Sure, I'm see him," the Mexican replied unexpectedly.

"Hell! Why didn't you say so? Can't you get it through your thick skull that I —"

"You deed not ask if I'm see him."

"You're *loco*, Mex —"

"You are ask eef he deed not pass this way. I'm tell you no. But I'm see him, eef that is what you wish to —"

"Cripes A'mighty, yes!" Hannan snapped. "Where did you see him? Hurry it up. I ain't got much time."

"Theese man you look for, ees hees name Jenkins?"

"That's the hombre."

"Hees work for the Ladder-A Ranchero?"

"Goddlemighty yes! Where did —"

"The Señor Jenkins hav' go to the T-Bench Ranchero . . ."

158

"He did! You sure?"

"That is what he tol' me, señor. Look you, I am return from the selling of my wood which I am peddle to the Señor Mayor and the Señor Hodkins, who operate the general shop of all stock, and the Señor Parker who hav' the livery of the Blue Star —"

Hannan swore. "Cut it short. I don't give a damn where you sold your wood. Where did you see Jenkins?"

"I am jus' leave Padre Wells and my poor burro is much relieve that he no longer has of the wood to pack on hees back, and we are thinking of home and of the res' —"

"To hell with you and your burro and your rest. I asked a question and —"

"But I am explain." There was an injured tone in the Mexican's words. "We are jus' leave the town when up rides the Señor Jenkins. He walks his horse by my side and we speak of the weather and of the cattle that are raise in theese country and I'm tell him of my small man-child who will one day be chop the wood in my place and —"

"Oh, my Gawd," Hannan exploded exasperatedly, "will you please get on with your story?"

"That is all there is to tell." The Mexican looked surprised. "Did you expec' more? When we come where the trail makes the fork to the T-Bench he says 'Adiós,' and that he goes to talk with the Señor Thompson about rustlers who has steal from the Ladder-A and pairhaps get the help of some vaqueros to catch the thieves . . ."

"He told you that?" Hannan demanded excitedly.

159

"Eet ees as I say. And that is all I can tell you."

"Goddamit! You'd saved me time if you'd told me this in the first place."

"But I hav' tell you . . ."

Hannan swore at the Mexican, whirled around and climbed back into his saddle. In an instant he was gone around the bend, headed back in the direction of the trail to the T-Bench.

The Mexican chuckled. A fat, beady-eyed Mexican woman thrust her black-haired head through the doorway. "Pascal! Your guest he does not remain to have the *frijoles* with us?"

Pascal shook his head. "That one," he said dryly, "is no guest. Think you I am *demente* that I should ask a coyote into our so fine *casa?*"

And with more throaty chuckles, Pascal slumped back to the porch to finish his interrupted dozing. The children continued their play in the house yard. The chickens still scratched. Life flowed on as before.

Back on the trail leading to the T-Bench, Hannan pushed his pony furiously. By this time, Jenkins must have approximately an hour lead on him. Furiously, Hannan cursed the Mexican for the wasted time. "Damn muddle-headed greaser," Hannan muttered. "If he'd only told me in the first place where Jenkins went, 'stead of all that beating around the bush."

He calmed down after a time when he thought of the news he'd have to bring Dave Scarab. "So the Ladder-A is havin' trouble with rustlers, are they?" he laughed sarcastically. "Now ain't that just too bad. And Jenkins is hoping to get some help from the T-Bench.

160

Well, Mister Jenkins is due to be stopped, plumb sudden. Get rid of him and the Ladder-A won't have only a couple of old fools, a girl and a wounded man to fight their trouble. Maybe I should ride straight to Dave and tell him what's what. No, Dave said to keep on Jenkins' tail and learn what he's up to." Hannan laughed again. "I'll be smart and follow orders. Dave will be plumb delighted when I get back and tell him he doesn't have to worry over Jenkins any more. I'll square up for Steve Franklin, I will."

He was sending his pony along in a space-devouring lope by this time. The trail was easy to follow and led toward a long ridge running north and south. Hannan knew that the opposite side of the ridge swept down to lower ground as it approached the T-Bench holdings.

On either side of the trail were rolling grass lands, dotted here and there with clumps of prickly pear and yucca. Overhead, the sky was a huge, inverted sapphire bowl. The sun had swung to the west and was already splashing the Truculento Range with bright gold above the purple ravines and hollows.

Eventually, Hannan's horse slowed pace of its own volition. The beast was tiring; its withers were foam-flecked. Hannan allowed it to drop to a slower gait.

"Anyway," he mused, "I've made up some of the time I lost. Damn the luck, I didn't use my head. When Jenkins headed east out of Padre Wells, I took it for granted he was going to Greyville. I never dreamed of him going to the T-Bench. That should teach me to use my head and not jump to conclusions. There's just one thing for me to remember if I'm to down Jenkins: I've got to get smart. If I'd given it a thought or two, I could have examined the T-Bench trail where it forks from the main road. Yep, I've got to get smart when I'm dealing with a fox."

His pony was climbing the steep grade to the top of the ridge now. There was a lot of scrub oak and piñon scattered about, and the horse's gait was a twisting one. By this time, Hannan had left the lower trail that wound around one end of the ridge to reach the T-Bench, and was making his way up the steep ridge-side.

When nearly to the top, Hannan dismounted, allowing his pony's reins to dangle on the earth. Then the man made his way forward on foot. Reaching the top of the ridge, he threw himself down on his belly and wriggled forward through the scanty brush that lined its backbone. From this point, he could see far down the opposite declivity to the T-Bench buildings. Now and then he could even hear the faint clanking of the windmill and the whinnying of ponies in a saddlers' corral. The roofs of the buildings were almost beneath his nose.

Hannan's eyes roved from building to building, finally settling on the Thompson ranch house with its wide front porch. There was a roan-colored horse tied to the porch railing. It was likely Jenkins was seated on the porch with Thompson, or in the house.

"He's there, all right," Hannan muttered. "I wish he'd get started back. When he leaves, I'll drift back down this ridge and wait for him at the T-Bench trail.

Then, we'll see what we'll see." He corrected himself with a nasty smile: "*I'll* see what *I'll* see. Jenkins' seeing isn't going to last long."

Fifteen minutes went by, then twenty. Hannan commenced to grow impatient. He drew out his cigarette tobacco and papers, rolled a cigarette. With a match poised to strike on his boot, Hannan paused, then returned the match to his pocket.

"Nope, that might not be smart," he told himself. "I'm not sure smoke could be seen up on this ridge, but it might be. Jenkins might not look up this way, either, but I can't take any chances of him seeing smoke and growing suspicious. I'm aiming to outsmart that jasper, I am."

He felt very virtuous over the relinquishment of his smoke and well satisfied that his mind was sharp and clear. He rolled on his back, taking his comfort and gazed up at the broad expanse of blue sky. A small wispy cloud floated high overhead and against the white background a soaring buzzard was cleanly silhouetted. After a moment, with a lazy flapping of wings, the buzzard moved off, out of eyesight.

Hannan rolled back on his stomach, eyes again focused on the ranch house below. A tiny form he made out to be Jenkins' had just moved out from the porch, accompanied by old man Thompson. Jenkins was untying his pony and preparing to mount. In one hand Jenkins held what appeared to be something wrapped in newspaper. Hannan wondered what it was. He saw the two men shake hands, then Jenkins climbed into his saddle and turned his pony.

Hannan started to move back to get his own horse. "I'll wait for him at the bottom of the ridge, where the T-Bench trail curves around —" Then Hannan stopped and considered. "I've jumped to conclusions once today," he cogitated. "I reckon I'd better wait and make sure he hits the T-Bench trail."

A slow smile dawned on Hannan's hard-bitten features as he saw Jenkins turn his pony directly toward the south. "Damn!" Hannan ejaculated triumphantly. "I used my head that time. He ain't hitting the T-Bench trail back to town. I wonder what he's heading south for." Then a new thought struck Hannan: "Say, mebbe he's going to the 9-Bar spread. It might be he's going to all the outfits in this neck of the range and asking 'em to lend a hand or so. Say, I'll bet that's what he's doing. The 9-Bar lays directly south. Jenkins is heading south. Mister Jenkins, I'll outsmart you yet."

Now that he was certain of the direction taken by Jenkins, Hannan moved back down the slope to get his own horse. The pony looked a trifle fagged. "Cripes," Hannan grunted, "I should have watered you at that greaser's. Oh, well, I reckon it won't kill you to go thirsty a spell." He swung up into the saddle and started down hill. "Get along, hawss, we're headin' toward the 9-Bar, to out-fox a fox."

Once at the bottom of the ridge, Hannan swung his pony toward the south and east. For the remainder of the afternoon, he followed Jenkins, staying almost opposite him and keeping low rises of ground between himself and his prey, that he might not be seen.

164

Hannan approached the crest of each hill cautiously, and made sure of Jenkins' position before going on.

The sun swung farther to the west and commenced to dip behind the highest peaks of the Truculentos. The continually blowing range wind died down somewhat. The shadows in the distant mountains were deep purple by now.

"Dammit," Hannan growled, "he'll probably reach the 9-Bar just about time for chow, if he gets a move on. And what's going to happen to me? I'm commencing to get hungry myself. If I have to hide out near the 9-Bar while that hombre stuffs his belly full, I'll throw an extra slug into him, just to get even."

The 9-Bar Ranch was still some ten miles to the south. The course Jenkins was now following bordered the foot of a huge mesa known as Topango Mesa. Where level range met the sheer, upright rock walls of Topango Mesa was a thick growth of brush, mesquite and cottonwoods. It was toward this clump of trees and brush, Jenkins was now heading.

From a slight rise of range, Hannan saw Jenkins dismount and unsaddle his pony. "What in the devil is he up to now?" Hannan frowned. While he watched, he saw Jenkins produce his knife and start to cut small limbs from trees and brush. Here and there, larger limbs of dead wood lay about. These too, Jenkins commenced to gather.

"Dam'd if it don't look like he was throwing up a brush shelter," Hannan muttered. "He's camping there for the night. Well, I'll be danged. You'd think he'd go on to the 9-Bar, rather than that."

Jenkins wasn't more than three hundred yards away. Even while he watched, Hannan saw Jinglebob's brush shelter take form. Forked limbs were set up in the earth; other small limbs were employed as miniature rafters; loose brush was placed on top, the roof slanting somewhat toward the growth and precipitous rock wall of Topango Mesa. Hannan saw Jenkins carry saddle, saddle-blanket and other gear inside the shelter, after pegging out his pony.

"Yep," Hannan mused elatedly, "he's making camp for the night. What a break for me. I sure got smart when I trailed him, thisaway."

He crept swiftly back to his horse, mounted and rode wide in a hill-concealed arc that carried him toward Topango Mesa. By the time Hannan had reached the high rock wall and the brush below, the sun had dropped back of the Truculento Range and the sky overhead was darkening.

The point at which Hannan dismounted among the trees and brush was at least a half mile from Jenkins' camp. Here, Hannan staked out his pony, which peacefully commenced to crop the sparse grass and leaves of stunted trees, and went forward on foot.

Ever keeping in mind how smart he was, Hannan employed unusual caution in working his way through the brush. Like an Apache he stole nearer and nearer to Jenkins' camp. Not a twig crackled under foot; there wasn't a swish of branch or tree limb.

It was dark by this time, but only a short way ahead Hannan saw the bright gleam of a campfire. Again, he moved stealthily on. Now, Jenkins' cheerful whistling reached his ears. Hannan crept in several more paces.

Peering through a screen of leaves and brush, he saw Jenkins crouched before the fire, his back toward the shelter he had thrown up. In his hand, Jenkins held the newspaper-wrapped package he had carried away from the T-Bench. Now he unwrapped it carefully, and Hannan saw that the package held several smaller packages. He learned what the packages contained, when he saw Jenkins broiling strips of beef on small sticks over the glowing coals of the campfire. Biscuits followed. Jenkins held a can of beans now, which he opened with his knife.

A slow fury grew within Hannan's breast. "Damn it," he mused, "here I'm going without my supper while you eat in comfort."

It had been Hannan's plan to meet Jenkins face to face, when they drew guns on each other, but now, for no reason Hannan could conceive, there arose before him, in his mind, a picture of Marshal Steve Franklin as he dropped before the thundering roar of Jenkins' Colt gun.

"Mebbe I'd better stay smart," Hannan muttered. "That hombre may be faster than I think. There's no use of my taking any chances. I can beat him to the shot, all right, but his slug might wound me. Nope, I can get him from here as well as not."

Carefully, Hannan drew his gun and drew a bead on the man eating before the fire. He was just about to pull trigger when Jenkins suddenly moved back out of range and entered his brush shelter. Within a minute he was

167

back, carrying a water canteen, but now he was continually on the move it seemed, and never remained still long enough to provide a good target.

He spilled some water into the can that had held the beans, rinsed it out, then poured in fresh water. He sifted something into the can from a small newspaper package and placed the can on the embers of the campfire. It wasn't long before the aroma of coffee reached Hannan's nostrils.

Hannan cursed bitterly to himself. This was adding insult to injury. Coffee! And already Hannan's stomach was commencing to crave its regular food. In a sudden wave of fury, Hannan again raised his gun.

At that instant, Jenkins abruptly turned his head and gazed intently in Hannan's direction. Hannan dropped down, lowering his six-shooter. He wondered if he had made some sound which Jenkins had heard. No, he couldn't have. He'd been too careful. Still, it would be best not to take chances. He'd better wait until Jenkins had gone to sleep and then make sure. That was the smart thing to do, not take any chances.

A slow bitter anger burned through Hannan as he watched Jenkins drink his coffee and follow it with three cigarettes, one after the other. Above stars commenced to blink into being in the indigo sky. In front of the brush shelter, the fire was gradually dying down.

Finally, Hannan emitted a slow, careful breath of relief, as he saw Jenkins turn and enter the shelter. He heard the sound of a saddle being arranged for a pillow.

There were other sounds, as Jenkins flattened down brush for a bed. Then fell silence.

Hannan sat quiet while fifteen minutes dragged by. Beyond the shelter he heard the sounds made by Jenkins' staked-out pony. Off to the left, some insect of the night made a soft, whirring noise. That was all. Time drifted past. Impatient to move, Hannan still held the same position. His limbs commenced to cramp. Then, at long last, came the sound he was waiting for: the long, heavy drawn breath of a sleeper. It was almost a snore. Then quiet again.

"It's time," Hannan whispered to himself.

Carefully, he eased his cramped position. Until the blood was again flowing normally through his limbs, he didn't make a move. Then, six-shooter gripped in right fist, he made his way noiselessly toward the brush shelter.

The campfire was almost out now. Occasionally a small flickering flame would dance momentarily above the dying coals, throwing light into the brush shelter. Still moving with caution, his body in a crouching position, Hannan moved to the front of the shelter, stepping past the campfire as he did so.

He stooped a little more, peering inside. The flickering flames of the fire gave but little light, but it was enough to throw dim highlights on boot-toes at one end of a long form stretched beneath a spread saddle-blanket. Hannan saw a saddle, and resting against it a sombrero.

He's got his hat over his face, was the thought that ran through Hannan's mind. He raised his gun, leveling the barrel toward the sombrero, then changed his mind and shifted the aim: it would be smarter to throw a slug through Jenkins' body first; the head would do for a finishing shot.

The gun in Hannan's hand was pointed directly at the saddle-blanket now. It was a Navajo blanket, with alternating red and gray stripes. Hannan squinted at the stripes, trying to decide which one covered Jenkins' heart. Finally he nodded with satisfaction.

His finger quivered on trigger, then tightened.

Two deafening reports shattered the night silence as Hannan yelled triumphantly, "I'm smart, I am!"

CHAPTER
FOURTEEN

Outguessed

The echoes of the yell and the twin explosions of Hannan's six-shooter were still sounding across the hills, when he rushed inside the brush shelter to throw in a finishing third shot.

Gun raised, ready to throw down, Hannan paused abruptly. Something was wrong here. At the back of the shelter was a second opening, large enough to permit a man's exit. Too, there had been no movement from the form beneath the saddle-blanket, no dying groans nor any of the sounds Hannan had expected to hear.

Sudden, stark fear carried the blood from Hannan's face as he kicked aside the blanket and sombrero. Beneath was only a pile of twisted brush. The boots he had seen were empty.

"Gawd!" Hannan gulped. "Where — where is he?"

He started to turn frantically toward the entrance to the brush shelter, when a sharp command halted the movement.

"Hold it, Hannan!" came Jenkins' voice.

Hannan stiffened, slowly raising his hands in the air, his body crouched above the blanket, saddle and empty boots.

From beyond the dying campfire, again came Jenkins' voice: "Did I hear you bawling something about being smart, Hannan?" There was cool laughter in the tones now.

Hannan cursed futilely and started some sort of stammering explanation.

Jenkins laughed again and kicked some loose brush and dry sticks on the fire embers. Within a few moments, the fire blazed up, throwing light on the scene.

"Dammit," Hannan commenced again, "it's like this, Jenkins, I didn't know you were in here . . ."

"I'm not," Jenkins chuckled.

"You know what I mean . . ."

"Sure, I do. I know what you intended to do, too. Nope, I haven't been inside that shelter for quite some time. I slipped out the back way and then worked around to here. Ain't you ashamed of yourself?" Jenkins was laughing scornfully. "This isn't any way to treat me. I'll bet you put a couple of holes in my blanket, too. And this morning, in the Acme, you smoked my cigar and I thought sure we were friendly all around. That was before I shot Steve Franklin, Hannan. Remember Steve Franklin, do you?"

"Now, look here, Jinglebob, you got me all wrong. I didn't know it was you camping here. There's been a lot of rustlers on this range and —"

"Hold it, Hannan. Don't turn around. Just keep your back to me like before. I know you're holding your gun in your hand."

172

Hannan swore a savage oath. He'd been hoping that Jenkins wouldn't notice that.

Jenkins went on, "Just so there won't be any accidents, Hannan, you lower that gun carefully and toss it back of you, out here. And don't try any tricks. The fire's between you and me. You wouldn't be able to see me well, in case you suddenly turned around and tried a shot."

And that was exactly what Hannan had been planning. Hot rage welled up in his throat, but with an effort he held his voice steady.

"All right, Jenkins, you got me," he said hopelessly. "I'm dropping my gun . . ."

"I said to throw it out here."

Gun in hand, Hannan whirled around with the speed of light. His plan almost worked, but just as he turned, his spur became entangled in some loose brush and he tripped. He threw up one hand to keep from falling, but it was no use. He sat down heavily. The gun flew out of his hand and landed beyond the fire almost at Jinglebob's feet.

A roar of laughter burst from Jinglebob's lips. "Well, you certainly obey orders. Do you always have to sit down when you throw? Seems like you make a lot of work of it."

A lurid flow of profanity burst from the brush shelter. Jinglebob stooped and retrieved Hannan's gun, shoving the weapon into the waistband of his overalls.

"You know," Jinglebob chuckled gravely, "I feel one of my poems coming to a head. I reckon it'll go something like this:

173

"A Bridle-Bit puncher named Hannan,
Indulged in some very shrewd plannin';
    But he made a bad slip
    Which caused him to trip,
And he found himself facing a cannon."

There! How does that sound to you?"

There were more curses from Hannan. He was on hands and knees, in the entrance of the brush shelter. Beyond the fire he saw Jenkins grinning widely, in his sock feet, with a forty-five clutched in his right hand.

"What! You don't like my poetry?" Jinglebob laughed. "Well, you got one consolation — you agree with nearly everybody else on that score. Mebbe we could change the poem around a mite, say the third and fourth lines. I could say:

    But he made some bad slips
    And came down on his hips . . .

Only it wasn't your hips you came down on, was it, Hannan? 'Course, hips is more polite. Either way you change it, the end would have to come out the same, because you're still facing a cannon, and if you got what you deserve, you skunk," and Jenkins' voice had suddenly turned hard and cold, "this forty-five cannon would explode right sudden. Now, cut out that cursing. Get my boots and Stetson and come out here. And move plumb careful."

Hannan fell silent. By the time he emerged from the shelter, carrying Jinglebob's boots and sombrero,

174

Jinglebob was seated near the fire. Hannan would have liked to have hurled the boots at Jenkins' head, but the steady-leveled six-shooter pointing toward him immediately banished any such ideas. Sullenly he tossed hat and boots on the earth, within reach of Jenkins.

"Well, sit down," Jinglebob ordered. "You're not going any place, not until I get ready to move."

Muttering baffled, enraged oaths, Hannan dropped to the ground and watched with lowered lids while Jenkins drew on his boots and donned his sombrero. Jenkins had shoved his Colt gun back into holster to accomplish this, but Hannan didn't quite dare an attempt to escape or overpower his captor.

Jenkins laughed softly, threw some more fuel on the fire and drew out his tobacco and papers.

"Want a smoke, Hannan?"

"Go to hell! I got my own makin's."

"I hope your makin's are better than your ideas. Your ideas aren't worth a hoot in Hades. All right, go to it, then we'll talk. And don't get any ideas, Hannan. I'm watching you close every minute. You're only a couple of paces away, but a lead slug can travel a heap faster'n you can. I don't like killing. That's why I took this way. But I'll kill if I have to. Remember Steve Franklin, Hannan?"

"Goddlemighty! You keep asking me that . . ."

"I just want you to keep remembering what happened to him."

Hannan didn't say anything. Both men rolled cigarettes and lighted them from small twigs at the fire. Jinglebob smoked in silence for a few minutes.

Finally, Hannan burst out, "You can't do this. Wait until Dave Scarab hears of this —" He checked himself suddenly.

"Yeah? What's Scarab got to do with this business? I don't suppose he put you on my trail."

"Certain he didn't. I didn't even know it was you. I been chasing cowthieves —"

"Would you like me to make a poem of that one too?" Jinglebob asked pleasantly.

"T'hell with you and your poems!"

"Uh-huh," placidly, "I reckon that's all they're good for. Hannan, just why does Scarab want the Ladder-A so bad?"

"What you asking me for? Pro'bly what any man would want it for, who wants to increase his holdings."

"That one don't go down either, Hannan . . . How'd you know I was at the T-Bench?"

"Why, I —" Hannan halted. "The T-Bench? Who said anything about the T-Bench? Were you there?"

"You know damn well I was. So were you."

"Me?" Hannan blustered. "You're crazy!"

"You were on T-Bench holdings, leastwise. I was sitting on the porch with Thompson. You were spying on my movements from that high ridge that overlooks the T-Bench buildings . . ."

"All right," Hannan said sullenly, "have it your way." He was curious to know how Jenkins had discovered the fact. "I admit it. I don't see how you saw me, though."

"I didn't," Jenkins said dryly.

"But, how the hell —?"

176

"I saw a buzzard soaring just over the top of the ridge. He started to swoop down once. That showed there was something up there. You must have moved, because it sudden flew away. I figured it was a human . . ."

"It might have been a jack-rabbit," Hannan pointed out.

"It might have been," Jenkins conceded with a chuckle, "only it wasn't. Jackass is a better word."

"Aw, go to hell," Hannan growled.

"How did you know I went to the T-Bench?" Jenkins persisted.

"I stopped for a drink at a Mex shack on the Greyville road. The Mex told me," Hannan snapped angrily. "That satisfy you?"

"Yeah, it does, particularly after you telling me you didn't know it was me in that brush shelter. I knew you'd slip, some place in our talk, Hannan, if I could only get you mad enough. That puts the deadwood on you for fair."

Hannan bit his lip. He hadn't meant to say so much.

Jenkins went on. "It proves that my dollar wasn't wasted, too."

Hannan didn't reply for a moment, then his curiosity gained the upper hand. "What dollar? What are you talking about?"

Jenkins chuckled, "I gave that Mex a dollar to tell you. You see, Hannan, after I finished Franklin, I figured some of you Bridle-Bit hombres would be trying to get me. I saw you and Raymer standing in front of that barber-shop in Padre Wells. I kind of

177

thought then, one of you might be sent by Scarab to trail me."

"Scarab ain't had a thing to do with this."

"I'll say one thing, Hannan, you're loyal to your boss. He'd probably make it tough for you, if you weren't."

"Scarab's a white hombre. He'll get me out of this. He'll furnish bail. Hell, Jenkins, you ain't got nothing on me. I haven't done a thing —"

"Except," Jenkins cut in, "shoot a couple of holes in my saddle-blanket. I know, it don't hurt the blanket much, but you figured I was under it. That makes it look like attempted murder."

"We'll see what Scarab has to say to that."

"Anyway," Jenkins went on, "I figured I'd be trailed. There was another attempt due on my life. If it happened in town, I'll sure have to kill somebody else. I don't like killing Hannan, so I planned to have that next attempt happen out here. So I told that Mex if anybody rode up asking about me, that he was to tell 'em I went to the T-Bench to talk about rustlers. You see, I hated the thought of a Bridle-Bit man riding clear to Greyville just to blow holes in my hide and then discover he was mistaken. But with these dumb Bridle-Bit waddies, you have to make everything clear and easy for 'em. They can't think for themselves —"

"Aw, cripes! You think you're damn smart, don't you?"

"Uh-huh — smarter than one Utah Hannan leastwise. I knew if I said I was going to the T-Bench to talk about cowthieves, whoever was following me would tag along to see where else I went and to try and bump

178

me off . . . Nice hombre, Thompson. I didn't once mention cowthieves to him. Just told him I rode over to get acquainted, though I did ask him if he'd ever found any of his cows hamstrung. He said no, he hadn't, so it looks like the Bridle-Bit is concentrating on Ladder-A stock . . . at present . . ."

"Aw, we never hamstrung no cows."

"Don't tell lies, Hannan. Little boys who tell lies don't escape the bad place . . ."

"Goddamit, Jenkins! You ain't funny."

"I can't say the same for you, Hannan. You're downright comical at times, like for instance this afternoon when you were trailing me. You didn't use your head. I could tell from the way my bronc acted, somebody was on my tail. The wind was coming from your direction, y'know. And then, when I stopped here to make camp, I happened to glance toward that rise of ground yonderly, and I saw a bunch of quail whirl up like they'd been startled off'n their feeding. It wasn't natural, so I guessed somebody must have been sneaking through the tall grass . . ."

"Aw, shut up, you give me a pain," Hannan growled.

"And after I had my supper I sort of prepared things for your visit," Jenkins chuckled. "You sure walked into it, Hannan. From now on, though, you won't be taking such long walks."

"What do you mean?" Hannan demanded.

"You're smart. Figure it out, waddie. If you can't guess the correct answer, let me know and I'll furnish it."

Hannan fell into a glowering silence. Jenkins tossed his cigarette stub into the fire and threw on some more brush and twigs. The flames leaped high, picking out crimson highlights on the leaves of the surrounding brush and on Hannan's harshly lined features, now marked with concern. Silvery light commenced to glow along the eastern horizon and the stars began to pale before the rising moon's advance.

"It'll be a nice night for our ride," Jenkins commented idly at last.

"What ride? Where we going?"

"Some place you're not going to like, Hannan. Where did you leave your horse?"

Hannan snapped, "None of your damn business. If you want my horse, go hunt for him."

"It's you that's going to want him. I don't care. You're going to get almighty tired walking, though, before you reach Padre Wells."

"You taking me to Padre Wells?"

"I hope you didn't think I aimed to deliver you to the Bridle-Bit, Hannan."

"What you figuring to do in Padre Wells?"

"I'm going to turn you over to Sheriff Clem Wagner."

Hannan laughed sarcastically. "A hell of a lot of good that will do you. Cripes! The minute Scarab learns I'm in the hoosegow, he'll arrange bail so fast it will make your head whirl."

Jinglebob yawned. "It's too damn bad I haven't my concertina here. We could pass a couple of mighty pleasant hours before you start walking to town."

180

Hannan said fervently. "That's one break I get anyway."

"You never heard me play," Jenkins said reproachfully.

"Cripes! I don't have to hear you to know it's lousy . . . Look, Jenkins, I left my bronc about half a mile south of here. Let's get him and get started."

"I'm in no hurry. I don't want to get to town until everybody's gone to bed."

"Huh!" scornfully, "Afeared some of the Bridle-Bit crew might be in town, eh? Figuring they'd make it tough for you?"

"Something like that, mebbe."

Hannan laughed contemptuously. Now that he knew he was headed for Padre Wells, he commenced to feel better. Once Scarab had heard of this, everything would be fixed up pronto. This Jenkins hombre was a damn fool if he thought Utah Hannan was going to spend more than a few hours behind bars. Leave it to Dave Scarab. Good old Dave. He could fix anything.

"Commencing to feel better, eh?" Jenkins commented.

"I ain't worrying."

"You feel like telling me everything you know about Scarab's activities?"

"I don't know anything and I never did know anything," Hannan sneered. "What's more I don't intend ever to know anything. That suit you, Jenkins?"

"It's about what I expected," Jinglebob said carelessly. "But don't hold that thought too long, Hannan. You're likely to change your tune plumb pronto one of these days, when you see Scarab roped and thrown like a cow critter for branding . . . But I'll try and be patient. I won't crowd you any."

"Damn right, you won't," Hannan blustered.

"Would you like to hear some poetry to pass the time?"

"You know what you can do with your poetry, don't you?"

"Keep your temper, Hannan."

"I'm sick of sitting around here. Come on, let's get started."

"If you knew what was ahead of you, you wouldn't be so anxious. But all in good time. When that time comes I'm going to hold my gun over you and watch you saddle my horse. Then, you'll walk down to your horse and I'll tie you into your saddle. Then we'll go see Sheriff Wagner. But it's a mite early to start yet. I wish I could think of some pleasant way to pass the next couple of hours. Say, Hannan, did I ever ask you if you knew a rhyme for Saskatoon?"

"No, and I don't want to be asked. Soon is a good word if it means when we start."

"It don't. Just hold your horses, Hannan, hold your horses. Once you get started and on your way, you're going to wish you hadn't been in such a hell of a hurry."

"Aw, I ain't worryin'."

"I don't suppose you are," Jinglebob said pleasantly, "not yet."

CHAPTER
FIFTEEN

Bucky Starts a Trip

It was about two in the morning, when Bucky Malotte, asleep in one of the rooms adjacent to the jail, was awakened by the sounds of gravel pattering against his window. Grumbling, he rubbed the sleep from his eyes, went to the window and opened it a little.

"Yeah? What do you want?" he growled.

"It's me, Bucky. Jinglebob."

Now Bucky could make out the lean form blending into the shadows between buildings. Bucky's voice took on a different tone: "Hello, there. What's up?"

"Come around to the front and open the door. I want to talk to you a minute."

"I'll be right out."

Bucky slammed the window shut, reached for his sombrero and then drew on overalls and boots. He buckled his gun and belt on and was rolling a cigarette by the time he left his room and walked along the corridor, past the closed door of the sheriff's office and on to the front door of the building.

Stepping to the porch that fronted the building, Bucky saw two horses at the hitch-rack. A man sat in one of the saddles; Bucky judged his hands were bound to the saddle horn. Jinglebob stood near the other horse.

Padre Wells was wrapped in silence, the wide main street bathed in blue-white moonlight and black shadow. There wasn't a light in a building anywhere.

Jinglebob left the hitch-rack and came up the steps to the porch. "I'm sorry to get you up, Bucky, but I knew you slept here and I —"

"Shucks, Jinglebob! Don't let that worry you —"

"I want to see the sheriff. I didn't know where he lived, so if you can rout him out for me, I'll be much obliged."

"Sure. But why all the secrecy? Who's the hombre you got tied to his horse, out there. It looks from here like Utah Hannan, but being in shadow like he is —"

"You're right. It's Hannan. He associated with Steve Franklin so long, he took on Franklin's shootin'-in-the-back habits. I expected something of the sort, so I camped out last night, over near Topango Mesa and was all ready when Hannan made his attempt."

"The dirty sidewinder! Did you wound him?"

Jinglebob chuckled. "It wasn't necessary to fire a shot."

Bucky swore. "You should have plugged him plumb center."

"I've got a better idea than that. Dead men tell no tales, you know. Before we get through with this business, we may want Hannan to do some talking. I'll explain when you get the sheriff. There's no use repeating the same story."

184

"You're right. I'll get started to once. Clem only lives a short jump and two bucks from here. I'll be back with him pronto."

"Good."

Bucky hurried down the steps, followed more slowly by Jenkins. As the deputy passed the hitch-rack, Hannan said, "What the hell, Malotte! Do you have to keep me sitting out here all night? Come on, put me in your hoosegow. I'm gettin' sleepy."

"From what I understand," Bucky chuckled harshly, "you ain't been very much awake all evenin'."

Hannan swore at the deputy, but Bucky only laughed and hurried on, his boot heels clumping hollowly on the plank walk along the silent, deserted street. At the first corner, Bucky crossed over and made his way down a side street.

Jenkins, meanwhile, had come out to the hitch-rack and stood leaning his slim form across the crossbar.

"Want me to roll you a cigarette, Hannan?"

"I'll roll my own, if you'll untie my hands."

"And your feet from the stirrups and the horse from the tie rack, eh?" Jenkins laughed. "Yep, you'd sure roll all right — if you had the chance, which same you haven't."

"Dammit, Jenkins, how long have I got to wait out here? Why couldn't Malotte have put me in a cell? So help me Gesis —!"

"Not so loud, Hannan. Do you want to wake the town?"

"I don't give a damn about the town."

"Well, I do. I'm telling you to keep your voice hushed."

"Why should I?"

"That's for me to know. You'll learn soon enough."

"I'll talk as loud as I damn well please."

"That'll be your tough luck, then."

Jinglebob drew his six-shooter and carelessly slapped the barrel against the palm of his left hand two or three times.

"Did you ever," Jinglebob asked pleasantly, "have one of these forty-five barrels bent over your head, Hannan? It's a sure-fire method of quieting a hombre who gets noisy. Now, just go ahead, make all the noise you like — try to make all the noise you like. It'll be an experience you won't forget in a hurry. I'm telling you to keep quiet. What's your views in the matter?"

"You wouldn't dare hit me with that gun!"

"You craving to put that idea to a test?"

Plainly Hannan wasn't. He started cursing again, but he kept his tones low. Jenkins laughed softly. Hannan eventually became silent. Jenkins rolled two cigarettes, lighted both of them and stuck one between Hannan's lips.

"Say 'thank you' to the man?" Jinglebob prompted with a grin.

Hannan grunted something unintelligible.

"I suppose that'll have to do," Jinglebob sighed. "Hannan, you're tamed down quite a bit."

"If I am," Hannan said bitterly, "it's because I got sense enough not to argyfy with my hands tied. But, when Scarab hears of this, he'll get me out. And when I get out, the first thing I'll do —"

"When you get out," Jenkins cut in, "the first thing you'll do is notice how the world has changed the last decade or so . . . maybe longer. You'll notice how nice it is not to be wearing stripes and you'll wonder how long it will take for your hair to grow out again. Where you'll be coming from, the haircuts will be free . . . and close. Or you might even be bald-headed by that time . . ."

"Why, blast your hide, Jenkins, I'll —"

Jinglebob commenced slapping his forty-five barrel against the palm of his left hand again. Hannan promptly fell silent, the smoke from the cigarette in his mouth curling up past his scowling features. Five minutes had passed since Bucky's departure. Another five drifted by, with no conversation between the two, though Hannan kept shifting uneasily in his saddle.

"Look," Jinglebob said suddenly, "you know that Saskatoon poem of mine?"

"I don't, thank Gawd," Hannan said fervently — still keeping his voice low.

"Well, you've heard of it, leastwise." Jinglebob had adopted an injured tone.

"Too damn much of it."

"I wish everybody didn't feel that way," Jinglebob said sadly. "But, look, I just thought of another verse. Want to hear it?"

"No."

Undaunted, Jinglebob commenced,

"Las Vegas Mabel's hard to beat,
    And so is Red Lodge Rose;
Topeka Lilly's mighty sweet;
    In Boise, Becky grows."

"Rotten," Hannan growled.

"Uh-huh, maybe it is," Jinglebob sighed. "That last line will need some fixing up and polishing. It sounds like Becky was a plant, or something."

"Why narrow your limits to the last line?" Hannan said insultingly. "They all sound lousy to me."

"Maybe you're right for once tonight," Jinglebob conceded. "I wish I could get a rhyme for Saskatoon, though, then I could finish the whole poem. But until I do, other verses keep popping into my head."

"I knew there was something wrong with your head. The sooner you get a rhyme for Saskatoon, the better, says I, if it will stop your runnin' off at the mouth."

"Now, that's what I'd call unreserved criticism," Jinglebob commented genially.

The sounds of booted feet carried along the sidewalk. Sheriff Wagner and Bucky Malotte took form in the moonlight. Within a few moments they had come up to the hitch-rack where Jenkins and Hannan waited. The sheriff's sombrero had been hurriedly placed on his tousled hair and his night-shirt was stuffed into trousers.

"Howdy, Jinglebob."

"Howdy, Clem."

"I hear you caught yourself a backbiter."

"He done his best, anyhow —"

188

"Dammit, Wagner," Hannan burst out, "how long am I to be kept waiting here?" He paused abruptly, as Jinglebob commenced slapping his gun barrel into his palm. Jinglebob didn't say anything. There was no need. Hannan fell silent.

"And stay that way," Jinglebob laughed softly, "while I *habla* a spell with the sheriff. Don't get impatient, Hannan, you'll be taken care of pretty quick now."

Jinglebob quickly drew the sheriff and his deputy away several paces, out of Hannan's hearing, while he told the two what had happened that night. Hannan sat his saddle, glowering at the three men, wondering what was to take place. He commenced to feel a trifle nervous. Evidently, his being placed in a cell wasn't to be just a routine matter.

When Jinglebob had finished his story, Wagner said, "The dirty skunk. I'll slam him in a cell to once."

Jinglebob shook his head. "Not here, Clem. That's what I wanted to see you about."

"What you got on your mind?"

"It's like this, Clem," Jenkins explained, "it's quite evident Scarab set Hannan on my trail with orders to wipe me out. If you put Hannan in jail, here, Scarab will get him bailed out, as soon as he hears about it, tomorrow."

"Right," Wagner nodded. "That's what I was just thinking."

"All right," Jenkins continued, "suppose we let Scarab worry a mite. If Hannan was suddenly to disappear and I was to be around as usual, Scarab would do some wondering. At first, he'd probably think

I killed Hannan, but when I didn't say anything, Scarab would start racking his brains to figure out just what had happened."

"C'rect," Wagner nodded tersely.

"Here's another slant. If we did manage to keep Hannan in jail, and Scarab knew he was in jail, Scarab would just hire another man to take his place. But so long as Scarab is expecting Hannan to show up, he won't do any extra hiring. I aim to keep the Bridle-Bit crew whittled down as long as possible, and in case we come to open warfare, every man counts."

"C'rect again," Wagner said. "I get it you want Hannan to just plain disappear for a spell."

"You get the idea, Clem."

The sheriff pondered a few minutes. Finally, "I've got a damn good deputy stationed over at Greyville. His name's Mike Sullivan. He's as big as a house, strong as a bull and will do what I say. I can trust him to follow out orders."

"I was hoping you'd think of something like this, Clem," Jinglebob nodded. "It's what I had in mind."

The sheriff turned to Bucky. "It's forty miles to Greyville, Bucky. You should be able to make it before noon, if you get saddled up at once. You can deliver the prisoner to Mike. I'll write a note to Mike explaining what we want and that Hannan isn't to send any word to anyone."

"He mustn't be allowed to talk to any outsider, either," Jenkins put in.

"I'll take care of that in my note," Wagner said. "I think you've got a good idea, Jinglebob. So long as

190

Hannan can't get word to Scarab, they can't get together on any stories that may have to be told later."

"And once we've cornered Scarab," Jinglebob said, "I think we'll find Mister Hannan mighty eager to do any talking we want to hear."

"Let me see," Wagner pondered, "what charge can we put against Hannan?"

"Disturbin' the peace," Bucky chuckled.

"Attempted murder," Jenkins said. "I'll make a formal charge any time it's necessary."

"I'll go saddle up," Bucky said. "I'll be back in a jiffy." He hurried off through the passageway between the building in which the jail was housed and its neighbor.

"I'll go in the office and write that note to Mike," Wagner said.

He and Jenkins came back to the waiting Hannan.

"Utah Hannan," Wagner said, "I arrest you for attempted murder —"

"Aw, cut out the legal business, Wagner," Hannan growled. "I know what you're going to say. Just put me in one of your cells so I can get to sleep. Then send a rider to Scarab and —"

"I'll go write that note," the sheriff cut in, and left the hitch-rack to go to his office.

"Hey," Hannan protested to Jenkins, "why don't he take me in to his damn jail?"

Jenkins laughed softly. "Attempted murder is a pretty serious thing, Hannan. We talked it over and got to thinking it would be pretty dangerous keeping you here."

191

"What do you mean . . . dangerous?" Hannan asked suspiciously.

"Why, think how it would be if a mob formed to lynch you and took you away from the law officers . . ."

"Aw, cripes! Nothing like that is going to happen."

"We can't take chances, Hannan. Bucky Malotte is going to deliver you to the jail in Greyville."

"What! Sa-a-ay, you can't do anything like that to me."

"We're doing it, Hannan. And don't raise any fuss. Just remember what I said about a gun barrel over the conk being a good remedy for a noisy hombre. And I wouldn't be a bit surprised if Bucky Malotte could hit harder than I can. He's got his orders, and it's up to you whether you want to walk into that Greyville jail or be carried in."

"Aw, look here, Jinglebob . . ." Hannan commenced to whine.

"The name's Jenkins, to you. And don't try to get tough with that deputy over in Greyville. I understand he's a right stiff customer when he's riled, and he'll have instructions from Wagner on just how to handle you. When the right time comes, I'll ride over and pay you a visit, one of these days. Until then, you'll get farther by sitting tight and not squawking."

"This ain't legal, Jenkins. I got a right to see Scarab. I want a lawyer. You can't do this. It ain't legal," the words flowed nervously from Hannan's lips.

"Of course, it isn't legal," Jenkins laughed softly. "We've taken that into consideration. But since when have the dealings of any of Scarab's crew been legal?

We're just meeting you on your own ground now . . .
and giving you a damn sight squarer shake than you'd
give us."

A horse pushed out from between buildings carrying
Bucky Malotte. He turned the animal and came up to
halt beside Hannan.

"I understand we're taking a little ride, sidewinder,"
Bucky said.

Hannan swore at the deputy.

Jenkins said, "You don't have to take that, Bucky. I've
explained to Hannan what a gun barrel can do to a
skull. You use your own judgment."

Bucky laughed. "I reckon Hannan will be a heap
tamed down by the time we reach Greyville. He'd
better be. Mike Sullivan won't take any lip of that sort.
Mike hits fast and sudden . . . and then when he gets
around to it, calls the doctor . . . sometimes the
undertaker. Mike's tough, he is. And he hates a crook's
guts."

Hannan slumped dejectedly in his saddle, saying
nothing more.

Within a few minutes, the sheriff appeared and after
locking the door behind him, came out to the
hitch-rack. He handed a long envelope to Bucky,
saying, "The papers are here, properly made out,
Bucky. I put in a note for Mike too, so he'll know how
to handle Hannan."

"Look here, Wagner," Hannan made a last attempt,
"I demand to see Dave Scarab."

"Demand and be damned!" Wagner growled.

"Anytime," Jenkins said, "that you're ready to tell us what you know of Scarab's activities, Hannan, we'll arrange for you to see Scarab . . . in the same cell."

"I've told you a dozen times, tonight, I don't know nothing," Hannan protested. "I just work for Scarab. He didn't have nothing much to do with me —"

Bucky Malotte's scornful laugh cut in on the speech. Hannan again fell silent.

"Here, Bucky," Jenkins said, "you'd better take Hannan's gun that I took off him tonight. You can clout a heap better with a gun in each hand."

"That," Bucky grinned, "is one elegant idea. I hope to have the chance."

"Get going, Bucky," the sheriff said.

Jinglebob untied Hannan's horse. A minute later, Bucky Malotte was herding his charge along the main street, on the way to Greyville.

The moon was swinging farther to the west by this time. Except for the soft thudding of hoofbeats, moving out of Padre Wells, the town was as silent as it had been when Jenkins entered with Hannan riding ahead.

"Well," Jenkins said at last, "that's that."

The sheriff leaned against the hitch-rack and nodded. "Hannan's pretty well tamed. I don't expect Bucky will have any trouble with him. Bucky's pretty cautious and he won't stand for any tricks."

"It's not bothering you, any, is it, Clem?" Jenkins asked.

"What you talking about?"

"This illegal way of keeping Hannan prisoner."

194

The sheriff swore softly under his breath. "It's no hide off'n my teeth," he said quietly.

"Because if it is," Jinglebob said, "I'm taking all the responsibility. You can take my word for it that I'll square any trouble that might come of this."

Wagner looked sharply at Jenkins. "You mean that?"

"Nothing else."

"Feel like saying any more now?"

"Not right away, Clem."

"That's all right with me."

Jinglebob said, "What happened after I left town today — shucks, yesterday, I mean — after I killed Franklin?"

"You mean, what did Scarab do?"

Jinglebob nodded.

"Him and Raymer hung around town for quite a spell. They were in the Acme. Raymer mentioned two or three times that he'd sent Hannan and Hank Wooley — Hank's the other Bridle-Bit puncher who was in the Acme when you downed Franklin — back to the ranch."

"Probably establishing alibis of some sort in case my dead body was found."

"That's the way I look at it — oh, say, I nearly forgot to tell you. A hombre named Jerrold — D. C. Jerrold — arrived on the evening stage and asked where he could find Scarab. He registered at the hotel first. The clerk sent him down to the Acme. I was in the Acme at the time. I was wondering who the hombre was, so I went down and looked at the hotel register."

"Do you know what he wanted to see Scarab about?"

"I haven't the least idea. They stood talking on the street a spell, then Scarab hired a buggy at the livery and Raymer drove this Jerrold hombre out of town . . . I reckon they went to the Bridle-Bit, because they stopped at the hotel to pick up Jerrold's suitcase. Jerrold looks sort of citified, like a banker, or somethin'."

"Didn't Scarab go with 'em?"

Wagner shook his head. "Scarab got on his horse and took the west road out of Padre Wells."

Jinglebob frowned. "The west road, eh? I wonder if he was heading for the Ladder-A?"

"You got me. He didn't come back to Padre Wells. I was on the lookout for him. If he did go to the Ladder-A, he pro'bly cut straight across the range for his own outfit when he left there."

Jinglebob didn't say anything for a few minutes, then, "Maybe this Jerrold hombre will bear investigating."

"Maybe so. It's beyond me. You figuring to head for the Ladder-A now? Oh, by the way, Bucky rode out there yesterday afternoon, and told 'em about you shooting it out with Franklin, as you asked him to."

"Good. I forgot to say anything to Bucky about that . . . No, I don't figure to go out there this time in the morning. I'd only wake up the bunkhouse. I'll drift down to the livery stable and crawl up in the hayloft."

"I've got a better idea than that, Jinglebob. You come along to my place and make use of our spare bed. You deserve a good sleep after tonight's work. Then you can

196

meet my missus in the morning and see what a good breakfast she dishes up. You'll be right welcome."

"That's mighty nice of you, Clem. I'll be glad to do it."

"Let's get going then. This night air ain't none too good for my rheumatics, sometimes."

"You can't start too soon for me, Clem. I'm commencing to feel plumb weary."

"Get your hawss and come ahead."

Side by side, Jinglebob and the sheriff walked along the silent street, Jinglebob leading the roan gelding behind him.

CHAPTER
SIXTEEN

Jinglebob Reaches a Decision

It was close to nine-thirty the following morning when Jinglebob reined his pony into the Ladder-A ranch yard. He was watching for a sight of Lorry Alastair, but the girl's raven-dark locks weren't in evidence. He didn't see anyone else, either, at first, but when he turned his pony toward the corral, he heard a loud whoop of welcome and old Tarp Jones and Matt Alvord came running from the bench where they had been seated in front of the bunkhouse. The two old cowmen reached the corral just as Jinglebob dismounted and commenced unsaddling.

"Jinglebob!" old Tarp Jones yelled his delight. "You long-legged, red-headed cow-nurse. It's good to see ye agin!"

"You downed Franklin, didn't you?" Matt Alvord panted.

"By the great palpitatin' prophets!" Old Tarp exulted. "I'll say he did. Them Bridle-Bits will l'arn not to buck us Ladder-A buckaroos. We're pizen to crooks and thieves."

They were both pumping Jinglebob's hand enthusiastically. He was laughing at the pair, as they fired questions at him faster than he could answer them. A second yell of welcome sounded as Chris Kringle came galloping across the yard to extend one gnarled, flour-covered paw: "Jinglebob! You shootin' galawampus! It's a sight fer sore eyes to have you back. Say, tell us about —"

"Hey, wait a minute," Jinglebob grinned. "Why all the reception? You'd think I'd been gone a couple of years, instead of only since yesterday morning. What's the idea?"

"Ye killed Steve Franklin, didn't ye?" Tarp Jones exclaimed. "Ye finished that back-shootin', murderin' sidewinder what killed Mitchell and like to done the same to Breck Alastair —"

"And was plumb foxy about runnin' him down," Chris Kringle put in. "Oh, we know all about it, Jinglebob. Bucky Malotte rode out to tell us — said you asked him to — yestiddy afternoon . . ."

"Yore brain was shore workin' fast, son," Matt Alvord was saying. "It took brainwork to down Franklin like you did —"

"And say, Jinglebob," Tarp Jones interrupted, "right after Bucky left, Dave Scarab came out here. He must have met Bucky on the road."

"So Scarab was here, eh?" Jinglebob frowned. "No, I don't reckon Bucky saw him. I saw Bucky early this mornin', and he didn't mention it."

"Bucky didn't follow the trail straight home," the cook cut in. "I ast him to stay to chow, but he said he was going to head over south on his way back, to look over that old Indian burial grounds for arrer heads.

199

Bucky's got a nephew, or somethin', in Denver, that collects such things."

"What did Scarab want?" Jinglebob asked.

Tarp Jones shrugged his bony shoulders. "I dunno. He went to the house and talked to Lorry and Breck. Didn't stay long. Lorry didn't tell me what was said. That gal never tells me nothin' no more. We tried to rib Scarab about Franklin gettin' killed, but he wouldn't rise to the bait. Tell us about it."

"Here," Matt Alvord proposed, "you talk, Jinglebob. I'll unsaddle yore hawss."

Laughing, evading questions he didn't feel ready to answer, Jinglebob finally managed to get the saddle from his pony's back. He turned the beast into the corral after Matt had promised to water it for him.

"And look here, Jinglebob," old Tarp said reproachfully, "ye didn't mention one word to me of your suspicions regardin' Franklin. Ye're gettin' as bad as Lorry. By all th' long-sufferin' ol' maids, we was sure surprised when Bucky brought us the news. But ye might have let us know what was goin' to happen."

"I sure would have, Tarp," Jinglebob said soberly, "only I wasn't sure how things were going to work out. After I got to Padre Wells, other things came up, and —"

A sudden hail from the house cut in on the conversation: "Jinglebob! Will you please come here, when you've finished talking to those youngsters. Tarp! It's high time you and Matt got busy at something. Chris! Don't forget there's dinner to get."

200

The four men near the corral paused and glanced toward the ranch house where Lorry Alastair stood framed in the rear doorway. Even at this distance, Jinglebob could see the bright spot of angry color on the girl's cheeks. He wondered what was wrong.

"I'll be right with you, Lorry," he called.

"Hey, Lorry," Matt Alvord said peevishly. "I'm going to water Jinglebob's horse, first, and then —"

"Water it then," the girl snapped back, "and then see if you can't find something to do. If you can't, I'll find it for you. And that goes for Tarp as well."

The girl retired inside the house, slamming the door behind her.

"Huh!" old Tarp grunted. "Youngsters, she called us. Plumb sarcastical, ain't she? By the seven palpitatin' prophets! I be damned if I know whut's got inter thet gal. She's been plumb peevilish, all mornin'. An' last night she was snappy as all get out. Whut's she got ter be mad about?"

"Whatever it is," Jinglebob smiled, "you cowhands had better get busy. I'm keeping you away from your work, maybe. I'll drift up to the house. Tarp, take my rig and stuff to the bunkhouse, will you?"

"Sartain, boy."

Jenkins left the three men and trudged up toward the ranch house. At the back door he paused a moment to knock, then turned the knob and entered, closing the door behind him.

Lorry sat near a window, at a table in the kitchen, the morning sun streaming through to shine brightly on her blue-black hair. She wore a neat green-and-white checkered gingham dress, with something white and ruffly low at her throat. The girl looked at Jinglebob, then quickly glanced away as he entered.

Jinglebob said, "Hello, Lorry."

Lorry nodded and her dark eyes came back to survey him. Her lips quivered a little as she said, "Back at last, are you?" Her voice was low and husky.

"Yes, I'm back." Jinglebob crossed to the table and stood looking down on the girl. Across the room, the door leading to the front of the house was closed. "Sure, I'm back," Jinglebob went on. "Say, what's wrong? What have I done?"

"You? Why, nothing," the girl said loftily. "Nothing at all. What makes you think —"

Jinglebob removed his Stetson and hung it on the back of a kitchen chair. "All right," he said quietly, "out with it. Something's wrong. There was no need for you to snap at Tarp and Chris and Matt, just because I've done something —"

"They needed snapping at," the girl retorted crisply. "They've just about refused to stir, until they knew what you were doing and where you were. Old Tarp and Matt have spent all morning cleaning their guns, saying you might be needing them. And here I'm trying to keep Breck peaceful and quiet and not let him know what was going on . . ."

"Why, that's foolish, Lorry. I mean, what you said about Tarp and Matt. I don't see why they —"

"Jinglebob Jenkins!" Lorry's velvety-dark eyes went hard and flashed angrily. She rose suddenly from her

202

chair, confronting Jinglebob almost menacingly. "I won't have it!" she exclaimed.

"You won't have what?" the man puzzled.

"You know very well, or you should. Do you think you have any right to worry your friends this way?"

"What way?"

"What way! Going off the way you did, yesterday morning, and then sending Bucky Malotte out to tell us what had happened in town, and that you wouldn't be back, and — and —" Lorry's voice broke.

"But I asked Bucky to come out here, so you'd know about Franklin and —"

"Yes," Lorry snapped, "and do you know what that old fool, Tarp Jones, has been saying?"

"I couldn't even make a guess," Jinglebob said, somewhat grimly. "I don't know yet what all this fuss is about, but s'help me, I'm going to know —"

"Tarp Jones said," Lorry interrupted, "when you didn't come back here, last night, that you'd probably gone to the Bridle-Bit to shoot it out with Dave Scarab, and — and —"

Jinglebob smiled suddenly. "And you believed him?"

The girl evaded the question. "Then, Chris and Matt got to saying the same thing, and I started to think maybe —"

"But that was foolish."

"Foolish? Foolish!" Lorry's face went crimson with anger. Hot words spilled in a torrent from her lips. "Foolish! And *you* can say that to me? You fool, Jinglebob Jenkins!" she said furiously. "Oh, you fool!

Haven't you any sense at all? I've never in all my life seen such a man. Taking chances like that —"

"What are you talking about?"

"You know very well I'm talking about that fight with Steve Franklin. Don't you think such things worry me — us? You could have had him arrested . . ."

"There wasn't quite time enough for that," Jinglebob said dryly.

"You know what I mean. There was no necessity for you to risk your life for us, putting us under further obligation . . ."

"Lorry Alastair! Don't forget I had a score of my own to square with Steve Franklin . . ."

"I don't care whose score it was. You had no right —"

"Lorry!"

The girl didn't answer.

"Lorry," Jinglebob said again, "were you worried about me?"

"Certainly we were."

"Were *you* worried about me?"

"No, I wasn't," the girl flashed, but her eyes dropped before Jinglebob's steady gaze. "Why should I be?"

Jinglebob laughed softly. "Lorry, you can't look at me when you say that."

The girl raised angry, disturbed eyes to meet the man's. Suddenly, Jinglebob's arms went about her and he kissed her full on the lips. Crimson banners waved in Lorry's cheeks. Her right arm lifted and her open palm smacked loudly against Jinglebob's jaw. Jinglebob kissed her again. Again, Lorry slapped his face.

"Three times and out," Jinglebob said, drawing her close again. His voice shook a trifle. "Oh, Lorry Alastair, are you going to put me out of your heart?"

"I — I guess not," came the shaky reply.

And then, there was quite a long silence.

After a time, Jinglebob smiled, "And you were worried about me?"

Lorry moved back, tucking stray strands of black hair once more in place. "A little, just a little," she conceded lightly. "But, oh, you make me so *damn* mad, at times, Jinglebob Jenkins, I could cheerfully wring your neck. Yow don't give a gal any peace of mind. Honest, my heart nearly stopped beating when I heard about Steve Franklin. And then, old Tarp commenced talking about how he'd bet you'd gone to the Bridle-Bit to clean out the Scarab crew, well . . ."

"But why did you call me a fool, Lorry?"

The girl laughed, mischievous lights in her dark eyes. "Maybe I was mad and maybe it was because you risked your life. You know, there are any number of gun fighters, Jinglebob, so why should a poet risk life for —"

Jinglebob gathered the girl in his arms. "Lorry, darlin' Lorry, I'm no poet . . ."

"You admit that?" Lorry's voice sounded half smothered.

"Willingly! I'm not even a good rhymester. I just write jingles, and not very good ones at that."

"When did you decide you weren't a poet, Jinglebob?"

"When I tried and tried and tried to write a poem about you and I found I didn't have the words. And you do deserve a real poet to say the precious things about your hair and your eyes and the sweet husky voice of you —"

"Lorry!" came Breck Alastair's voice faintly from the front of the house. "Has Jinglebob come in yet?"

Lorry said, half under her breath, "Oh, damn." She raised shining eyes to Jinglebob and took his hand. "I promised to let him know the instant you came in. Come and see him, Jinglebob. He wants to hear all about it. Come."

She opened the door into the front of the house and Jinglebob followed her into the main room where Breck Alastair was seated in an easy chair, wrapped in blankets. There was more color in the invalid's face today. He put out his hand as Jinglebob crossed the big room.

For a moment, Alastair didn't speak as he gripped the other's hand. Then, a faint rueful smile stole across his face. "Well, young fellow, you took a job off my shoulders. I don't know whether to thank you, or get mad for cheating me out of squaring my account with Franklin."

"Forget the thanks," Jinglebob smiled. "As for taking the job from your shoulders — well, that was one job that couldn't be put off any longer."

"I've been waiting to hear about it . . . And, Lorry, look around and see if you can find that bottle of bourbon, again. I think I'm strong enough to stand a little snifter, and Jinglebob deserves a drink for a job well done."

"I'll get the bottle, then you two can talk while I'm starting our dinner. I don't want to hear any more of that fight. Jinglebob, you stay up here for dinner, and talk to Breck. I'll slip down and tell Chris you're eating with us."

Smiling at her two men, Lorry left the room.

Dinner had been finished and the two men were still talking, Jinglebob having told Breck and Lorry of his encounter with Utah Hannan. Lorry had shaken her head accusingly at Jinglebob when he related briefly how Hannan had crept up to the brush shelter and attempted a killing, only to be captured a few minutes later.

"If you aren't a man to take chances," Lorry sighed exasperatedly, "I never saw one. I'm glad I didn't know this last night."

"It was pretty dang clever," Breck chuckled. "You handled that coyote right, Jinglebob. Sending him off to Greyville, thataway, was smart. Now we'll let Scarab do some thinking."

Jenkins changed the subject: "Just what brought Scarab out here, yesterday, anyway?"

"I've been looking for a chance to tell you," Lorry smiled, "but you and Breck have been talking like a couple of old hens and I haven't had an opportunity to get a word in edgewise."

"His visit wasn't any different than usual," Breck Alastair growled, sobering suddenly. "He's still trying to buy the Ladder-A and I'm still saying no to his proposition."

"He's raised his price, though," Lorry said. "This last is the highest he's ever offered. Not nearly so much as the Ladder-A is worth, of course, but I think we'd have taken him up on it, if he'd offered so much before you came, Jinglebob."

"Yep, you've brought us a new lease on life, boy," Alastair said slowly. "I'd give a lot though to learn just why Scarab is so blame anxious to get hold of my spread."

"You and me both," Jenkins nodded. "You said he seemed in a rush to close a deal. I'm just wondering if D. C. Jerrold has anything to do with it."

"Who's D. C. Jerrold?" Lorry frowned. Alastair was also looking questioningly at Jenkins.

"Never heard of him, eh?" Jinglebob said. "I was wondering if you had. Why, this Jerrold arrived on the stage yesterday. Sort of a citified individual, according to Clem Wagner. Scarab hired a buggy to send him to the Bridle-Bit, then came out here to make you a new offer. I'm wondering if there's any connection."

"Might be, at that," Alastair frowned worriedly. "A citified cuss, this Jerrold, eh? I wonder if Scarab is bringing in some law sharp to make trouble. The Ladder-A could never stand any court litigation, now. It'd break us." The haggard lines commenced to creep back into the invalid's cheeks as he spoke.

"Now, Breck," Lorry said, "don't you start worrying again. You don't want to retard your recovery. You've had too much talk of Scarab and gun fights. That's not good for you. Maybe Jinglebob will sing us a couple of songs, just to change the subject."

208

"I'll be glad to oblige," Jinglebob laughed. "I can stand it if you can. I'll go get my concertina from the bunkhouse."

"It isn't every outfit that can boast a troubador of their own," Alastair brightened, as Jinglebob left the room. "We're lucky."

Within a few minutes, Jenkins returned bearing his concertina. He took a seat not far from Lorry and her father and drew out a few wheezy chords. "Danged if this thing doesn't sound more all the time like it had caught asthma," he grinned. "Maybe it's caught the heaves from one of the horses. It sounds sort of wind-broken . . . . Let's see, what'll I sing . . . ?"

"Any of those you gave us the other night," Alastair said. "They were all good."

"I can't give you the same program twice," Jinglebob chuckled. "I'll have you know I have a very extensive repertory." He pondered a minute, then, "I don't think I gave you 'The Ballad Of Kansas Kate, or Marry In Haste and Repent at Leisure, If You Have Time'?"

"Good grief, no," Lorry laughed. "You've never stayed long enough to even say a title that long."

" 'Kansas Kate' wins," Alastair chuckled. "Hop to it, son."

Jinglebob drew the accompanying notes from his instrument and commenced to sing:

"Come gather around, all you cowboys,
    I'll sing you a song hard to beat.
Your heart strings will rend at the terrible end
    That happened to poor Pecos Pete.

"Pete rode into old-time Dodge City,
    A-trailin' a herd he had brought;
He met his last fate when he saw Kansas Kate,
    And wed her right off, without thought.

"Now Kate was a hardboiled young hussy;
    More a man than a woman was she:
Forked her bronc on the run, while she toted a gun,
    According to all history-y-y."

"By cripes," Breck Alastair chuckled, "I knew a woman down in Tombstone, once, just like that. We called her Bull-Neck Belle. Couple of the boys gave her a razor and a corncob pipe one Christmas, and she shot 'em both. She could rassle down a steer like any man —"

"Hush, Breck," Lorry smiled. "I want to hear what happened to Pete's and Kate's wedded bliss."

Jinglebob manipulated sounds from the concertina and continued:

"But love wrought a change for the better;
    Pete gained more a wife than a pal;
Till a serpent-like lad made their Eden plumb sad —
    A galoot named Chuck-Wagon Cal.

"Cal laughed as he told all and sundry,
    'Poor Pete has shore married in haste:
'No home will Kate make, for she can't even bake;
    'Calf-branding is more to her taste.'

210

"Then Kate rose up sorely indignant.
    'Cal's a dod-blasted liar,' quoth she.
'I'll bake Pete a pie and prove to Cal, I
    A wife was intended to be.'

"The pie from the oven came steaming,
    And Cal was invited right in,
To eat of his fill and test Kate's expert skill
    At all that was pure feminine."

Jinglebob paused. "Now tragedy creeps into the
scene," he said solemnly. His listeners exchanged
delighted glances. Jinglebob sawed at the concertina
and the tempo quickened as he sang on:

"Cal snapped at his pie like a coyote,
    Then, sneering, arose from his seat,
'I'll admit that it's hot, but pie it is not —
    This mess is not fitten to eat.'

"Pete's face became black at such insults,
    As he gobbled the rest of the pie;
Then his gun flashed in view and he said to Cal,
    'You
    Eat them words mighty quick or you die!"

"Though Cal was sure fast on the trigger,
    All bullets flew wide of their aim,
Till Pete clutched his heart with an agonized start,
    And dropped to the floor all the same!

"Now, Cal was not guilty of murder;
  Indigestion had reaped its grim toll.
Pete breathed out his last on a sad, choking gasp—
  'Twas Kate's pie that had taken his soul-l-l-l."

As the concluding words drifted from Jinglebob's throat, he changed the time and drew from the concertina the doleful strains of a funeral march. Breck Alastair roared with laughter, the lines of fatigue and worry gone from his face. Between smiles, Lorry glanced at her father and cast grateful looks in Jinglebob's direction.

Jinglebob swung from one song to another, and before the three realized it, the afternoon had vanished, and for the time being all thoughts of Dave Scarab had been driven from Breck Alastair's thoughts. Jinglebob refused with thanks Lorry's invitation to supper, and when Chris Kringle's beating on a dishpan sounded, announcing the evening meal, the red-headed troubador quickly gathered up his concertina and headed toward the bunkhouse.

All the time he had been engaged in entertaining Breck Alastair that afternoon, Jinglebob's mind had been occupied with other, more serious thoughts. Finally, he had reached a decision: he would saddle up and ride for the Bridle-Bit. Once there, there was a chance he might learn just what brought D. C. Jerrold to the Scarab outfit, and learn what, if any, was the connection between Jerrold's arrival and Scarab's most recent visit to the Ladder-A.

As outlined in Jinglebob's mind, the plan was a dangerous one, but once he'd reached his decision, he was determined to carry it out.

CHAPTER
SEVENTEEN

"You're Covered!"

The western sky, back of the Truculento Mountains, was still showing faint streaks of crimson, after supper, when Jinglebob drew old Tarp to one side, in front of the bunkhouse, though overhead night was already settling down.

"What's on yer mind, Jinglebob?" Tarp asked curiously.

"Two or three things. Right now I'm heading for the corral to get my horse. I want to take him over to the blacksmith shop. I've got a hunch he might have a loose shoe."

"Want me to peg it on for ye? No? Well, I'll go along with ye and show ye where the nails is. The Ladder-A has got an A-1 shop and I'll bet a pretty ye can't name a tool we ain't got."

"No, I won't need any help fixing a shoe, Tarp. In fact, I'm not sure it does need fixing. You're heading up to the house to see Breck, aren't you?"

Tarp looked narrowly at Jinglebob, then said shrewdly, "Now that you speak of it, I reckon I am. I drops up every day, to ask Breck how he's feeling, anyway."

214

"Good. When you go up there, just drop it sort of casual, that I'm busy in the blacksmith-shop."

Tarp frowned and studied the evening sky for a moment. Then he said slyly, "Just to sort of explain yer absence, ye might say. Is that it?"

"You get the idea, Tarp. I've got something in mind, and if I have to stop to make explanations, I'm afraid Lorry won't agree with me. I don't want to waste time in arguing."

"I know, I know," Tarp was shaking his head. "That gal's a caution for finding out things. What ye aimin'?"

"Don't stay too long, Tarp. I'll be waiting with my horse at the blacksmith-shop, and I'll be much obliged if you'll bring me my rig and bridle."

"Where ye headin' for?" Tarp asked curiously.

"Run along now. I'll tell you when you come to the blacksmith-shop."

Tarp nodded and trudged up toward the house. Jinglebob entered the bunkhouse and strapped on his belt and gun. He could hear Chris Kringle and Matt wrangling over something in the kitchen. It was dark in the bunkhouse, but Jinglebob had no trouble locating what he wanted. He drew his bed-roll from under his bunk, unrolled it and felt among the folds where he kept various personal effects. When he had once more spooled the bed-roll and restored it to its place under the bunk, he straightened to his full height. Now, he held in his hand a second cartridge belt and holstered six-shooter, a twin to the weapon already buckled at his waist.

This second gun he donned on his way to the corral. Opening the corral gate, he whistled for his pony. With a low whinny of recognition, the roan came trotting up. It followed at his heels like a dog, when he closed the gate and headed back toward the blacksmith-shop.

As he passed the bunkhouse again he glanced up toward the ranch house to see Lorry standing in the window, her slim form silhouetted against the yellow lamplight in the kitchen. The girl was looking out toward the ranch yard. Jinglebob struck a match and held it near his face. In an instant, he caught the girl's answering wave. The match went out and he strode on, out of sight of the ranch house and around a corner of the barn.

"I sure don't like sneakin' away, like this," Jinglebob muttered, "but if Lorry knew what I planned, I'm afraid she'd put up some objections."

He strode on, the pony walking at his back, and a moment later, drew to a stop before the Ladder-A blacksmith-shop. Five minutes drifted past, then ten, before Jinglebob's ear caught old Tarp's step. Jinglebob was standing near his pony, smoking a cigarette when Tarp arrived, carrying the cowboy's saddle and other equipment.

"Thanks, Tarp." Jinglebob commenced to saddle the pony.

"Lorry was washing dishes when I went in," Tarp's voice came low through the darkness. "She asked what we were doing. I got a hunch she was more interested in you, though. Pro'bly wants you to give 'em some more entertainment. I told her you was intendin' to fix

216

yer bronc's off-shoe, or somethin' like thet. I was plumb short with her. Then I went in and made *habla* with Breck a few minutes. Say, he's lookin' better every day."

"I'm aiming to see the improvement continues, Tarp. That's why I'm sloping off in this fashion. Breck couldn't stand a setback now. I'm going to see if I can't learn just what's going on. If we can get this business settled, you'll see Breck get well fast."

"Where ye headin' fer?"

"The Bridle-Bit is located northeast of here, isn't it?"

"Great palpitatin' prophets! Ye goin' to the Bridle-Bit?"

"Over that way. Northeast, isn't it?"

"C'rect . . . 'bout twelve or fourteen mile. Ye can't miss it. Just line out, due northeast, and ye'll hit the trail that runs from Padre Wells to the Scarab outfit. Turn left on the trail and about a mile or so farther, ye'll strike a plank bridge that's built over the north fork of Sleepy Horse Creek. Half a mile beyont the bridge is the Scarab outfit. What ye aimin' to do?"

"Look around a mite." Jinglebob tightened his cinch another notch. "Just sort of spy out the land and see if I can learn anything new."

Tarp put out one gnarled hand in the darkness and slapped Jinglebob's left gun. "Spyin' out the land, eh? Thought I heard a sort of a gun-and-leather squeak. What's that yer spyin' with, some new-fangled type of telyscope?"

Jinglebob laughed. "That's just extra precaution, Tarp. I'm not figuring to use it, nor the other gun, either. But I want to be prepared for the unexpected. Nope, I won't take any chances." He moved up near his pony's head. "I'm just going to see how near I can get to any windows that might be open and learn if Scarab's conversation is worthwhile. I'm not a fool enough to tackle that whole outfit."

"Come to think of it," Tarp said slowly, "the Bridle-Bit's sort of hard to find. I reckon me and Matt had better go along with you."

"Nothing doing."

Tarp nodded innocently. "I figured ye wouldn't want Matt, but I'll go saddle up and grab my hawglaig . . ."

"You'll do nothing of the sort, Tarp. This is my job. Your job is to stay here — and keep your mouth shut regarding my whereabouts. Don't you go running to the house, now, the instant I've left."

"What do ye think I am?" Tarp demanded indignantly. "But I reckon I'd better go along with ye and —"

"That's out, Tarp. I'm going alone. I've got my mind made up. Now, you drift back to the bunkhouse and act like everything is just as usual."

There were further objections on Tarp's part to be silenced, but Jenkins finally convinced the oldster — or thought he had — that Tarp's place was at the ranch. A minute later he had gripped Tarp's hand and swung up to the saddle.

"*Adiós*, Tarp."

"S'long, ye bull-headed, mule-minded, ornery —"

Jinglebob laughed as he dug in his spurs and sent the pony off at a brisk lope. He glanced back once and

218

could just faintly make out, through the gloom, old Tarp's skinny form shuffling back through the darkness. Then he straightened in the saddle again and urged the pony on its way.

It was about two hours later that Jinglebob reached the plank bridge over Sleepy Horse Creek. He reined the pony across, slowing its clattering hoofbeats to a walk. From this point on, old Tarp had said, the Bridle-Bit was only a half-mile farther.

Now, Jenkins swung his pony from the well-beaten trail and pushed the animal quietly through the lush grass that grew on either side. A low hill lay ahead. Here and there was a scattering of mesquite bush. Reaching the crest of the hill, Jenkins saw points of yellow light gleaming through the night. He was less than a quarter-mile from the Scarab domain now.

Gradually, as he drew nearer, the blocky forms of buildings commenced to take shape against the lighter, nocturnal surroundings. A cottonwood tree rustled in the soft breeze, and close to the buildings the sounds of a windmill could be heard. Three cottonwood trees, close together, grew not far from where Jenkins was passing. He swung the pony beneath the limbs of the largest tree, dismounted and tethered it to a low branch.

"Horse," Jinglebob muttered, "if you get to kicking up a fuss of any sort, you'll tip off those skunks that there's strangers around. Just take it easy and quiet and I'll be back in a short spell."

Now the Bridle-Bit buildings were only the distance of a city block away. Jenkins moved silently on foot through the grass. Before long the sounds of voices fell on his ears. He drew nearer and made out the outlines of a ranch house, bunkhouse, corrals, barns and other, smaller, miscellaneous buildings. The buildings were of 'dobe construction with flat roofs. Light shone from two of them, the ranch house and bunkhouse. It was from the bunkhouse, the voices came.

Approaching cautiously from the rear, Jinglebob moved up close to an open mindow at the back of the bunkhouse, and crouched close to the wall. The voices were louder now, though Jinglebob didn't recognize any of them. There was a great deal of loud laughter and much profanity. The voices dropped for an instant. When they commenced again, two of the men were quarreling:

"I tell you it's my deal!"

"T'hell it is. You just dealt. I never do have any luck when you deal."

"Cripes A'mighty, cut the scrapping and get those cards on the table."

The voices of the bickerers were lost in further loud laughter. Jenkins straightened cautiously and peered in at one corner of the window. Five men in range togs sat about a table playing seven-up. They were a hard-looking crew, unshaven and none too clean. A partially emptied quart bottle of whisky stood on the table and every once in a while one of the card players would raise the bottle to his lips. None of the men had taken off their guns while they engaged in the game. Evidently, this Bridle-Bit crew believed in being always prepared for trouble.

220

Jinglebob gazed at the five men. Two of them he recognized as having been in Padre Wells the day of his fight with Gus Raymer. The others he had never seen before. Of Raymer, Scarab, and the man named Jerrold, there was no sign.

Jinglebob drew away from the window, then commenced a retreat from the rear wall of the bunkhouse. A few yards away from the building, he paused to consider the situation.

"There's a light in the ranch house," he said to himself. "Scarab must be up there."

He glanced toward the ranch house, which stood some fifty or sixty yards away. A lighted, open window was toward him, but Jinglebob wondered if it could be approached without the attention of someone in the bunkhouse becoming aware of the fact. He gazed across the intervening yards, separating the two buildings. Most of the way was well illuminated by the lights streaming from each structure.

"It's a long chance to take," Jinglebob mused. "If those hombres playing cards will only stick to their game, I can risk it, but if one of 'em ever happened to leave the game and come to the door, he'd spot me sure as hell. Well, I'm here. There's no use going back until I've had a look at Scarab."

Jinglebob circled widely to approach the ranch house. The boisterous voices of the card-players went on as before. Then, Jinglebob commenced to draw close to the house. Now it was inevitable that he must cross a broad patch of earth illuminated by a long yellow oblong of light pouring from the bunkhouse doorway.

Jinglebob stepped swiftly across the lighted rectangle and, momentarily, once more found himself in shadow. He moved on toward the house. A moment more and he was crouched down, hugging the wall, beneath an open window of the house.

Voices came to him now — Scarab's smooth tones, Raymer's harsher ones, and a strange voice that Jinglebob did not recognize. That must belong to D. C. Jerrold. The men appeared to be arguing about something. Now and then a loud whoop floated up from the bunkhouse. From time to time, Jinglebob glanced in that direction but the card-players seemed as intent on their game as before.

Scarab's quiet voice sounded through the open window above Jinglebob's head: "I've told you," Scarab was saying, "that I'm pushing my end all that's possible. If you can only stall things off a little longer, D. C., we'll win out."

"I've stalled things off all I can," came the nervous reply. "Dave, you've got to do something. Why not ride over there tonight and make it clear you won't offer more?"

"That would be a waste of time," came Scarab's reply. "So long as the Alastairs think Jenkins is backing them up, they refuse to listen to me. If you'll just be patient and wait until Hannan returns, maybe we won't have to bother about Jenkins any longer. I don't know why he hasn't returned —"

"Cripes!" Raymer cut in. "Hannan's all right. He probably had to trail Jenkins all over the county before he caught up to him and finished him."

222

Jinglebob chuckled mentally and slowly straightened to his full height. Peering cautiously around the edge of the window frame, he found himself looking into what was probably the main room of the ranch house. It was sparsely furnished with bare walls. To all appearances, the house wasn't used to any great extent; Scarab probably lived in the bunkhouse with his crew.

Jinglebob saw Scarab first, sitting sidewise at a round, bare wooden table. Raymer sat with his back toward Jinglebob, only a few yards from the window. Across the table from Raymer was the man named Jerrold. Jerrold was a rather gaunt individual with thinning gray hair, a harshly lined face and quick, nervous movements. He held a cigar in one bony hand and drew on it impatiently from time to time. He was clothed in a dark, neatly pressed suit, starched collar and black necktie. He was hatless at the moment; Raymer and Scarab wore their sombreros.

A sudden burst of laughter from the bunkhouse drowned out Jerrold's next words. Jinglebob was suddenly conscious that his head, near the window, might easily be seen, should any of the Bridle-Bit men in the bunkhouse glance toward the house. Again, Jinglebob crouched low in the shadows. From within the house the voices went on as before:

"It seems to me, Dave," Jerrold remarked irritably, "that you've bungled the whole business. I demand some action."

Scarab replied softly, "You don't know range conditions, D. C., the way I do, or you'd never say that.

With Jenkins on the job, we've got to move carefully. We can't crowd things."

"For two cents," Jerrold snapped, "I'd drop the whole business."

A coin rang on the table, then came Scarab's easy tones, "There's your two cents and some over. Take it and get out, D. C. I'll handle the business myself and take all the profits . . ."

"Dammit!" Jerrold's voice sounded peevish. "I won't have that. I wish I'd never gone into this thing, but now that I'm in, I'll stay long enough to take out my profits."

"Then cut out your belly-aching," Scarab said, and a chill breath had crept into his tones. "It was your proposition in the first place. You came to me. I've kept my part of the bargain. Now, you keep yours. If Jenkins hadn't showed up, we'd owned the Alastair place by this time. You can stall off things a little longer."

"I tell you I can't," Jerrold protested. His voice was high-pitched, nervous. "The railroad won't wait forever on my say-so. I have only so much influence. The oil people are getting mighty impatient, I can tell you. Every time I suggest a postponement, my brother directors look at me as though I were crazy. It's been all I could do to convince them . . ."

Myriad thoughts were racing through Jenkins' head. What was it all about? Jerrold had mentioned a railroad and oil. Something big was afoot.

"Dang it," Jenkins said to himself, "I wish I knew what those skunks are planning. That Jerrold talks like a big gun of some sort. It must be big money. Cripes! If I

224

could only get Jerrold off to myself for about ten minutes, I'll bet I could bluff him into making a few explanations . . ."

Jenkins paused suddenly as a sudden, bold idea commenced to take form in his mind. For just an instant he hesitated, then a slow grin creased his tanned features. "It might work, it might work," he mused delightedly. "The unexpectedness of it might carry it through. Shucks, I reckon I'll give it a try."

Still crouching low, he moved away from the window and worked along toward the end of the building, where a door gave into the room where Scarab and his companions were seated. Jenkins rounded the corner of the building, then drew both guns. He approached the door softly and saw, by the long crack of yellow light, that it was unlatched. He lifted his guns. There came an almost noiseless double-click as the hammers came, back. Then, with his foot, he gave the door a push inward. Slowly, it swung open and Jinglebob stepped inside, a leveled gun in either hand.

Raymer was seated on the right; Jerrold on the left. Now Dave Scarab's back was to Jinglebob.

Raymer was first to spot the cowboy. "Cripes A'mighty!" he gasped, starting up.

"Sit right where you are, Raymer," Jinglebob said coolly. "All of you, put your hands in the air. Quick! You're covered and I'm not taking any chances. I just thought I'd take a hand in this game and learn just how the cards are stacked. That's right, get those hands high. Now, we'll get down to business."

CHAPTER
EIGHTEEN

Cornered!

Raymer was the first to get his hands into the air. Scarab followed more slowly. He had just stiffened a trifle at the sound of Jenkins' voice, but had made no move to turn around. Raymer mouthed a bitter oath. Jerrold had hesitated a moment before putting his hands in the air, then, after a glance at his companions, he followed suit, his face hardening as he glared at the interruption.

"This is an outrage," Jerrold fumed. "Scarab, if you can't keep your men in check —"

"Take it easy, D. C.," Scarab cut in coolly. "That's no Bridle-Bit man throwing down on us, if I recognize the voice. How about it, Jenkins, did you come here looking for a rhyme for Saskatoon?" Scarab's voice was level, easy.

"Something more important than that, Scarab," Jinglebob said quietly. "I've heard too much —"

"Jenkins!" Jerrold snapped nervously. "Jenkins? Is this the fellow —?"

"Jinglebob Jenkins," Scarab replied somewhat wearily. "The well-known thorn in the flesh, D. C. Right now he's apparently holding high cards in the game. You'd better do what he says, D. C."

"You're taking it sensible, Scarab," Jinglebob said.

"It's the only wise course," Scarab drawled, "with your gun at my back. This string isn't played out yet."

Jinglebob nodded. "Take out your gun, easy, Scarab. Put it on the table before you. No tricks, now." Scarab complied with the order. Jinglebob went on, "You're next, Raymer."

Raymer cursed, but did as he was ordered to do.

"You, Jerrold," Jinglebob continued, "gather up those guns and take 'em to the other end of the room, where they can't be reached easy. Have you got a gun on you?"

"Certainly not," Jerrold snapped indignantly. "I'm no common gun-fighter, to be carrying a weapon."

Jinglebob felt from Jerrold's manner that the man was speaking truthfully. "All right, pick up those guns and get busy."

"I'll do no such thing," Jerrold refused testily. "I'm not the man to be at the beck and call of every thug who wants —"

"You do what Jenkins tells you, D. C.," Scarab cut in. "He's not to be trifled with, right now. Later, we may change things around, but at present he holds the upper hand. We've got to admit that. And you'd better move fast."

"Much obliged, Scarab," Jinglebob nodded, "You show sense."

"Don't thank me," Scarab scowled. "I'm just thinking of my own skin. With that gun of yours pressing against my backbone, I aim to be plumb amenable to reason. Get busy, D. C."

Jerrold rose from the table, his gaunt features working with anger, his mouth voicing futile protests. He gathered Raymer's and Scarab's weapons from the table-top and started with them toward the far end of the room.

"And don't get to monkeying with those triggers," Jinglebob cautioned the man. "I'd hate to hear a gun go off, 'cause that would sure as hell precipitate other explosions. Somebody might get hurt."

Silence fell on the room. A moth entered the open window and fluttered aimlessly around the oil lamp suspended on one wall. Finally it swooped down inside the glass chimney and became quiet.

Jerrold deposited the guns on a chair at the far end of the room, then returned to the table, still voicing protests.

"Sit down," Jinglebob said. Jerrold resumed his seat. Jinglebob holstered one gun, moved up behind Scarab and patted the man's shoulder to see if he carried a hide-out gun.

"No, I don't," Scarab replied to Jinglebob's unspoken thought. "Neither does Gus. But you probably won't take my word for it."

"Nope, I won't," Jinglebob answered. He moved cautiously around the table, gun swinging in a short arc to cover the men, and examined Raymer in the same manner. Raymer started to curse again, but Scarab told him to keep quiet. For just a moment, Jinglebob saw the smoldering fury working in Scarab's features. Scarab was restraining his temper with an iron will, but

Jinglebob realized the mam was only awaiting the slightest opportunity to reverse the situation.

Jinglebob returned to his position back of Scarab. "All right, take it easy, hombres. You can lower your arms now, but keep your hands where I can see 'em." He drew his other gun, and kept his weapons trained on the three. Scarab shifted around so he could face Jenkins, but kept his hands on the table before him.

"All right, Jenkins," Scarab said calmly, almost too calmly. "You've won the first hand. What do you want?"

"Information." Jinglebob spoke the one word quietly.

"Regarding what?"

"I want to know why you're so anxious to gain control of the Ladder-A, and just how Jerrold is mixed into this business."

"Dave, maybe we'd better tell Jenkins the whole story," Jerrold said nervously. He was somewhat shaken at the manner in which Jenkins was controlling the situation.

Scarab said, "You keep your mouth shut, D. C."

"But look here, Dave, we can probably show Jenkins how to make some money."

Scarab laughed harshly. "You don't know Jenkins, D. C. He's not one of the bribable kind."

"One of you is going to talk plenty pronto," Jinglebob said. "I've risked too much to leave without getting what I came for. Come on, Jerrold, Scarab, start talking."

"You didn't happen to run across Utah Hannan, did you?" Scarab said smoothly, ignoring Jinglebob's words.

Jinglebob smiled. "Yeah, I did, Scarab."

Scarab considered that a moment. "I take it," he said at last, "Hannan got the worst of the argument."

"You take it correct, Scarab. You can quit worrying about him now. He's all taken care of. Now, you get busy and answer my questions."

"It wouldn't do you any good if I did," Scarab stalled. "You'd never leave here with any information I might give you. I've got men in the bunkhouse. The instant you left, I'd sound the alarm. Before you could get back to your horse, wherever you left it, you'd be captured or shot down. Don't try to bluff me, Jenkins. I don't bluff easy."

"I could stop you from giving that alarm." Jinglebob suggestively tilted one of his guns.

Scarab shook his head. "That don't go either, Jenkins. I know your type. You'd never shoot an unarmed man." He laughed scornfully at Jinglebob. "It's not looking so good, is it, Jenkins? It sort of appears to me as though you'd caught the tiger by the tail and didn't dare let go."

Jinglebob was realizing with a sinking heart there was a good deal in what Scarab said. But he decided to keep up the bluff. He laughed coolly. "I've got a lot of cards up my sleeve that you don't know about, Scarab." His voice suddenly went hard and cold, "You, Jerrold, you'll do the talking. What brings you here?"

"Don't answer him, D. C.," Scarab snapped.

"You'll answer plenty quick, Jerrold, before I let daylight through you," Jinglebob scowled.

"He's trying to bluff you —" Scarab commenced.

"I'm through bluffing," Jinglebob cut in. "You don't seem to realize I mean business. I came here to get certain information. I'm not leaving without it. Talk fast, Jerrold, if you don't want your soul blasted to hell."

"My God, Dave!" Jerrold turned pleading eyes on Scarab. "What'll I tell this —"

"Tell him nothing," Scarab swore. "He won't hurt you."

Raymer snarled, "Don't let him bluff you, Jerrold."

One of Jinglebob's guns jerked toward Raymer. "One more word out of you and it's the end, Raymer." Raymer quailed back in his chair and fell silent. Jinglebob's eyes shifted to Scarab's. For a moment Scarab glared back at the cowboy, then something cruel and hard seemed to appear in Jenkins' gaze, something Scarab had never noticed before. Scarab inhaled a quick, sharp breath, then,

"All right, D. C.," he said, and his tones sounded beaten, "you'd better tell Jenkins what he wants to know."

"I — I felt right along we should," Jerrold quavered. He turned his gaze toward Jenkins. "What is it you wish to know?"

Raymer was muttering curses under his breath. Scarab said nothing. His head dropped on his chest. From the vicinity of the bunkhouse came another burst of laughter. The card-players were still occupied with their game.

"Jerrold," Jinglebob said sternly, "you mentioned a railroad a spell back. What road was it?"

"The T. N. & A. S.," Jerrold replied meekly.

"What's your connection with it?"

"I'm — I'm on the board of directors and have certain responsible duties. My authority is considerable —"

"Never mind your authority," Jinglebob cut in. "You mentioned some oil company also. What company is it?"

"The Napache Petroleum Corporation."

Jinglebob thought a moment, then nodded, "The Napache is located at Wyattown, isn't it, over the other side of the Truculento Range?"

"That — that's it," Jerrold said nervously. He kept glancing toward Scarab, but Scarab didn't say a word.

"All right. What's the connection?"

"I can't say there's any particular connection, Jenkins. The railroad wants to carry the Napache's freight. I can't see how that can concern you."

"Cut out the stalling, Jerrold," Jinglebob said coldly. "I want the truth."

Jerrold paused and glanced toward Scarab. "I guess I'd better tell him, Dave."

Scarab didn't raise his head. "Go ahead," he said listlessly. "You're in this deeper than I am."

Jerrold sighed. "Well, here's the situation. The T. N. & A. S. is planning to extend its rails as far as Padre Wells —"

And that was as far as Jerrold got, when Scarab made a last desperate effort. With a lightning-like, panther movement, Scarab whirled sidewise from his chair, diving at Jinglebob's body. He dove low, coming in under Jinglebob's guns, hoping when Jinglebob fired, his wound would be only a minor one, and at the same time that the sound of the explosion would bring the men from the bunkhouse.

Just in time, Jinglebob saw Scarab leave the chair. One swift step took Jinglebob to one side. Scarab plunged on, through space. As he passed, Jinglebob rapped one gun barrel smartly across the man's head. Scarab went to the floor, groaned a moment and lay quiet.

"Help-p-p!" Jerrold bawled. "Help-p-p!"

"Cut it!" Jinglebob snapped.

Raymer was half out of his chair, but he sank down again, as one of Jinglebob's guns swept around to cover him. Jerrold cowered back under the threat of the other gun.

"I don't want a word out of either of you," Jinglebob jerked out.

But the damage had been done: from the bunkhouse came a sudden silence, then a loud clamoring of voices. A man yelled, "Something wrong up there, Dave?"

Raymer looked at Jinglebob. Jinglebob said, "Go to that window, Raymer. Tell those hombres nothing is wrong. Tell them Jerrold got scared at a tarantula. Go on, hurry!"

"What's the matter up at the house?" another call floated up from the bunkhouse.

Jinglebob's forty-five tilted savagely. "Get busy, Raymer," he snapped.

Raymer went to the window. "No, nothing wrong," he called back. "Jerrold just got scared of a tarantula. He ain't used to seein' 'em crawl around."

A burst of laughter came from the bunkhouse, and the men returned to their game.

Raymer drew his head back out of the window. "That satisfy you?" he growled sullenly.

"That was plumb elegant," Jinglebob smiled thinly. "You can sit down again."

Jerrold's horrified gaze was fastened on Scarab's silent form. "You've — you've killed him," he said.

Jinglebob laughed. "Cripes! He'll be on his feet again, inside fifteen minutes. But I don't reckon, Jerrold, you'll be here to see it. You and I are leaving, but first, you're going to take that rope hanging on that hook on the wall yonder, and tie Mister Raymer up secure."

"I won't go —" Jerrold commenced.

"Oh, yes, you will," Jinglebob contradicted, "If you know what's good for you. There's too many interruptions here for our little talk. You're coming with me. Go on, get that rope. You'd better stuff your handkerchief in Raymer's mouth too. It won't do much good, but it'll help some."

"Now, look here, Jenkins," Raymer started a protest, "you can't do this —"

"Jerrold's doing it for me. I'm just taking him away. My horse isn't far from here and —"

Jinglebob paused and started to turn around. Too late his ear had caught a soft step at his rear. Then he stiffened as he felt a gun barrel jabbed against his spine.

"Drop those guns, Jenkins. Quick, or I'm boring you!"

It was Utah Hannan's voice!

234

There was nothing else to do. Jinglebob lowered his guns, allowed them to drop from his hands to the floor. Then he heard Hannan laugh cruelly.

"Talk to me about usin' a gun barrel on a head, will you?" Hannan sneered. "Try it yourself and see how you like it."

Something descended with crushing force on Jinglebob's head. He felt himself falling, then a heavy black curtain enveloped his fading senses . . .

CHAPTER
NINETEEN

Crooked Plans

Jinglebob regained consciousness slowly. He hadn't been out long from the force of Hannan's blow: his heavy felt sombrero had softened considerably the violent impact of Hannan's gun barrel. There was a blur of voices in the room. Jinglebob didn't open his eyes at once. His head throbbed. He moved his wrists, then his ankles a trifle. Things came clearer after a moment, and he realized he was prone on the floor, bound hand and foot. Scarab once more had control of the situation.

The room was full of men. Jinglebob opened his eyes a thin crack and saw Scarab seated on a chair a few feet away, bathing his head with cold water. Jerrold and Raymer were nearby, Jerrold looking nervous and pale. Utah Hannan and the puncher known as Hank Wooley were talking to Scarab. Jinglebob recognized the men who had been playing cards in the bunkhouse. Scarab and Raymer had their guns once more. Jinglebob wondered what had become of his own guns. He remembered dropping them to the floor, and that was all.

Another thought struck Jinglebob: where was Bucky Malotte? Hannan's presence meant that he had escaped from Bucky. But how? And what had become of Bucky? Perhaps, though, Bucky had delivered Hannan to the deputy in Greyville and Hannan had escaped afterward. A few moments later, Jinglebob's thoughts were answered.

Scarab was talking to Hannan and Hank Wooley. "But I don't see what kept you hombres away so long," Scarab frowned. He reached to a pail of water at his side and soaked up a rag which he lifted to the spot on his head where Jinglebob's gun barrel had landed.

"I been telling you," Hank Wooley answered. "I'd gone all the way to Greyville —"

"I don't see what you did that for?" Scarab cut in.

Wooley laughed shortly. "I reckon that wallop on the conk must have spoiled your memory, boss. Don't you remember, when Utah didn't show up, last night, you told me I'd better head toward Greyville and see if I couldn't see some sign of him. 'Member? You'd figured that Jenkins must have gone to Greyville and that Utah was on his trail, and —"

"Don't be a fool, Hank," Scarab interrupted. "I remember all that clearly. After the way Jenkins outguessed Utah and took him prisoner, I reckon it's a good thing I did get anxious about him. But that's all clear. There's nothing wrong with my memory. You went to Greyville. On your way back, you spotted Bucky Malotte with Hannan, heading toward you."

"And, like I told you," Wooley put in. "I plugged Malotte and untied Utah. Malotte was carrying Utah's gun and —"

"Dammit, yes," Scarab said impatiently. "You said all that. But where've you two been all day? You should have been here long ago. Here it's getting along toward midnight."

"I explained where we'd been," Utah took up the story. "I'd been arrested. I was an escaped prisoner. It didn't seem good sense to come back in daylight. I didn't know but what Jenkins or Sheriff Wagner might be riding around and spot me. So me and Hank hid out in a dry wash all day. When it commenced to get dark we started for here. Now is it clear?"

Scarab nodded. He smiled thinly. "That's what I wanted to know. There was so much noise here I didn't get it the first time, I reckon. What did you do with Malotte's body?"

"We dragged it off'n the road and left it in some brush. I tied his horse in the brush too, so it wouldn't come wanderin' home," Utah said.

"Good work," Scarab nodded. After a minute he said, "You're sure no one noticed you, Hank?"

"Hell, there wasn't a soul within miles."

"No doubt about Malotte's being dead, is there?"

Wooley laughed scornfully. "Cripes! I knocked him off his horse with a slug in the back. Then, just for good luck, when we were leaving him, I thrun another slug at his head. That bull-headed deputy is dead as a doornail."

Jinglebob's heart sank. So that was the end of Bucky Malotte. Plucky Bucky was dead and, in one way, Jinglebob was responsible for his death. Right then,

238

Jinglebob made a mental vow if ever he escaped from this situation alive, he'd avenge Bucky's murder.

Scarab was again doing things to his head with water and a rag. He swore. "Damn, but my head aches!"

"Just take it easy, boss," Raymer suggested.

"How in the devil can I take it easy with a gang all around me and everybody talking at once?" Scarab said iritably. "Come on, clear out of here, you hombres. The excitement's over. I want a mite of peace and quiet. I'll let you know if I need you. Go on, clear out!"

The five punchers who had been playing cards in the bunkhouse were quick to follow their boss's order. Jerrold sank down on a chair with a long sigh. Raymer, noticing Hannan and Wooley remaining behind, said, "Go on, get out. Didn't you hear what Dave said?"

Wooley scuffed out of the room and closed the door behind him. Utah Hannan made no move to leave.

Scarab raised his head. "Cripes A'mighty, don't close that door. Let some fresh, air in. My head's splitting."

Hannan swung the door open again. Then he came back into the room. Scarab looked coldly at him. "Didn't you hear what I said about getting out, Utah?"

Hannan nodded. "I heard you," he said coolly. "I want to talk to you a minute."

"What's on your mind?" Scarab asked.

"I'm asking for a square deal," Hannan replied.

"What do you mean?"

Hannan said, a trifle uneasily, "I'll put it up to you, fair and square, Dave, and leave it to your own judgment. There's something big under way — big money."

"What if there is?" Scarab said coldly.

"I'm asking for an in."

Scarab swore softly and studied Hannan. "Do I understand you're demanding a share in what Gus and D. C. and myself are planning?"

Hannan shook his head. "Not demanding. Asking. Leaving it to your judgment."

"Just how do you figure," Scarab said, "that you're entitled to any more than the rest of those waddies in the bunkhouse?"

"I've done more than them. I risked my life against Jenkins."

"He outguessed you, though. You didn't outsmart him."

"The fact remains," Hannan said hastily, "that I took risks they didn't. I figure I'm a notch ahead of them. It was all right before. You paid good wages for hamstringing Ladder-A cows and running them off and so on. There wasn't any danger in that. Whether I succeeded with Jenkins or not, you've got to admit that I tried. I took chances them others didn't take."

Scarab laughed sarcastically, "Yes, and if Hank hadn't rescued you from Malotte, where would you be? Maybe Hank is entitled to something else too."

"He didn't act like he'd thought of it," Hannan pointed out. "That proves he ain't got the brain I got. You need brains, Dave. This business ain't all cleared up yet. You'll mebbe have something else for me that requires brains and nerve too. I'll be more valuable if I know what it's all about . . . and get a cut on the profits. You realize that as well as I do."

240

Scarab eyed Hannan a moment. Hannan met the gaze boldly, then added, "Remember, I'm not demanding a thing. I'm leaving it to your own sense of what's fair and right. Besides, you've got to admit, Dave, that I squared accounts with Jenkins for that wallop on the conk he give you. Am I in, or ain't I?"

Scarab smiled a trifle. "You got nerve, I'll say that for you." He turned to Raymer and Jerrold. "How about it, do we let him in for a small share?"

"Whatever you say, Dave," Raymer replied.

Jerrold shook his head. "I'm against it. Why divide the profits? This man is well paid and —"

"Yes, you would be against it," Scarab sneered. "All you had was an idea. We're doing the work. To hell with you, Jerrold. You're shaky right now. I figure Hannan deserves more than his wages. We may need him bad before we get through."

Jerrold's shoulders gave a shrug of resignation. "I withdraw my objections . . . though I still don't like it."

"You're in, Utah," Scarab said shortly. "But don't expect more than a small cut."

"Thanks." Hannan glanced triumphantly at Jerrold, then back to Scarab, "What do I do?"

"Nothing right now. Maybe I'll have something for you when Jenkins regains consciousness. You must have walloped him plenty hard, Utah. He hasn't stirred."

"They stay hit when I hit 'em," Hannan smirked. "Say, Dave," and there was a new familiarity in the man's voice, "can you tell me what this game is you're playing? I knew something big was under way, something bigger than just getting control of the Ladder-A, and I've been plumb curious."

Scarab hesitated a moment. "I reckon there's no harm in telling you," he said shrugging his shoulders. "Keep it quiet from the crew in the bunkhouse. There's not much to tell. The Napache Petroleum Corporation, over in Wyattown, have been shipping their crude oil, as it comes from the wells, on the Desert Central Railroad."

"The Desert Central is just a jerkwater line," Hannan said contemptuously. "I used to know a brakeman on that string of rusty rails."

"What you say is true," Scarab nodded, "but it's the only connection between Wyattown and the larger lines up north. Consequently, the Desert Central is charging exorbitant rates. The Napache people are getting plumb sick of being robbed. Now, the T. N. & A. S. road, of which our little pal, D. C. Jerrold, is a director, wants the job of carrying Napache oil —"

"But the T. N. & A. S. rails only come as far as Greyville," Hannan interrupted. "Wyattown is clear the other side of the Truculento Mountains —"

"I know all that," Scarab said. "Keep still while I do the talking. Now, it is planned to bring the T. N. & A. S. road as far as Padre Wells. So far, our worthy friend, Jerrold, has succeeded in keeping those plans secret from the country hereabouts. Mr. Jerrold has explained very patiently, to his business associates, that until the rails actually commence to be laid, nothing should be said. You see, Utah, the T. N. & A. S. will have to buy certain property in Padre Wells and the Napache people

242

will construct tanks there. If the plans were known, the holders of such property would immediately increase the purchase price of their holdings. At least, this is the excuse D. C. has used to keep the plans secret. Now, both the road and the oil people are getting impatient to start operations."

Hannan shook his head blankly. "It's too deep for me, Dave. Even with rails to Padre Wells, Wyattown is still some twenty miles distant, through the Truculentos. Danged if I see —"

"I'll make it clearer," Scarab nodded. "The contract between the T. N. & A. S. and the oil people, calls for the railroad to lay a pipe line to carry the oil, from Wyattown to Padre Wells where it can be put into tank cars —"

"Pipe line?" Hannan frowned.

"To pump the oil through," Scarab explained impatiently.

"I never heard of such a thing," Hannan said, shaking his head.

"You will in the future," Scarab said. "They've been using pipe lines in the eastern states for quite some years now. Until the T. N. & A. S. puts its rails straight across country, it's the sensible way of handling the proposition."

Hannan considered a moment. "I suppose this pipe line will go through Sabre Canyon, in the Truculentos?"

"Exactly," Scarab replied. "It's the only pass through for miles around. It would be a hell of a job to carry a line across the mountains at any other point, too expensive to be thought of, in fact."

Light suddenly dawned on Hannan's face. "Sabre Canyon is part of the Ladder-A holdings," he exclaimed.

"That," Scarab said dryly, "is what has been bothering us for some time. To carry out its part of the contract, the T. N. & A. S. has got to get a right of way through Sabre Canyon and across the Ladder-A property. The railroad would pay Alastair a nice chunk of money for that right. However, D. C. and I feel that Alastair wouldn't have sense enough to get as much cash as he could. The idea being for me to get hold of the Ladder-A and then boost the price Alastair would probably accept."

"You mean hold 'em up — stick the railroad with a big price?"

Scarab smiled thinly. "You put it rather crudely, Utah, but you get the general idea. Then Jerrold and I, and my men, split the profits."

"My Gawd!" Hannan looked respectfully at Scarab, "what an idea. It's plumb elegant. You're smart, Dave. So that's why you're trying to scare the Ladder-A into selling to you."

"That's it — but don't credit me with being smart. D. C. gets the credit. He had the idea long before he negotiated the contract with his road and the oil people."

"But — but," Hannan floundered, "where do you come in? Why didn't he buy the Ladder-A himself?"

Jerrold smiled sourly at the question. Raymer grinned and said, "You ain't smart in big business workin's, Utah."

Scarab chuckled, "Can't you see, Utah, it wouldn't look well for D. C. to be holding up his own company?"

"By Gawd!" Hannan exclaimed, suddenly indignant. "That's what he *is* doing! He's robbin' his own pals, ain't he? I call that downright crooked!"

Scarab turned to Jerrold with a soft laugh. "You see, D. C.? There is a difference in the various moral planes. Now Utah would never think of cheating a pal."

"It's lousy dirty," Hannan insisted earnestly. "Holding up his own company." He shot a look of moral indignation at Jerrold.

Jerrold returned the gaze with a poisonous sneer. "You'll be glad enough to share in the profits, Hannan, when this deal goes through. Let's hear no more of such talk . . . Dave, I think you've said too much as it is. I saw Jenkins move, just now. I think he's regaining consciousness. It wouldn't do for him to hear what you've said."

"That," Scarab replied coolly, "wouldn't make the slightest difference. Jenkins isn't going any place where he could tell our plans. His course is run."

CHAPTER
TWENTY

Scarab's Proposition

Jinglebob lay motionless on the floor, his aching head teeming with thought. Now he knew the reason for Scarab's wanting the Ladder-A outfit. Inwardly he cursed his luck. With the knowledge he now possessed, Jinglebob could at once relieve Breck Alastair's mind of all its worries — providing he were free. But Jinglebob couldn't see how he was going to be free. His guns were gone; he was bound hand and foot. Victory was in Scarab's grasp and nothing, it seemed, could be done to prevent it. Jinglebob now had no illusions as to his ultimate fate were it left to Scarab to settle.

Hannan was still thinking over the plans that had been outlined to him. Now and then he shook his head and cast angry glances in Jerrold's direction. Raymer smoked a cigarette and said nothing, leaving the next move to Scarab. Scarab had gone on bathing his head with the wet rag. The five cowboys in the bunkhouse — six, including Hank Wooley — weren't making as much noise as before. Plainly the card game hadn't been resumed. Jinglebob counted the odds against himself. Ten against one. Even if his hand and feet were free and his guns at reach, the odds were too big. It looked like the end. Jinglebob knew he could expect no mercy from Scarab.

Scarab rose suddenly and moved across the floor to Jinglebob's side. He nudged Jinglebob's ribs with one booted foot. "Come on, Jenkins, come awake. You've stalled long enough."

Jinglebob groaned and moved a trifle. He opened his eyes slowly and gazed around with a vacant expression in them.

"Cut it," Scarab said impatiently. "We've had enough of bluffing for one evening, Jenkins. I've been watching you. You've been conscious for some time. There are certain tremors of a man's eyelids that give him away, when he tries to fake unconsciousness."

Jinglebob opened his eyes and forced a smile. "You, win, Scarab," he said, "for the present."

"Hell," Scarab sneered, "I win for all time —"

"Look here, Dave," Jerrold interrupted excitedly, "do you mean to say Jenkins heard everything you told Hannan?"

"Sure, he did," Scarab admitted, "as well as anything you hombres might have mentioned. I figured Jenkins might be interested in my reason for wanting the Ladder-A. I knew he was listening."

"But, Dave," Jerrold looked horrified, "that was a rash thing, a very rash thing to do. Jenkins may —"

"Jenkins," Scarab smiled thinly, "isn't going to have any opportunity to spill what he's learned. He's finished, right now. He realizes that as well as I do . . . Want to get up, Jenkins?"

"Suits me," Jinglebob replied from his prone position on the floor. "These boards aren't any too soft."

Scarab said, "Bring a chair over here, Hannan."

Hannan brought a straight-backed chair. Scarab reached down, grasped the front of Jinglebob's shirt and easily lifted him to the chair. A wave of dizziness swept through Jinglebob's head. When his mind cleared he found himself seated on the chair, his bound hands before him on his lap, his bound feet resting on the floor.

"Take it easy a minute," Scarab's voice came through a rapidly clearing fog. "I've got a proposition to make, when you feel able to talk. There's a bottle here. Do you want a drink, or a cigarette?"

"A drink of water and a cigarette," Jinglebob replied.

"Hannan!" Scarab gave a brief order.

Utah Hannan brought a tin dipper of water and held it to Jinglebob's lips. He couldn't help taunting the captive. "Talk to me about a gun barrel over the conk, will you?" he jeered. "Guess I showed what I could do in that direction. How'd you like —"

"Shut up, Hannan," Scarab said briefly.

Jinglebob finished drinking, then asked for another dipper-full. Hannan brought it and Jinglebob drank half of that. Scarab took the dipper from Hannan's hand and dashed the remaining water in Jinglebob's face. "That'll help clear your mind," Scarab said. Jinglebob didn't reply. Scarab rolled a Durham cigarette and thrust it between Jinglebob's lips. He rolled one for himself, and lighted both with the same match.

Hannan took the dipper away and seated himself near Jerrold and Raymer, four or five yards away. Jinglebob inhaled deeply on the cigarette and glanced around the room. He saw his guns on the table, where someone had placed them. So near and yet so far. He blew out the smoke and looked at Scarab.

Scarab said, "How do you feel?"

"You should know," Jinglebob forced a grin. "We both had a dose of the same medicine."

"I reckon," Scarab nodded, "though I think you were hit harder than I was. Your barrel just struck me a glancing blow."

"Maybe," Jinglebob proposed lightly, "we should be in the same hospital so we could compare operations."

"I see," Scarab nodded again, "you want to get down to business and hear what my proposition is. I was just making it clear, Jenkins, there's no hard feelings. We've played a game and you've lost. I've nothing against you personal . . ."

"Of course not," Jinglebob said sarcastically. "It's all a pure business proposition with you, just like getting the Ladder-A and selling it to Jerrold's company. He robs his own company and you do your best to practically steal a ranch. You can't get away with it, Scarab."

Scarab laughed confidently. "That's only your own opinion, Mr. Deputy U. S. Marshal."

Jinglebob had been looking at Jerrold. Now his eyes came back to meet Scarab's mocking gaze. "You know, then," Jinglebob said quietly.

Scarab nodded.

"I suppose you went through my pockets and found my badge."

Again, Scarab nodded. "I knew before that, though. I didn't need that gold badge to tell me."

Jinglebob said as quietly as before. "I'm curious to know where I slipped up."

"You didn't exactly," Scarab replied. "Ichy Wellman got careless."

"Ichy Wellman?"

"That clerk in the general store where they handle the mail. Ichy talked about you mailing out poems. It sounded sort of phony to me. I maneuvered Ichy into leaving the store to go to the storehouse, while I picked up one of your letters. I suppose you've been mailing reports to the U. S. Marshal. Anyway, that's what the letter I saw consisted of. It was smart using a double envelope that way, so your reports could be forwarded on to the U. S. Marshal, but it wasn't quite smart enough."

"I reckon," Jinglebob said ruefully, "we can't blame Ichy any more than myself. So you've added robbing the U. S. mails to your other crimes, Scarab."

Scarab smiled. "Guilty," he said, "guilty as hell. But that information isn't going to do you any good either . . . Do you know, for a time, I had you spotted as an Artexico Cattle Association detective."

Jinglebob puffed on his cigarette, thoughtfully. Well, it would do no harm to talk now. The longer he kept talking, the longer he'd keep alive. Something might happen — but Jinglebob didn't know what that something could be. He said, "Yes, I know a lot of folks suspected me of being an A. C. A. man. I was with the Association a few years back. That man they sent down in answer to Alastair's letter was a good friend of mine."

"You mean Mitchell?" Scarab asked.

Jinglebob nodded. "Mitchell, the man Franklin dry-gulched. After I heard he'd been murdered, I asked my office to put me on the case. The U. S. Marshal got in touch with the A. C. A. and explained the situation. The Association knew my work and consented to let me come down here instead of sending one of their own men. As a matter of fact, I guess they were glad to have the case in the hands of a government man. Mitchell had come down here openly; everybody knew he was a cattle dick —"

"Your way had us fooled for a spell," Scarab put in, "but after I'd read some of your poetry, I knew you were no poet."

Jinglebob grinned. "I call that plumb unkind. You've broken my heart."

"That's too bad," Scarab chuckled. "Of course, all I had to go on were those verses you wrote for Pat Hogan, but —"

"They were representative," Jinglebob smiled. "You're right on that point, anyway, Scarab."

"You might have fooled me if you'd come to me carrying that chunk of baling wire we found in your pocket. I might even have put you on my payroll to do some branding."

"I considered that and passed it up," Jinglebob replied. "Yes, I know, a lot of folks have suspected me of being a cowthief, when they saw that wire. Carrying that is an old habit I picked up when I was working for the Artexico people. We had branding to do now and then."

Jinglebob was keeping the conversation going as long as possible. Every moment meant added life.

251

Scarab said suddenly, "Jenkins, you don't need to keep glancing at your guns on that table. You can't get to 'em."

"I suppose not," Jinglebob said easily. "There's no law against trying, I suppose?"

"Only the law that might makes right," Scarab replied. "However, it's not going to be necessary for you to try. We're going to put 'em back in your holsters . . . just as we returned your badge and other stuff to your pockets. Then everything will be found on your body and folks will wonder who did this last killing."

Jinglebob stiffened just a trifle. "Like that, eh?" he said steadily.

"Just like that, Jenkins."

"There isn't any other way, I suppose?"

"Dam'd if I can see one, Jenkins. You know too much. I can't let you go now. I hate to have you rubbed out —"

"I'll bet you do," Jinglebob said scornfully.

"It's a fact. Dammit, I could almost like you, Jenkins. You've got brains. You've had me guessing two or three times. You've made this game I'm playing plumb interesting. But I can't see any other way. I'm in this too deep now to pull out even if I wanted to, which I don't. No, it's your finish, Jenkins."

"You figuring to do the job yourself?"

Scarab frowned. "I don't reckon. Utah Hannan was a score to square with you. You probably heard him asking for an in. I figure I'll give him the job —"

"I'll take it and glad of the chance," Hannan cut in.

252

Scarab cast a cold glance toward Hannan. "Nobody invited you to talk, Hannan."

Hannan shrank back from the chill glance in Scarab's eyes and kept silent.

Jinglebob said quietly. "You'll mebbe let yourself in for trouble, Scarab. There's people who know I was coming here."

Scarab nodded. "I reckoned as much. But your body will be found a long way from here. Nobody's going to be able to prove anything against us, and there's too many Colt forty-fives in the country to tie the slug they dig out of your body, to any particular individual. You see, Jenkins, it's all worked out. We're playing for big stakes and we can't afford to let one man's life — or even a half a dozen — stand in our way —"

"Dave," Jerrold cut in, uneasily, "you had a proposition to make to Jenkins. Seems to me you're wasting time, with all this talk."

"Don't get impatient, D. C. You're in my bailiwick, now, not in your mahogany-decorated director's office. I'm running things here."

"But, Dave, it's getting late."

"What if it is? Would you begrudge Jenkins a few more minutes of life? You're about as cold-blooded a fish as I —"

Jinglebob cut in, "Maybe your friend Jerrold is right, Scarab. I'm waiting to hear what your proposition is. Why not get to talking?"

Scarab shrugged his shoulders. "Just as you say, cowhand. Well, it's this way. The last time I visited the Ladder-A, I made Alastair an offer for his ranch."

"A pretty lousy offer if you ask me," Jinglebob said. "About a half what the outfit is worth."

"I'm not asking you," Scarab said coolly. "Under the circumstances, I believe you'll presently admit the price is fair."

"What are the circumstances?"

"Alastair is going to lose his ranch, anyway."

"How do you figure that?"

"You're going to write a note to Alastair, advising him to take my offer. I've a right strong hunch that Alastair will do what you advise. Right?"

Jinglebob laughed scornfully. "Maybe. But suppose I refuse to write such a note."

"You won't, if I've got you figured out correctly," Scarab said confidently.

"I suppose if I write the note, you'll give me my life . . ."

"I didn't say that."

". . . and if I refuse to write it, you'll kill me."

"Look here, Jenkins, you've got the wrong idea. Face the facts. Whether you write that note or not, you're due to be put out of the way. You know too much to be good for my health."

"That settles it," Jinglebob said grimly. "I'm writing no such note. You can't force Alastair to sell, whether I'm alive or dead."

"No, I can't," Scarab conceded readily, "and I don't intend to try any more along the lines I've been employing. It's time for action. If you refuse to write what I ask, then we'll be leaving to raid the Ladder-A within an hour or so. There's four men there and a girl.

254

It won't be hard to put them out of the way. We'll burn the buildings, at least the bodies —"

"Damn you, Scarab!" Jinglebob strained against his bonds.

"I thought that would get you," Scarab said cruelly.

"That won't give you the Ladder-A!"

"That's where you're wrong, Jenkins. D. C. will write out a bill-of-sale and sign it with Breck Alastair's name."

"You won't be able to make a forgery like that stand up —"

Scarab's cold laugh cut in on the words. "You don't realize what an artist D. C. is with a pen. I managed to get hold of a sample of Alastair's writing. D. C. can imitate it so Alastair's own folks wouldn't know the difference. Back about twenty years, D. C. was considered one of the cleverest forgery artists that ever served a term in the Colorado Penitentiary, and he's improved since then —"

"Look here, Dave," Jerrold cut in quickly, "there's no use raking up my past history. That's all gone and forgotten. Folks don't know —"

"Cut the piousness, D. C.," Scarab snapped. "We've got to make this fool see light. If he won't write that note, well, we'll be money ahead. All it will cost us is a short ride, a few cartridges and a lighted match here and there." He turned back to Jinglebob, "How about it, Jenkins, will you write that note and give the Alastairs half what their ranch is worth, or will you refuse and give them . . . death?"

"Damn you for a cold-blooded devil, Scarab!"

"Don't waste your breath with histrionics, Jenkins. They're not effective. Think, think fast. Will you write that note?"

And Jinglebob was thinking fast. By writing the note, he would at least save the lives of Lorry, Breck and the others. He slumped down in his chair. "All right," he said grimly, "you win. Bring on your paper and pencil and untie my hands."

"Good!" Scarab exclaimed. "I thought you'd listen to reason. And don't think when your hands are untied, you'll be able to start anything. You'll have plenty of guns pointed your way . . . Gus, get a paper and pencil."

Raymer rose to his feet. "I guess there ain't any up here. I'll slope down to the bunkhouse and tear a sheet out of the tally book."

"Hurry it up."

Raymer rose to his feet and started toward the door. Then he stopped short as a new voice interrupted the proceedings:

"Don't be in any hurry about that pencil and paper. You ain't going to need it. Just reach high and reach pronto!"

All eyes flashed to the doorway. A bloody apparition stood there, swaying a trifle, clutching the door jamb with one hand, a leveled forty-five gripped in the other, covering the men in the room. Slowly, four pairs of hands rose in the air.

"Bucky!" Jinglebob said unbelievingly. "Bucky Malotte."

256

CHAPTER
TWENTY-ONE

Powder Smoke!

It was a terrible looking Bucky who stood so uncertainly in that doorway. Only his bulldog courage had kept him going on the trail of his escaped prisoner. He was disheveled. His hat was gone and his blood-stained hair hung down over his glassy blue eyes. His shirt was stained darkly; the lower half of his face was a bloody mask.

He half stumbled into the room, closing the door at his rear. Through a supreme effort of will he managed to hold his gun steady on the men in the room.

"Get back, back, all of you," he said thickly. "Face the wall. Keep your hands in the air. Hannan, prisoners don't escape from Bucky Malotte."

His blocky body swayed uncertainly and the sturdy bulldog legs seemed no longer sturdy as he advanced farther into the room. Scarab and his companions were facing the far wall now, their arms elevated.

"Get me untied, Bucky," Jinglebob pleaded. "Quick. Don't make any noise. There's men in the bunkhouse. But shoot if you have to. They're planning to raid the Ladder-A."

He could see Bucky was nearly out on his feet. Bucky's eyes were growing vacant. The man was weak, nearly done. Jinglebob's words finally penetrated his mind.

"You, there, with the city clothes," Bucky mumbled thickly. "Get those ropes off —"

"That's you, Jerrold," Jinglebob cut in. "Hurry up. Get these ropes off, if you don't want to be plugged."

"Take your time, D. C.," Scarab advised, glancing over his shoulders. "Malotte's nearly finished now. He can't last. Take your time . . ."

"Dammit," Bucky growled, with a momentary return of his old spirit, "I'll show you if I can last or not. Get busy on those ropes, mister."

Jerrold came to Jinglebob and commenced fumbling at the ropes about Jinglebob's wrists.

"Don't you take Scarab's word for it, Jerrold," Jinglebob snapped. "I know Malotte. He'll last. He'll plug you sure as hell. Keep going."

"Stall it, D. C., stall it," Scarab said. "Don't let 'em bluff you."

"You, Scarab," Bucky managed to say, "I'll get you, anyway, if you don't shut up."

"Don't let him worry you, D. C.," Scarab spoke swiftly. "Stall along. He don't dare shoot."

Bucky swung one gun toward Scarab. Scarab flattened himself against the wall. He didn't say anything more.

Jerrold was working steadily at the knots now. Bucky swayed and nearly fell. With an effort he jerked himself

258

upright. "Hurry, hurry," he mumbled thickly. "Jinglebob . . . you'll have to . . ." Again he swayed.

"He's going!" Scarab yelled. "Stall, D. C."

But Jinglebob's arms were loose now. He jerked them free just as Bucky slumped to the floor. Scarab gave a cry of triumph, and swung away from the wall, jerking his gun.

Jinglebob gave Jerrold a shove to one side, just as Scarab fired. The bullet entered Jerrold's body. Jerrold groaned and crumpled down. Scarab fired again, as Jinglebob, his feet still bound, made one leap toward the table for his guns. His hands closed about the butts, as Scarab's second shot flew wide.

Hannan and Raymer had whirled around now, their guns flashing in the light. Two reports sounded almost together. Jinglebob felt something like burning hot iron pierce his side. With his feet tied together and his guns in his hands he couldn't save himself from falling. Even as he fired he crashed into the table, overturning it.

He heard Raymer give a yell of pain and heard a body strike the floor. Scarab swore suddenly and Jinglebob knew he'd scored hits with both guns. He heard slugs *thud-thud-thud* into the overturned table behind which he'd fallen.

Behind him, Bucky was sprawling on the floor, swearing at his inability to rise. He braced himself on one hand, released one quick shot at Utah Hannan. Hannan smashed back against the wall and crashed down. Bucky laughed and lifted his gun toward the lamp. There came a loud roar and a shattering of glass as the room was plunged in darkness.

259

There were wild yells from the bunkhouse now.

Jinglebob snapped, "Good work, Bucky," and crawled through the darkness toward the door. He reached it, felt for the knob and hauled himself upright. With his other hand he shot the bolt in place, locking it, just an instant before the men from the bunkhouse arrived. There came a loud pounding on the door and wild yells for admittance.

A crimson flash split the gloom and in the momentary light, Jinglebob saw Raymer's form. He fired again, and in a second moment of illumination saw streaks of fire spurting from Dave Scarab's vicinity. A choked, bubbling curse was torn from Raymer's lips as he crashed down. At the same instant, a second slug entered Jinglebob's body, knocking him to the floor again.

Scarab yelled, "Break down that door, boys!"

Jinglebob twisted around, sent two swift shots ripping through the door and heard startled, panicky yells and the sounds of retreating feet. A red-hot knife sliced across his left thigh. Again, he whirled back toward Scarab. It was too dark to see the man's position, but Jinglebob thumbed his right gun twice.

Only dull clicks sounded. That gun was empty. Scarab fired again. Jinglebob felt the breeze of the bullet as it cut the handkerchief at his throat. He lifted his left gun. Three spurs of fire spurted from the muzzle. In the light of the final shot, he glimpsed Scarab as the man was plunging down, and heard his body strike the floor.

Silence descended as the echoes of the roaring guns died away. The room was swimming with powder smoke that stung eyes and throat and nostrils. Jinglebob waited tensely. Outside he could hear men's voices, but he knew, for a few moments at least, the other Bridle-Bit punchers would keep their distance. He waited a moment longer, then reloaded his guns. He said quietly, alert for the first movement, "Got enough, Scarab?"

There was no reply. Jinglebob made a soft scraping noise on the floor. That didn't produce any shots either.

"Sounds like they're finished, Bucky," Jinglebob said low-voiced.

"Finish', finish'," Bucky said thickly. He sounded drunk.

Jinglebob put down his guns and untied the knots about his ankles. There was a dull ache at two spots in his body. His shirt felt warm and wet and sticky. His left thigh burned, but he judged that wound wasn't as serious as the others. He holstered one gun, then with the other in his hand, he made a painful course about the room, feeling for bodies in the darkness. He could only judge who they were from their positions when he had seen them last.

The survey didn't take long. Scarab was dead as was Utah Hannan. Raymer was still alive, but unable to speak or move. Jerrold was unconscious and, from the sound of his labored breathing, had taken a slug through his lungs.

Jinglebob stumbled about the room until he had found the bucket of water. He made his way back to

Bucky, on the floor, and dashed some water in his face. They both drank from the dipper.

From outside came a yell in Hank Wooley's voice, "Hey, Dave! Are you all right?" Footsteps were approaching the house again, more cautiously this time.

"Scarab's finished, you coyotes," Jinglebob yelled, or tried to yell back. His voice was little better now than a hoarse croak. "And so's the rest of your pals."

A sudden torrent of cursing sounded outside the house, then a rattle of gunfire. Bullets crashed through the door and open window to thud into the walls.

Bucky was struggling to rise, now. Jinglebob held him close to the floor. "Stay down, Bucky, stay down. We've cleaned up in here, but there's six hombres outside that want our scalps." He held more water to Bucky's lips.

Bucky's words came clearer after a moment. "I reckon I was sort of out," he said haltingly. "Hannan got away from me. He must have had a pal . . ."

"It was Hank Wooley. He followed you. They left you for dead, Bucky."

"Lucky they left . . . my horse . . . near. I followed their trail . . . when I come to . . ."

"Do you know how bad you're hit, Bucky?"

Another hurricane of flying lead swept through the door and open window. Jinglebob staggered to his feet, raised one gun. A stream of orange fire lanced through the window. A man yelled with pain and started off at a stumbling run that ended when he pitched to the earth.

There were wild yells of rage and more gunfire. Bullets thudded into the walls. Jinglebob had immediately dropped to the floor again and returned to Bucky.

"We've got to make a fight for it, Bucky, old son," he said unsteadily. "I'll load your gun for you. Are you too hard hit to fire?"

"Don't think . . . I'm hit . . . bad," Bucky mumbled. "I got a slug playin' around my left ribs, some place. It bled like hell. There's a furrow cut across the back of my head. It was close. When I woke up I was layin' on my face . . . and . . . the blood was running down across my nose. It . . . it tickled." He laughed rather light-headedly. "Sure, I'm . . . I'm all right. I been pullin' these faintin' spells . . . on arid off . . . all afternoon. Gimme my gun . . ."

He staggered to an erect position and stumbled toward the window. Jinglebob was up too, swaying queerly on unsteady feet. His head was swimming in a crimson fog. He felt dizzy.

"We'll give 'em hell, Bucky." He tried to make the words come steady, but his voice sounded faint and far away. He lifted his gun and nearly fell through the window when he fired it. He steadied himself against the wall. A steady stream of hot flame was jetting from Bucky's gun in the direction of the shadowy figures outside.

Bridle-Bit six-shooters commenced to bark again. Bucky and Jinglebob dropped to the floor as a hail of bullets swept above them.

"What do you say we open the door and rush 'em?" Bucky asked — and immediately fainted away.

"Bucky! Bucky!" Jinglebob said. "Did they get you, pard?"

Bucky didn't answer. Once more, grimly determined, Jinglebob staggered to his feet. His whole body seemed filled with pain. There wasn't any strength in his legs. He stumbled against the wall and crashed down again. Gamely he gritted his teeth and fought to arise, but the necessary strength wasn't there. The firing outside commenced again with renewed fury. There was a great deal of angry shouting, curses.

Then, for the second time that night, Jinglebob Jenkins lost consciousness . . .

CHAPTER
TWENTY-TWO

Conclusion

Gray dawn was filtering through the windows of the Bridle-Bit bunkhouse when Jinglebob opened his eyes. He was undressed, covered with blankets. His body felt stiff and sore. His leg throbbed unmercifully. He moved one arm. It moved freely.

"Nope, I'm not a prisoner," he muttered. "I wonder what's happened. Where's Bucky?"

A movement at his right caught his eye. He twisted around and his mouth fell open when he saw Lorry Alastair standing there. Lorry was wearing overalls; a six-shooter was slung at her right side.

"Hello, Lorry," Jinglebob grinned. "Welcome to our party. How did you get here?"

"So you're awake, are you?" Lorry shook her head exasperatedly. "Jinglebob, you'll be the death of me yet. Why do you insist on running off and getting into fights?"

"It's the nature of the beast," Jinglebob chuckled. His head was clearing fast. He didn't feel nearly so bad as he had when first awakening.

Lorry drew a chair next to the bunk and sat down. "How do you feel?"

"A mite stiff. Otherwise, all right. Sa-a-ay, what happened? The last I remember . . ." He paused, then went on, "Say, Lorry, I know now why Scarab wanted the Ladder-A — oh, say, he's dead —"

"I know he's dead and so is Gus Raymer. Utah Hannan may pull through. I guess that Jerrold man is going to live to serve a prison sentence. He told us the whole story about the railroad and the Napache oil people and all they'd planned."

"Sa-a-ay, you know as much as I do — hey. Where's Bucky Malotte? What happened to him?"

"Bucky's over in the cook shanty, propped up on chairs," Lorry replied. "He refused to be put to bed. Tarp's making some coffee and —"

"Coffee? Good. That's all I need. And a cigarette." Jinglebob started to rise from the bunk.

Lorry pressed him back. "You'll stay right there until the doctor comes. Matt has gone to town for him. Your wounds aren't really serious, but there's a couple of bullets to extract, then we'll move you to the Ladder-A."

"Hey, am I hit bad?"

Lorry smiled and shook her head. "Not bad, but you're going to require some nursing, after those bullets are out. Sheriff Wagner patched you up as well as possible until the doctor gets here. It was loss of blood that knocked you out, the sheriff says. And the same applies to Bucky, though his wounds aren't quite as bad as yours."

"Look, Lorry, how did you get here?"

"On horses."

"Dang it, you know what I mean. How did you know I was coming here, when did you arrive and —"

"Tarp Jones told me."

"Dang Tarp Jones. I told him not to say anything."

"Jinglebob Jenkins, you should know better than that. I could have told you, from my experience, that old Tarp only obeys the orders he wants to obey. And I can't say I like the way you slipped off without telling me."

"Lorry, I had to do it. It was the only way. This business had to be settled. Breck couldn't stand much more uncertainty. But, just what happened to bring you here?"

Lorry told him: "Last night, some time after you'd left, Tarp came to me and said he thought he and Matt should go to the Bridle-Bit and see if you were all right. That was the first intimation I'd had that you'd left. I didn't feel so good about that, Mister Deputy U. S. Marshal —"

"You know that, too, eh?"

"There isn't much now I don't know about you, cowboy. There'll be no more secrets between us from now on."

"I'm hoping there won't be any need for secrets," Jinglebob chuckled.

"I'm going to see to it there won't," Lorry said sternly, though there was a twinkle in her dark eyes. "Anyway, when Tarp said where you'd gone, my heart dropped into my shoes. Tarp bucked against me going along, but I couldn't be stopped then. We left Breck with Chris, then Tarp, Matt and I rode to Padre Wells, where we picked up Sheriff Wagner. He agreed with me that we'd better get here as soon as possible. Before we reached here we heard firing. Those Bridle-Bit cowboys were just getting ready to smash down the door. We came up on them from the rear and Wagner ordered them to throw down their arms. There was a little firing, but it didn't amount to much —"

"Lorry Alastair, are you admitting you were in a gun fight?"

Lorry frowned. "I don't know, Jinglebob," she said frankly. "I don't remember firing my gun, but after we'd rounded 'em up and taken prisoners, I discovered my gun was empty. Anyway," and she smiled, "I'm maintaining I forgot to load it before leaving home. And then we broke down the door to the house and found you and Bucky; and, Jinglebob, I was plumb scared, until the sheriff said you were both alive. Then the sheriff fixed you up and Matt rode to Padre Wells to bring the doctor. Bucky came out of his faint and told us what he knew and we talked to the others, and . . . and . . . I guess that's all."

There was a step at the door of the bunkhouse and old Tarp Jones entered, bearing two cups of steaming coffee.

"Hello, there, Jinglebob," he greeted. "Ye're awake, are ye? How about some Java?"

"Good, but, Tarp, you're an old scoundrel."

"Me," innocently, "what hev I done?"

"I told you not to tell I was coming here."

"Young feller," Tarp said seriously, "they's times when wisdom is above promises. I saw my duty and I took it, and it's a right good thing for you young squirts — meanin' you an' Bucky Malotte — that me'n Matt and Lorry done what we done. Ye'd been wiped out."

"I reckon, Tarp," Jinglebob grinned. "All right, you're forgiven."

Tarp placed the coffee on a nearby table. "I'll go tell Bucky and the sheriff ye're awake. They wanted to know."

"Don't be in too much of a hurry. I want to talk to Lorry a few minutes. Seeing too many people at once might bring me a rise of temperature," Jinglebob said gravely.

Tarp slowly winked one eye. "All right, I'll leave ye alone a spell, but I doubt yer temperature will stay down." And when Lorry gasped, the old cowman beat a hasty retreat.

"Well, Lorry," Jinglebob tried to keep his voice level, "I reckon the sale of a right-of-way to the T. N. & A. S. will put you and Breck on easy street."

"It'll help," Lorry nodded. "Look, Jinglebob, we want you with us. Breck wants a man to run the Ladder-A. I talked it over with him last night . . ."

"Now, wait a minute, Lorry —" Jinglebob started a protest.

"I'll do no more waiting, man dear. You're leaving that Deputy U. S. Marshal job. You're going to stay where I can keep an eye on you."

"But, Lorry, I can't live on your ranch . . ."

"I've got my own ideas about that. If it wasn't for you, we wouldn't have that ranch"

"I can't do it, Lorry" Jinglebob was shaking his head and reaching for her hands at the same time.

Lorry laughed. "Maybe I can bribe you."

"What's the bribe?"

"I'll give you a rhyme for Saskatoon."

"Lorry!"

"Jinglebob, did I ever tell you my name?"

"It's Lorry," puzzledly.

"That's my nickname. No, I know I never told you. You see, my mother named me. She'd read a book, when she was younger, she'd liked a great deal. She named me after the book. The title of the book was *Lorna Doone*. I'm Lorna Doone Alastair —"

"Lorry, it fits!"

"I reckon it does, cowboy."

"Now I can end that poem."

"Just how did it go, Jinglebob?"

Jinglebob sat a little straighter in the bunk. Forgotten now was the pain of his wounds. His eyes sparkled as he recited:

> "You ask which one I like the best,
>   From Miles to Saskatoon?
> The sweetest girl in all the West,
>   Is the one named Lorna Doone."

Lorry's eyes were misty bright. "It's grand, Jinglebob."

Jinglebob said ruefully. "You had that rhyme all the time and you never told me."

Lorry admitted the truth of his statement. "I — I wanted to make sure you were going to stay, first. I wasn't going to give you a rhyme to pass on to some other girl."

"Lorry, you little idiot, you sweet little idiot."

Jinglebob raised his arms as the girl leaned closer. He held her tight, murmuring, "Sweet little idiot." After a time she stopped his voice with her lips . . .